PRAISE FOR CARLENE THOMPSON

BLACK FOR REMEMBRANCE

"Gripped me from the first page and held on through its completely unexpected climax. Lock your doors, make sure there's no one behind you, and pick up *Black for Remembrance*."
—William Katz, author of *Double Wedding*

"Bizarre, terrifying…an inventive and forceful psychological thriller."
—*Publishers Weekly*

"Thompson's style is richly bleak, her sense of morality complex…Thompson is a mistress of the thriller parvenu."
—*Fear*

SINCE YOU'VE BEEN GONE

"This story will keep readers up well into the night."
—*Huntress Reviews*

DON'T CLOSE YOUR EYES

"*Don't Close Your Eyes* has all the gothic sensibilities of a Victorian Holt novel, combined with the riveting modern suspense of Sharyn McCrumb's *The Hangman's Beautiful Daughter*. Don't close your eyes—and don't miss this one."
—Meagan McKinney, author of *In the Dark*

"An exciting romantic suspense novel that will thrill readers . . . terrific."
—*Midwest Book Review*

IN THE EVENT OF MY DEATH

"[A] blood-chilling…tale of vengeance, madness and murder."
—*Romantic Times*

THE WAY YOU LOOK TONIGHT

"Thompson . . . has crafted a lively, entertaining read…skillfully ratchet[ing] up the tension with each successive chapter."
—*The Charleston Daily Mail*

Black for
Remembrance

Carlene Thompson

St. Martin's Paperbacks

Previously published by Avon Books, a division of Hearst Corporation.

BLACK FOR REMEMBRANCE

Library of Congress Catalog Card Number: 90-45095

ISBN: 0-312-98461-8

Printed in the United States of America

Avon Books edition / June 1992
St. Martin's Paperbacks edition / December 2002

St. Martin's Paperbacks are published by St. Martin's Press, 175 Fifth Avenue, New York, NY 10010.

10 9 8 7 6 5 4 3 2 1

To my family

Thanks to Casey Joe Smith

Black for Remembrance

Prologue

~

THEY CRESTED THE hill, a tall, slender man and a little girl carrying a clown doll, pale figures against a wall of trees turned blue-green by summer dusk. He held her hand tightly and bent to whisper something in her ear. They laughed. Pointing to a swing suspended by ropes from the limb of a towering oak, he asked, "Ready to ride?"

She nodded enthusiastically, then hesitated, her blue eyes growing troubled. "It's getting dark. Mommy'll worry."

"No, she won't—not if you only swing for a few minutes."

The little girl considered for a moment. Then she beamed. "Okay. Will you push?"

"Don't I always?"

She gently laid aside her clown doll, and he lifted her onto the swing, carefully locking her small hands around the old ropes. He circled behind, pushing her gently at first, then with more force until she arced through the air, her golden hair flying.

A grating, animal scream shattered the quiet darkness. The man blanched, his head snapping to the left. His arms fell to his sides, and the swing slammed into his abdomen, knocking him to the ground. The impact threw the little girl forward, onto knees and hands. She scrambled to the man. "What was it?" she quavered, cuddling next to him.

"Something screamed." He ran a hand over her shining hair. "Sometimes people set traps up here. Maybe a dog got caught instead of a rabbit. I should investigate."

She frowned over *investigate*, but she could feel his muscles tensing, his whole body leaning toward the direction of the scream. She gripped his shirt. "Don't go!"

"I have to see what it is." He rose, pulling her up with him.

"I'm scared. Maybe it's a woof."

He lifted her and set her on the swing, then placed the clown doll in her arms. "Hayley, there are no wolves up here. This is our magical forest, remember? Nothing here means you any harm." Her eyes were round. "I'll be back in a minute."

She gazed after him as his tall, spare frame disappeared into the shadows of the trees. At first she held rigidly still, gripping the doll against her chest. Then, very slowly, she relaxed. She inspected her knees, which were only slightly skinned. One was bleeding a little. She licked a finger to run over the scratch and winced at the sting of saliva on raw skin. Tiring of knees, she looked up. Even though the sky was not black yet, she could see a slice of moon and a bright star she knew was not a star but Venus. What a pretty name, Venus, she thought. She wished her name were Venus. In a few weeks, when first grade started, she could say to the teacher, "How do you do? My name is Venus" and the teacher would smile—

Something rustled in the trees. Her eyes strained through the shadows, but no tall, slim figure came toward her. Nothing but the deepening purple shadows of evening drew closer.

Then she heard the bells. Little bells jingling merrily, coming closer.

She gasped when a figure danced out from the trees. It wore a gleaming, baggy red-and-white satin suit, and its face was painted white, with big red circles for cheeks, black diamonds for eyes. The mouth was a huge red grin. Orange hair frizzed gaily from beneath a white hat dripping bells. A clown. She loved clowns.

The little girl's astonishment dissolved into delight. Daddy had said this was a magic forest. Now she knew he was right.

"Hi! You look just like Twinkle!" she called gaily, holding up her doll.

The clown turned a clumsy somersault and fell. She giggled as it quickly clambered to its feet and danced toward her, extending a big, red-gloved hand.

Still laughing, she reached for the hand. Its grip tightened as the clown pulled her from the swing and urged her forward.

She balked. "I'm sorry, clown, but I'm s'posed to stay here."

The clown nodded no, gesturing toward the trees.

Her pale eyebrows drew together and her mouth pursed in thought. Then she cried, "It's a surprise, isn't it? Daddy wants me to go with you!"

The clown's head jerked up and down, making the bells jingle happily. Its slippered feet two-stepped before it pulled firmly on her hand again.

This time she went easily. She was smiling as the clown led her into the gloom of the woods.

1

"**W**HY DID YOU give me peanut butter instead of cream cheese?"

Caroline Webb looked at her eight-year-old daughter, Melinda, who was peering critically between slices of wheat bread. "Daddy said cream cheese could spoil before noon."

"Jenny brings cream cheese sandwiches."

"Jenny also came down with a mild case of food poisoning two weeks ago." David Webb straightened his tie in front of the kitchen mirror, then turned to grin at his daughter, his craggy features creasing with homely amiability. "You don't want to get sick, do you?"

"I guess not." Melinda clumsily rewrapped her sandwich in Saran Wrap and poked through her Barbie lunch box. "Cherry Kool-Aid in my thermos?"

"Apple juice," Caroline said.

"Yuck. And where are my Reese Cups?"

"I gave you a granola bar instead."

Melinda groaned in agony, and her father swooped over her, his fingers digging into her thin sides. "Shut up and stop pestering your mom, kid."

"Daddy, *quit* it!" Melinda laughed.

4

"Not until you tell me how much you love granola."

"Never!" David tickled harder. "Okay, I love it, I *love* it!" Melinda shrieked. David let go and she fell into a gasping heap of giggles on the yellow-and-white linoleum floor. George, their black Labrador, rushed over to bathe her in kisses, which brought on a fresh attack of hysterics.

"What's all the noise?" Greg Webb, fifteen, ambled into the kitchen, his curly black hair still wet from the shower.

"Mommy gave me apple juice and granola," Melinda told him in injured tones as she struggled to her feet.

"Hippie food," Greg announced. "They ate that kind of stuff in the sixties."

Caroline cocked an eyebrow at him. "Around here we still eat it. And Melinda, if you want to be a ballerina, you have to eat healthy food. Reese Cups will make you so fat no one can lift you."

"Bafishnirof can."

"Baryshnikov. And he'll be retired by the time you're a prima ballerina."

"Oh, damn," Melinda muttered, then flushed and added hastily, "I mean darn."

"Sunday school's doing the child a world of good," David said, dropping a kiss on his daughter's chestnut hair. "Can you sue Sunday school teachers?"

Caroline put the last plate in the dishwasher and shut the door. "No, only doctors."

David grimaced. "Don't remind me. I just wrote a check for my malpractice insurance last night." He shrugged into his raincoat. "I'm getting out of this madhouse." He wrapped an arm around Caroline's slim waist. "What's on your agenda today?"

"I'm taking some things over to Lucy's, then going to the grocery store. Fidelia's coming."

David rolled his dark eyes. "Out of all the cleaning ladies in the city, why are we blessed with the one who practices voodoo?"

"Just because she's from Haiti doesn't mean she practices voodoo."

"Well, she's always messing around with tea leaves."

"Not tea leaves, Daddy," Melinda piped. "Tarot cards. Fidelia says I'm the Page of Cups."

"Reese Cups, no doubt." Melinda giggled, but David frowned into Caroline's eyes. "I don't know that I like all this hocus-pocus around the kids," he said in the fogyish tone that drove Caroline crazy.

"It's just for fun," she explained, keeping the irritation from her voice. "She's a perfectly respectable person. She even taught school in Haiti."

"So why is she cleaning houses here?"

"Something about not having the teaching credentials, and there was a sick father until a few months ago. They couldn't afford a nursing home, and Fidelia had to spend most of her time with the old man. But anyway, she cleans for six other families, not just for us. She's thorough and polite. She's even teaching Melinda a little French."

"And I'm an old sourpuss." David kissed her cheek. "I'm sorry. If you're happy with her, that's all that counts."

And it was, Caroline knew. Her husband adored her in his preoccupied way, and he did his best to tolerate her acceptance of people who were very different from herself, although he didn't understand it.

Caroline kissed David's cheek, which always showed an underlying shadow of heavy black beard that no longer matched his mostly silver hair. "Don't deliver too many babies today," she said affectionately.

"There's nary a one on schedule, but that doesn't mean a thing." He turned to the kids. "Who wants a ride to school?"

"Me!" Melinda clicked shut the offending lunch box. "When Greg walks me he always drags along looking at girls, and I want to get there early to check on Aurora."

David frowned. "Who in the world is Aurora?"

"My bean sprout. I told you already. I call her Aurora because that was Sleeping Beauty's name, and my bean sprout's still sleeping." She looked forlorn. "All the other kids' sprouts are growing."

"Maybe Fidelia can cast a spell on Aurora," Greg said, peeling a banana in spite of the massive breakfast he had consumed twenty minutes earlier.

"Bean sprouts," David sighed. "In my day we read Shakespeare."

"In the third grade?" Caroline asked dryly.

"I was a child prodigy."

"Don't let him kid you, squirt," Greg said to his sister. "When he was in the third grade, Shakespeare hadn't even been born."

David threw a dishcloth at him and Caroline laughed, knowing that age jokes didn't faze her husband, even though at fifty-six he was older than the fathers of Greg's friends. *"You* can walk to school." He took Melinda's hand. "Come on—by the time we finally make it to school, Aurora will be a foot tall."

"I'll see you guys after school," Caroline said.

Melinda shook her head in a violent negative. "I'm supposed to go to Jenny's after school, remember? Her mom's making spaghetti."

Caroline frowned. "Is her mother going to pick you up at school?"

"Sure. And she'll drive me home."

"I guess it's okay then, although I'd feel better if *I* were picking you up."

"But Mommy, it's all fixed."

"And I have basketball practice," Greg said, tossing away the empty banana peel. "Then I'm taking Julie for pizza."

"I want you home by eight."

"Eight! None of the other guys have stupid curfews like I do."

"It's a school night, and considering your grades—"

"Eight *is* a little early, Caroline," David said. "Eight-thirty."

Greg's face settled into the prickly lines that had become familiar since he reached adolescence. "Great. I ought to be safe from werewolves at that hour."

"Not if there's a full moon," Caroline said sweetly, and Greg grinned in spite of himself. She looked at David. "Looks like it's just you and me."

"Honey, it's Monday. I have evening office hours."

"Oh, David, I thought we decided you were only going to be in the office Tuesday and Friday nights. Three nights a week is too much."

"I know. I'll cut back as soon as I can get things squared away." Caroline had no idea what had to be "squared away." It was merely another one of David's excuses when he didn't want to argue about his work, which consumed him. She sighed and let the point go. "I promise I'll be back by nine," David said.

"Sure." Caroline forced a smile, knowing that meant ten at the. earliest.

The four of them trailed out the door into the garage. While David helped Melinda strap herself into the seat of the Mercedes, Caroline snapped on the automatic garage door opener and the big door whirred upward. With exaggerated teenaged nonchalance, Greg loped away without a backward look, but Melinda waved as if she were leaving on an ocean voyage while David backed out.

Thank goodness she's over those crying jags that sent her home from school at least two days a week last spring, Caroline thought. Lots of attention and time at home with her mother over the summer had eased whatever anxiety Melinda was feeling but refused to reveal. Now she seemed relatively content with school, although her teacher Miss Cummings said she had a tendency to cling. Maybe she picked that up from me, Caroline mused. I've always been overprotective with her and Greg. But what mother with my experience wouldn't be?

She smiled and waved back at Melinda. Then she shut the door, poured a second cup of coffee, and sat down at the kitchen table with George stretched out beside her.

They had moved into the house nine years before, when Caroline learned she was pregnant with their second child, and she had loved the place since the first day. But especially, she loved her big, airy kitchen with its island range and the huge antique maple table facing a floor-to-ceiling window. This morning she looked out on their acre of front lawn, still green beneath a wisteria-blue October sky. White and yellow chrysanthemums massed themselves in thick beds beneath the window, and a crimson cardinal perched importantly atop the wrought-iron lawn lamp.

"I'm a very lucky woman," she said aloud, listening to the thump of George's tail on the floor as he stared up at her. "I'm an incredibly lucky woman. If only I could forget . . ."

Her stomach was starting to tighten in that sickeningly familiar way, when someone tapped on the kitchen door and she ran to open it, absurdly happy to see Fidelia gazing back at her. "I'm early. Too early? I can go away for a while."

"Don't be silly. I'm glad you're here." Fidelia stepped in, her bare arms speckled with goosebumps. "I don't know when you're going to realize you're not in Haiti anymore and start dressing for cold weather. How about some coffee to warm you up?"

"Sounds good. Sugar, no cream." Caroline loved Fidelia's honeyed Caribbean accent an English-speaking, Ohio-born father and several years in the United States had done nothing to temper. She stooped, her faded red-print cotton dress flowing out around her thin, bare legs. "Hello dere, George, my handsome man!" The dog rolled on his back for a belly rub, which Fidelia laughingly administered. "Dis is de biggest baby in de house."

"You'd be surprised at how protective he can be, though," Caroline said, pouring coffee. "Last year a man broke in one night when David was gone, and George nearly took off his hand. Then the guy had the nerve to try to sue us, but of course he got nowhere."

"You should be glad you live in Ohio, not California. A judge might have listened to him out dere."

They sat down at the table, and Fidelia looked at

Caroline closely, her strange light-blue eyes sharp in her café-au-lait face. "You all right dis morning?"

"Of course." Caroline smiled. "Well, at least I was until about ten minutes ago. Then I started thinking about something sad."

"Your little girl—Hayley?"

Caroline looked at her in surprise. "You *are* psychic."

Fidelia shook her head. "You don't have to be psychic to know when a woman is grieving over a child."

"But I've never mentioned Hayley to you."

"I've lived in dis town five years. I've heard a lot of talk in all dat time, especially since I work for another lady who knows you."

Caroline's eyes drifted back to the gay chrysanthemums. "Yes, I should have thought of that. I think Alice Anderson's favorite topic of conversation is the kidnapping and murder of my little girl and my divorce from Chris."

"Yes, Mrs. Anderson she talks a lot. But why is Hayley on your mind today?"

"She's always on my mind. But last night I dreamed about her. It was a terrible, frightening dream about her death. It was very brutal."

"I know all de details," Fidelia said softly.

"And also, today is Hayley's birthday. I always put flowers on her grave on her birthday. She would have been twenty-five. That's how old I was when she died."

Fidelia wore beautiful dangling silver earrings that caught the light when she shook her head. "Hard to tink of you with a child dat old. You look tirty-five."

"You're sweet, Fidelia."

"I've been called many tings, but never sweet."

She laughed, a deep, smoker's laugh, her even teeth white against red lipstick. Caroline had never been able to guess her age—the glossy, undyed black hair said twenties; the leathery skin said sixty years in the sun. "Why don't you get out, cheer yourself up?"

"I was planning to go by Lucille Elder's place."

"Buying or selling?"

"Selling." Elder's Interiors was the most popular interior design studio in the city. "She commissioned six needlepoint pillows and eight crewel dining chair seat covers for Pamela Fitzgerald's new house."

"I don't know her."

"Her last name is really Burke now. She's married to Larry Burke. His father owns Burke's Construction Company." Caroline frowned. "Maybe that's part of what has me down today. Pamela was in Hayley's kindergarten class, but I'd forgotten her until Lucy started talking about her lately. I keep thinking that if things had been different, maybe Hayley would be the one married to a rich young man and decorating a big, new house."

"You can't second guess de fates."

"I've never believed in fate, Fidelia. Life's always seemed a matter of chance to me." She drained her cup. "Good heavens, now I'm waxing philosophical. It's definitely time for me to get out for a while."

"Go for de day," Fidelia said. "Enjoy yourself. I'll make de house sparkle for you, and lock up when I leave."

Caroline went upstairs, took a shower, washed her hair, and, after blowing it dry, wound it on hot rollers. She wore it shoulder-length and softly curled, although lately she'd been wondering if she shouldn't change to a more mature style, even though it was still a shiny chestnut, the gray limited to a few hairs she always quickly pulled out. She told herself she wore it long for David, but she knew he wasn't particular. It was Chris who years ago had loved her thick, then-waist-length hair, Chris who had painted her naked, sitting on the bed drawing a silver-backed brush through a half-concealing veil of russet-tinged strands.

She rubbed a window in the steam on the mirror. "Caroline, you are a melancholy soul today," she said, grinning. "You should be wearing flowing white robes and carrying a candle." Then the grin faded, and she peered closer. Fidelia was right—she didn't look her forty-four years, which somehow made her feel shallow. After all she'd been through, why should her pale forehead be only finely lined, her eyes as clear green and steady as they had been twenty years ago? Melinda will look like me when she's forty-four, she thought. Melinda is the image of me.

Half an hour later, wearing brown wool slacks, a bright yellow sweater, and a tweed blazer, she loaded the pillows in her Thunderbird and waved good-bye to Fidelia, whose long, still gaze followed her out the driveway.

Caroline rolled down her car window, drinking in the crisp air that tasted as crystal blue as the sky. The sun had turned the pale yellow of autumn, and the trees blazed gold and red. She passed the grade school and glanced over, zeroing in on the room where Melinda had third grade. Construction-paper leaf cutouts decorated the windows, and a jack-o'-lantern grinned at her. Which reminded her, Halloween was in two days. She would have to put the finishing touches on Melinda's costume and be sure to stock enough candy for the hordes of children who drifted up and down their street until nine, when the city decreed all ghouls must return home.

Caroline stopped for gasoline and oil, then headed for Elder's Interiors. As usual she pulled around to the tiny private lot in back, where Lucy's white Corvette and her assistant Tina Morgan's Volkswagen huddled in the building's shade. She angled the Thunderbird in beside a tree so she wouldn't block the other cars. She could easily move if anyone needed to get out, but she doubted that young Tina would ask—the store seemed to be her life. Lucy said she arrived at 7:30 in the morning, brought a sack lunch, and usually left well after six in the evening. Caroline had seen for herself how devoted Tina was when Lucy redecorated the Webb home two months earlier. Tina always seemed to be around—measuring, making suggestions, insistently poring over wallpaper and paint samples with Caroline until at last Caroline had simply closed her eyes and pointed to selections, telling Lucy to correct any major blunders she'd made. But for all her intensity, Tina was beautiful and lively. By the time she left, Greg had developed a crush on her, and Melinda announced that except for Mommy and Lucy, Tina was her favorite grown-up girl.

Caroline opened the back door and stepped into the storeroom, which was more dimly lit than usual. One fluorescent bulb set in the eighteen-foot-high ceiling was out and the other buzzed weakly, throwing the room into bluish pallor. For some reason Caroline suddenly felt uneasy with the gloom, and she picked up her pace, trying to skirt all the table legs she couldn't see clearly over the top of her sacks full of pillows and seat covers. She was nearly to the showroom door when she tripped over a hassock, tumbling sideways and landing heavily on her hip.

"Damn!" she muttered, grabbing up the pillows that had spilled and smiling when she saw they remained spotless. She was stuffing them back in the sacks when the crawling sensation of being watched spread up her spine and touched her neck. She sat still, looking around her. "Lucy? Tina?"

No one answered, but someone watched. She felt a presence in the room just as strongly as she felt the throbbing in her hip. The single fluorescent light hissed, then went out. Caroline blinked in the total darkness. "Is someone there?"

Whoever it was didn't intend to answer, and Caroline was as unnerved by her thudding heart and suddenly icy flesh as she was by the darkness. "Get hold of yourself," she muttered as, clutching her sacks, she got to her feet and began inching around furniture toward the crack of light where double doors opened into the showroom.

Then she heard it. A soft whisper. "Mommy?"

Caroline went rigid. She knew that voice, even if it was only a whisper. "Hayley?"

This time the voice rose. "Mommy, I need you!"

"Hayley?" Caroline looked around wildly, although she could see nothing but gray. "Hayley, are you here?"

Silence, but a compelling silence that thrummed in her ears and beat in her stomach.

Caroline's tongue touched her dry lips. "Hayley, darling, where are you?" she asked, while her mind said, This is insane. Hayley is dead.

The light flickered back on with a faint buzz.

Caroline stood trembling, her gaze shooting into every corner and up the wide back staircase leading to the second floor. But whatever it was had vanished. The silence once again turned empty, and eyes no longer trailed up and down her body. She let out a faint whimper and rushed headlong toward the shop.

The doors flew back and hit the wall as she burst into the showroom. A young woman in a stern gray suit turned to peer at her disapprovingly over outsized glasses. Caroline threw her a nervous smile and looked around the room.

"Ms. Elder is upstairs," the woman announced, gazing at her warily. "She and Ms. Morgan have gone up to get some cloth samples for me."

She emphasized *me*, letting Caroline know that even if she'd arrived in a flurry, she could just cool her heels until Lucy and Tina had finished more important business.

So it wasn't either of them in the storeroom, Caroline thought as she walked past the woman and laid down her sacks on a Hepplewhite dining table. But of course if it had been Lucy or Tina they would have answered her. And they certainly wouldn't have lurked around in the darkness saying *Mommy*.

In Hayley's voice.

Stop it! That was not Hayley's voice, Caroline told herself firmly. You're just imagining things because you had that awful dream about Hayley, and she's been on your mind all morning.

She sat down on a hard Boston rocker and took a deep breath, trying to calm down. Look at the shop, she commanded herself, ignoring the curious glances the woman in the gray suit was tossing her way. Look at all the pretty things in Lucy's shop and stop letting your wild imagination run even wilder.

She forced herself to gaze over the exquisite furniture artfully arranged in the big showroom. She remembered when Lucy started the business twenty years ago. Everyone had expected her to fail, certain that behind her off-beat, bohemian manner there wasn't a dash of business sense. And of course Chris had been appalled that she was going to "squander" her impressive artistic talents "selling living room suites and bric-a-brac to the up-and-coming."

What a snob Chris had been then, Caroline thought mildly. But of course he was riding high in those days when a major art critic had noted that "Christopher Corday will someday be the premier landscape painter in this country, if he isn't already." She had been thrilled for him, happy she could tell her parents, "I told you he was wonderful, even if you didn't approve of him or of my marrying when I was eighteen." And she had known the years she'd worked as a receptionist for David instead of going to college had been worth it. They had allowed Chris the freedom to paint, with none of the dross of humdrum employment to drag him down. Yes, they had been riding high when Lucy opened her first small store.

"Caroline!" She looked up to see Lucy poised at the top of the spiral showroom staircase holding an armful of material swatches. "I didn't know you were here."

"I think I'm a little early," Caroline said, noting that Gray Suit was heading determinedly toward the stairs, afraid the batty woman in the yellow turtleneck was going to claim her time. "Finish with your customer and I'll take you to lunch."

Lucy smiled. "Fabulous. I'm *starving.*"

Good old excessive Lucy, Caroline thought. She was never just hungry; she was *starving.* She was never tired; she was *exhausted.* And she was never afraid; she was *terrified*. Would she have been terrified in the dark storeroom where a long-dead child begged for help?

Caroline felt a tremor pass through her. She would tell Lucy what had happened, and Lucy would tell her all about the weird acoustics in the storeroom and describe exactly what sound had been distorted into something resembling a little girl's voice. Caroline had learned to count on Lucy's down-to-earth interpretations of life, which always surprised a lot of people because of the way she dressed. She glanced over at her friend, who was patiently showing the customer sample after sample of material. They looked ridiculous together, one all severe lines, sleek hair, understated makeup, a study in neutral tones; the other a rainbow of purple, green, and gold with shaggy copper-colored hair and lovely, heavily accented violet eyes in a slightly equine face. She was flashily attractive thanks to makeup and clothes, and she looked just as unconventional as she had twenty-three years ago when Chris introduced them.

Chris had brought Lucy home to dinner one evening, saying, "Caro, this is Lucille, an old friend of mine. I saw her today in Mallory Park, looking absolutely rapt while she painted that statue of old man Mallory. I thought, 'How could that sanctimonious buzzard inspire anyone to capture him on canvas, much less look so *ardent* doing it?' Then I came up behind her and I saw she was painting the old guy naked, of all things, and I said to myself, 'Lucy hasn't changed one bit. I've got to take her home to meet Caroline and the baby.' "

Lucy had laughed uproariously as Caroline gave her a tentative smile. "I'm really not a pervert, Caroline. It's just that my art teacher *made* me paint that hideous tribute to Mallory's ego, so I decided to shock him into letting me paint what I want to from now on." Instead she had received an F in the class, which she seemed to take with good grace, as she did most rejections, although Caroline had always felt the grade was partially responsible for her turning away from painting.

"I'm ready," Lucy was saying, then, "Caroline, are you all right?"

Caroline's gaze jerked up to Lucy, who stood five-nine barefoot. "Sure, I'm fine. Just a little jumpy today."

"We'll talk about it." Lucy touched Caroline's hair and smiled. Many years ago her little physical signs of affection made Caroline uncomfortable; now she was used to them. "Where do you want to eat?"

"How about Zeppo's?"

"That place with all the young people and guys sliding down the firepole with a cake when it's someone's birthday and huge greasy hamburgers? Sounds *wonderful.*"

Caroline noticed Tina coming down the stairs, her long, straight black hair gleaming under the lights, her slim figure outlined in sleek black slacks and a white silk blouse. Her features were classic, from the high cheekbones, slender nose, and large dark eyes to the perfect, rose-accented lips. Caroline had often wondered if she'd considered modeling as a career.

"Tina, Lucy and I are going to Zeppo's for lunch," she said on impulse. "Would you like to go with us?"

Tina's quick smile flashed. "Thanks, Mrs. Webb, but I have to mind the store," she said in her slightly husky voice that always reminded Caroline of Kathleen Turner's.

"I don't think we'll go bankrupt if we shut the place down for an hour," Lucy said, looking encouragingly at her. "Come on, it'll be fun."

"Lucille, in that hour we're closed Jackie Onassis could come here wanting us to redecorate all her homes."

Lucy made a face. "Sure. And Queen Elizabeth will be right behind her. But if you're determined to devote your life to business, there's nothing I can do about it. Want me to bring you back something?"

"No again. I brought a lunch."

"Probably something wonderful like tuna fish and hardboiled eggs," Lucy said to Caroline. "She eats nothing."

Tina winked at her. "We're not all naturally thin like you."

"Skinny, you mean. And believe me, if eating hardboiled eggs would give me a body like yours, I'd never touch a hamburger again. But unfortunately . . ." Her eyes shot to the front of the store. "Oh, hell, there's old Mrs. Edwards, and if I'm not mistaken, she's carrying that horrible moth-eaten swatch of brocade with her. It's about a hundred years old, and she's been in here at least five times trying to match it, but nothing ever suits her. She can't even remember she's brought it before."

Tina grinned. "You two go have fun. I'll handle Mrs. Edwards." She strode to the front of the store, delight edging her voice. "Why, Mrs. Edwards, how lovely to see you. Have you brought something with you?"

"Cloth, my dear," the old lady quavered, holding out a faded square. "I've just come across it. I thought perhaps you could find a match and make some draperies for me just like the ones we had in Grandfather's house."

"We'll go through the sample books and see what we can come up with. My goodness, isn't it beautiful? Now you just sit down here in this comfortable chair and I'll bring down my books. And how about a cup of tea?"

Lucy shook her head in wonder. "She's an absolute gem, Caroline. Not only talented, but unbelievably patient with our most tedious customers. And speaking of tedious customers, did you bring the stuff for Pamela?"

Caroline had almost forgotten why she came. She retrieved the sacks from the dining table and pulled out pillows and seat covers all stitched in peach and turquoise.

"Oh, Caro, these are exquisite!" Lucille held them up. "Just beautiful. You do gorgeous work."

"Let's just hope Pamela likes them. You said she's a real nitpicker."

"I believe I called her worse than that. She's impossible, but I don't know how even she could find fault with these. Why don't you come with me to drop them off? We'll go before lunch, and that will give me a good excuse to leave in a hurry. She's a great one for thinking up things to complain about if you don't make a fast getaway."

Little Pamela Fitzgerald. Caroline hadn't seen her since she was in kindergarten. Even then she hadn't liked Pamela, and according to Lucy, time had done nothing to sweeten her personality. Still, it would be interesting to see her—she had been a beautiful child. And she knew Lucy wanted her to see the Burke home she was decorating. "Okay," she said finally, "but remember we're both hungry. I don't want to linger around there for hours, and I *don't* want to invite Pamela to lunch."

"Easier said than done," Lucy laughed ruefully. "The girl has a way of getting what she wants."

2

PAMELA FITZGERALD BURKE swung back the carved teakwood door of her magnificent hillside house and smiled graciously. "Hello, Lucille."

"Hi. I brought a friend along. This is Caroline Webb."

Pamela blinked, long, curled lashes sweeping over eyes like brown velvet. "Mrs. Webb?"

"Yes. We met a long time ago, Pamela, at your kindergarten picnic in the spring."

Caroline wondered if she imagined the color heightening in Pamela's face. "I remember you now."

"You do? That's amazing."

"I have a good memory. Besides, you look the same. Only your last name used to be Corday." She hesitated, then smiled again. "Won't you come in? I've just made tea."

"We can't stay long, Pam," Lucy said. Even when she was a child the girl had hated to be called Pam. Lucy told Caroline shortening the name was one of the few ways she could compensate for enduring Pamela's high-handed manner. "If we weren't making a small fortune on this job, I'd tell her to take a leap," Lucy had confided. "As it is, I have to settle for petty revenge."

Pamela led them into a sprawling living room with

a soaring cathedral ceiling. Gleaming oak floors stretched to a stone fireplace large enough to hold an ox, and walls of windows allowed a panoramic view of autumn-colored hills and the city beyond. They padded over a flax shag rug that must have cost the earth, Caroline thought, and Pamela motioned them toward chairs before carefully arranging her whip-slim body in an S pattern on the incredibly long vanilla sweep of couch just opposite, resting a peaches-and-cream cheek on her hand and knowing exactly how pretty she looked.

"Pamela, your house is beautiful," Caroline told her.

"My husband designed it. He's very talented, not just a construction worker like everyone thinks."

"*I* never thought the heir to the Burke Construction Company was just a construction worker," Lucy laughed. "But let's get down to business. Caroline's finished the things you ordered." Only Pamela's eyes moved, sliding down to the sacks where Lucy was plunging her hands. "Just look at these pillows," she said excitedly. "The turquoise exactly picks up the color of this velvet wing chair." She tossed one of the pillows to Pamela. It smacked the young woman in the face and fell on the floor. Lucy flushed. "I'm sorry. I thought you'd catch it."

Even Caroline could hear the genuine contrition in her voice, but Pamela regarded her coldly. "I don't like playing catch. I prefer being handed things."

"I see...." Lucy leaned forward, picked up the pillow, and placed it gently in Pamela's outstretched, beringed hand.

"Thank you," she said stiffly. She studied the pillow. "Quite nice."

Caroline had the impression she was supposed to fall to her knees in gratitude before the queen. She felt faintly amused and very sad. Obviously Pamela had simply grown into an adult version of the gorgeous, uppity little girl who had made fun of Hayley for living in a log cabin and "accidentally" poked a hole in the painting of Canadian geese in flight that Chris had done for their kindergarten teacher at the end of the year.

"I love the colors," Lucy persisted.

"Yes," Pamela said languidly. Then her arched eyebrows drew together fretfully. "But I wonder if we shouldn't have gone with brown and burnt orange."

"Brown and orange!" Lucy snapped. "But you said you loved these colors. Our whole color scheme is based around them."

"I know. But now I'm just not *sure* . . ."

Lucy took a deep breath and looked earnest. "Earth tones are out of style, Pamela. *Really* out."

"They are? Oh . . . well." Clearly that settled the matter for Pamela, no matter what her tastes. Caroline caught Lucy's fleeting smile of triumph. "At least these colors are interesting," Pamela said magnanimously.

Lucy's lips compressed in irritation. "As I said, we can't stay. Tina will come by to attach the dining chair covers."

"Oh, but I wanted to ask you about the color of the carpet in the master bedroom. The Bahama Tan is restful, but I'm not sure I won't get tired of it after a while."

"But you're not tired of it yet, so let's leave it alone for now, shall we, Pam?" Caroline looked down. When Lucy said things like *shall*, she was quietly angry. She stood. "Caroline and I really have to be going."

Pamela rose from the couch like a cat uncurling in the sun. "Well, I guess we can talk about the carpet later. There's also the paint in the second guest bedroom . . ." She looked from one to the other. "Are you going to lunch?"

"No, the doctor," Caroline said quickly. "Ophthalmologist. Lucy's driving because I'll get drops in my eyes."

Did I have to go completely overboard? Caroline wondered as Pamela's velvet gaze found hers and seemed to ferret out the lie. "I see," she said flatly. Then, "By the way, Mrs. Corday, I have one of your husband's paintings I haven't hung yet. It's an oil of sun slanting through a broken barn roof onto a pile of snow on a rusty barbed-wire fence. I don't much like it, but Lucille says it's tasteful."

"It's beautiful! The play of light and shadow. The attention to detail. The mood of serenity . . ." Lucy's voice, too high, broke off unhappily after her last cliché.

Caroline smiled. "Chris and I haven't been married for a long time, but you're very lucky to have one of his paintings, Pamela. He's a brilliant artist."

"She'll still be a brat when she's eighty," Lucy fumed as they pulled away from the house. "She brought up Chris for pure spite because we didn't invite her to lunch."

Caroline looked at the acres of brilliantly hued trees spreading around them. The house was really isolated, she thought, almost like the place where she and Chris used to live. "I suppose it isn't all her fault,

Lucy. From what I've heard her parents gave her everything except their time. Her father is obsessed with business and her mother belongs to every club in the city except the bowling league."

"Her mother *couldn't* belong to the bowling league. She's big as a whale," Lucy said acidly. "I hope Pamela looks just like her in a few years."

"Lucy, you're awful!"

"I just say what you're too nice to say. But honestly, I feel a little sorry for her, too, try as I do not to. She's such a jerk she doesn't have any friends. It's a miracle she found Larry."

"I guess there's someone for everyone."

"Leave it to Pamela to find a rich someone."

Caroline laughed and Lucy looked over at her. "Well, at least you're in a better mood. Want to tell me what was wrong earlier?"

Caroline suddenly drew inward. In Lucy's bright company, Hayley's voice in the storeroom lost its reality. "Earlier I thought I heard a child in the storeroom."

Lucy frowned. "A child? In *my* storeroom? I know I should be more careful about locking those doors! I just go so busy after this morning's delivery."

"There wasn't a child, Lucy. It was my imagination. The lights went out, and then I thought I heard . . . Hayley."

"Oh." Caroline saw Lucy's hand tighten on the steering wheel.

"It's her birthday, Lucy."

"I know. I put flowers on her grave this morning."

"Yeah, well . . . the mind can play funny tricks, can't it?"

"Especially on a day like this." Lucy's eyes slewed

toward her. "But Caro, if you thought you heard Hayley, it *was* your imagination. You know that, don't you?"

"Of course. I said so, didn't I?"

"Yes, you did. Without much conviction."

"Well, it wasn't you or Tina."

"No, I don't usually hang around storerooms trying to scare you. And Tina was helping me when you arrived."

"Then unless there really was a child hiding in the storeroom, I *know* I imagined it."

"Well, just to make sure, I'll call Tina as soon as we stop for lunch and ask her to check the storeroom and lock the doors. I don't want to find half-eaten lollipops down in the cushions of my antique settees."

"You also don't want to have something stolen." Lucy took a deep drag on the cigarette she'd lighted as soon as they got in the car, and Caroline said quickly to change the subject, "I wonder how Pamela remembered I was married to Chris?"

"He's pretty well known around here, Caro. And so are you because you were his wife at the time of Hayley's death."

"I guess you're right." Her nose was starting to tingle from the cigarette smoke. "Is Chris painting a lot now?"

"More than he has for years. I've started handling some of his stuff, but he really belongs in galleries. I feel better about him these days, and if he can just leave the women alone, he might be on his way back up."

Caroline sighed. "Chris and his women."

"They became his escape after Hayley died."

"I know. It's just hard to believe he was once a faithful husband. Is he seeing anyone in particular?"

"He *never* sees anyone in particular. Whoever's available in the singles' bars is good enough for him." She cast a sideways glance at Caroline. "But that doesn't still bother you, does it?"

"No, except that I hate to see him make such a waste of his life and his talent, not to mention the risk he's taking with his health. I hoped the AIDS scare would slow him down."

Lucy crushed out her half-smoked cigarette. "You're awfully generous, considering how he treated you."

"I wasn't always this forgiving. You know that. I spent years inwardly raging. I even got to the point where I'd catch myself talking out loud, telling him off, saying all the things I was too shattered to say when we divorced."

"He was hurting a lot back then, too."

"I know. That's why I couldn't hang on to my bitterness." She looked over at Lucy. "I'm glad you remained his friend, even if I couldn't remain his wife."

"Chris and I are both misfits. Oddballs. We understand each other."

"You want to be an oddball, Lucy Elder, but you're not really. Sometimes I think you're a lot more conventional than I am."

Lucy raised her eyebrows derisively. "I doubt if anyone would agree with you on that one, but believe what you like."

At Zeppo's Lucy urged Caroline to have a daiquiri with her lunch. "Well, just one," Caroline said reluctantly. "I still have some errands to do." An hour later, when her third drink arrived, she looked at

Lucy seriously and said, "To hell with the grocery store and dry cleaner. Would you consider going to see that new comedy showing at the two o'clock matinee?"

"I would absolutely love it! I'll go call Tina again and ask her to hold the fort. She'll probably be relieved to get through an extra two hours without having me around."

Caroline was surprised. "You were just telling me what a gem she is. Are there problems?"

"She seems edgy lately. Distracted. Something's on her mind."

Caroline nodded knowingly. "And you've been trying to pry it out of her."

Lucy drew back, acting hurt. "Why, Caro, you know I'd never do such a thing." She grinned. "Besides, I already know. She's seeing Lowell Warren."

"The lawyer?"

"Senior partner of Warren, Tate and Stern."

"He seems a little old for her."

"Late forties. The trouble is, he's also a little married. Of course, Claire is usually off campaigning for one of her causes like Save the Three-toed Sloth or whatever might get her a shot on some rinky-dink talk show, so it's hard to tell she *is* his wife, but if there's been a divorce, I don't know about it."

"Are you sure he and Tina are involved?"

Lucy nodded. "He's called the store three or four times for her that I know of. He didn't leave his name, naturally, but once you've heard that deep, cultured voice you don't forget it. Also, one evening I passed them together in his car." She looked away and sighed. "I just hope she doesn't get hurt."

"She seems very self-reliant to me, Lucy. And who

knows—maybe Lowell is finally planning on a divorce."

"In any case, Tina Morgan is a grown woman whose life is absolutely none of my business. So why don't we just forget about her and go have some fun?"

At the theater Lucy and Caroline bought giant Cokes and two barrels of heavily buttered popcorn, pretending they hadn't just finished a substantial lunch. "I'm eating like Greg," Caroline said when they settled into the dark, half-empty theater and dug into the popcorn. "Today ought to put ten pounds on me."

"More likely twenty," Lucy said gravely, "and all in your hips."

They giggled hysterically as if Lucy had said something amazingly witty, and a middle-aged man down the aisle turned and glared at them, which set them off again.

When they emerged from the theater a little before four o'clock, Caroline smiled happily. "You've made my day, Lucy. Thanks so much for going with me."

"I had more fun than you did. I just hope David doesn't get mad if his dinner's ten minutes late." She said the last with a wink, knowing that David rarely got mad at anyone, much less his wife. The two had become fairly good friends after David got over his initial wariness of a woman he said dressed like a beatnik. Caroline reminded him that beatniks had not existed since the fifties, but he refused to update his vocabulary, clinging doggedly to the phrases of his youth.

Caroline did not go back into the store with Lucy, claiming she was in a hurry to get home. Actually, she wanted to stop at a florist's before five o'clock closing time. She could not let this day pass without putting flowers on Hayley's grave. She chose a bouquet of pink carnations and baby's breath trimmed with lace and a pink bow, and drove to the isolated hillside cemetery where Chris had insisted their daughter be buried. "You can look out over the whole city from up here," he'd said as they stumbled in their grief over the grounds the day after Hayley's body had been identified. They were so young, they'd never thought about buying cemetery lots. Then suddenly they were in immediate need. "I bet it's beautiful up here at night," he went on. Caroline could remember thinking of her baby lying on the cold hillside throughout the long dark hours of night and bursting into violent sobbing for the first time since Hayley had disappeared a month before. Chris had held her for nearly an hour, until she could see clearly enough to walk back to the car.

Today the hillside looked desolate, with fallen leaves blowing over the graves in a cold wind that had sprung up when the sun abruptly faded ten minutes earlier. Caroline shivered, buttoning her blazer as she walked through the overgrown grass. At the time of Hayley's burial, the cemetery was perfectly maintained. Management had changed since then, though, and in the past few years Caroline noted with despair the growing shabbiness of the grounds. When she complained about the neglect to David, he suggested moving Hayley to a nicer cemetery nearer their home, but the idea of disinterring her child bothered Caroline. Hayley had been through enough without having her final rest disturbed.

As Caroline drew near Hayley's grave, tears sprang up in her eyes. The angel Chris had lovingly carved from pink Italian marble and set atop her tombstone had been desecrated, its delicate bowed head broken off and thrown a few feet away. Caroline sank to her knees, picking up tiny chips of marble scattered around the sunken plot. They looked raw and fresh, as if they had only just been hacked from the angel. Was it possible someone had done this today? She sat back on her heels, wiping tears from her cold cheeks and asking herself who would do such a thing. Vandals was the obvious answer, but it didn't feel right. None of the other gravestones had been touched. Besides, the destruction seemed too studied, almost as if the violator knew Hayley had been decapitated.

Slowly Caroline realized she had dropped her bouquet when she spotted the broken angel. She retrieved it and laid it near the tombstone, looking at the cheerful red and white roses Lucy always left on Hayley's birthday and the familiar bunch of violets from Chris. But among them rested a third offering—a cluster of black silk orchids tied with a black velvet ribbon. Puzzled, Caroline picked up the flowers, peering at the round, childish printing on a small card attached to the ribbon:

> To Hayley
> Black For Remembrance

"Black for remembrance," Caroline breathed. "What on earth?"

She dropped the bouquet as if it burned her hand. The sky had turned a bruised purple and mauve, and a sharp wind blew up, rocking the pink angel's head so that its dead eyes gazed at her.

A voice in a deserted storeroom. A shattered angel. A black bouquet. Caroline let out a tiny cry, suddenly breathlessly afraid. She scrambled to her feet and ran to the car, ignoring the gaping old couple slowly making their way to a grave just beyond Hayley's. Spraying gravel behind her, she tore down the steep road and didn't slow down until she hit the rush hour traffic streaming from the city.

Usually heavy traffic got on her nerves, but this evening she was grateful for the cars on either side of her. They were filled with people—some laughing together, some cursing the traffic, some singing along with the radio—but all looking ordinary and unafraid, as if their days had held no ghostly voices or desecrated tombstones. "Enjoy yourself," Fidelia had told her that morning. Caroline laughed mirthlessly. "Well, I tried, Fidelia," she said aloud. "I guess the stars weren't on my side."

She got home at six o'clock, and because they had gone off daylight saving time, darkness was already closing in. The dusk-to-dawn light glowed over the driveway, turning everything blue-white, lifeless.

She let herself into the house and immediately put on a pot of coffee, feeling she needed something to clear her head. Fidelia had left a note in her spiky script on the kitchen counter:

Hope your day went well. George is chained on the back porch. Didn't know when you would be home and thought he might make a mess.

Poor George. He would explode before he made a mess in the house, but Fidelia could not be convinced of this. Caroline decided to change into jeans and an old sweater before she braced herself for one of his rowdy greetings. As the coffee began to perk, she walked through the dining room and entrance hall, turning on lights as she went. Tonight she felt like having every light in the house blazing. She had just reached the staircase when from somewhere in the darkness above came a voice:

"The weather will be clear and dry tonight with a low of forty-seven. Sunshine tomorrow with a high of sixty. And now we return to music with a golden oldie by Peter Frampton, 'Baby, I Love Your Way.' "

The music began, loud and tinny, as if it were coming from Melinda's transistor radio. "Greg, Melinda, are you home?" Caroline called, although she could feel the house's emptiness. The radio hadn't been on this morning, and Fidelia never listened to it. In fact, it had been stored in Melinda's dresser drawer since she received a portable radio/cassette player last Christmas.

Caroline went slowly up the stairs to Melinda's closed door at the end of the hall. When she threw the door open, music blared. The hall light glowed into the room as she walked to Melinda's vanity where the transistor lay, going at full volume. She turned it off and stood staring at it in confusion. Who would turn the radio on so loudly and leave it playing in an empty house?

For the first time Caroline realized how cold the room was. She glanced over to see Melinda's dotted-swiss curtains stirring with the wind as moonlight shone on shards of glass lying on the blue carpet.

"How did that window get broken?" she muttered,

turning on the overhead light to get a better look. Then she screamed.

On Melinda's bed grinned Twinkle, the clown doll that had disappeared with Hayley nineteen years ago.

3

1

"**I** WOULD LOOK exactly a million times better in a ballerina outfit," Melinda announced, staring at herself in Caroline's full-length mirror.

"Melinda, it's forty-five degrees out tonight. Do you know how cold you'd get in a tutu and tights? And besides, you wouldn't look a million times better. You look darling."

"I look like a nerd." Melinda whirled on Caroline, making her big fuzzy rabbit ears sway back and forth. Caroline had to bite the inside of her mouth to keep from laughing. "I'll have to resign from third grade."

"Melinda, you're being ridiculous. You look wonderful, and you'll be warm."

"Warm! I'll be a baked rabbit when I get home. It's four hundred and fifty-six degrees in here." Melinda was always precise with numbers. "Mommy, *please* don't make me go out like this."

Greg had come to stand in the open doorway, and he winked at Caroline, his dark eyes twinkling like his father's. "Wow, what a terrific costume!"

Melinda turned. "What did that mean?"

37

"What's the matter—can't you understand English anymore? I said that's a great costume."

"It is?" Melinda studied herself in the mirror once more, as usual influenced by her adored older brother's approval. "You don't think I look nerdy?"

"Are you nuts?" He walked over and tweaked the huge bunny tail. "That is *really* sharp."

"Yeah? Would you wear it?"

"Well, it seems more like a girl's outfit, but if I were a girl I'd sure wear it."

Melinda pursed her mouth at her reflection, black-eyeliner whiskers twitching. "And you won't be embarrassed taking me out trick-or-treating tonight?"

"Jeez, no. I hope everyone sees us."

"Okay." With one of her lightning mood changes, Melinda smiled radiantly and ran over to kiss Caroline's cheek. "Thanks for making the outfit, Mommy."

"You're welcome, punkin pie. And be sure not to eat any of your candy before you bring it home to let Daddy and me have a look at it. And Greg, take—"

"Very good care of your sister. Okay. I won't even steal any of her loot."

The doorbell rang downstairs, and Melinda shrieked, "They've already started! Halloween'll be over before I even get outside!"

"Then let's get a move on," Greg ordered. "Got your sack?"

Melinda held up her bag. "Check."

"Remember your lines?"

"Trick or treat! Thank you!"

"Awesome. The kid's got talent all over the place, Mom."

"I always suspected it," Caroline laughed.

She sat on the bed, watching the two of them race

down the hall, Melinda trundling along in her bulky suit. For just a moment she saw Hayley on her last Halloween, dressed in a clown suit identical to Twinkle's, insistently saying "Treats or tickles" to the bafflement of her and Chris. "Did you teach her that?" Chris had asked. "No. Maybe it was Lucy." Hayley stubbornly refused to tell where she learned the phrase, but it had become hers, repeated over and over as Caroline and Chris trooped up and down residential streets with her, carefully watching as she rang doorbells and begged for candy with her dimpled smile.

And now, so many years later, she was sending another little girl out to beg candy, this time under the protection of her muscular teenaged son. It was impossible for her to imagine so much time had passed. Particularly after recent events.

Two nights before, Caroline had hidden the clown doll and managed to assume a false calm by the time Melinda returned from Jenny's. The child was excited by the broken window and insisted all her stuffed animals and dolls be moved to the guestroom so they wouldn't catch cold or be snatched by the burglar she was sure had invaded the house. Caroline lied. "Someone just threw a rock through the window, Lin. I found it on your floor. Nothing has been disturbed. No one was in here."

"Are you sure?"

"I'm sure."

"Did the police come?"

"Yes," Caroline was able to say truthfully.

"Are they sure no one was in the house?"

"Yes," Caroline hedged again.

"Okay, but I'm sleeping with you."

She was sound asleep in the king-sized bed with

George on the floor beside her when David got home at 10:30. Greg was in his room supposedly doing homework but really on the phone. Caroline sat rigid on the living room couch.

"It's Hayley's," she insisted, holding the doll out to an amazed David. "She had it with her the night she was kidnapped. It was never found, not even with her body."

"Then it isn't her doll," David said firmly. "It just looks like it."

"David, I *made* Twinkle for her. I'm not mistaken. Can't you see how old and dirty this doll is? I'm telling you, it's Twinkle."

"Caroline, you made a lot of dolls like this twenty years ago. I bought one to give to my niece. I think you said Lucy had one. Hell, dozens of people could have a doll like that."

"All the other dolls I made had red hair. Only Twinkle had orange."

"Couldn't red wool turn orange after all that time?"

"Yes, I suppose," Caroline said reluctantly.

"So this doll could be any one of the dolls you made years ago."

"I don't think so. There's something about the facial expression . . ."

David had gently taken the doll from her. "Caroline, you haven't seen Twinkle for a long time. You can't remember exactly what its expression was. Don't let imagination get the best of you."

"But who put that doll on Melinda's bed? And why?"

Finally David had given her a tranquilizer and sat beside her until she fell asleep on the big bed beside Melinda, then went off to the guestroom with the stuffed animals and the dolls. Dear David, who had ended up delivering two babies that day, one of which died, and who had come home to no evening snack and a half-hysterical wife. And now he was standing down at the door in the cold, handing out candy to droves of kids after working all day while she sat brooding about the past. Giving herself a mental shake, she hurried downstairs.

"You go fix yourself a drink. I'll handle the trick-or-treaters," she told him as he was tearing into another bag of miniature Mounds bars.

He smiled. "I just got started. I'm good for another hour yet."

"I said to go relax, and if you don't, I'll throw a tantrum." She took the plastic bag from him. "Now go."

David sighed. "Whatever happened to meek, sub-servient women who never said a harsh word to their husbands?"

"They exist only in Victorian novels." The door-bell rang, and she shoved two candy bars in his hand. "Eat these and watch TV. Pretend you're one of those detectives who drives a sportscar and has a beautiful woman falling all over him."

"I do have a beautiful woman falling all over me."

"Why, thank you, honey."

"Oh, I meant my nurse at the office," David called as he disappeared into the family room.

"On second thought, *you* can hand out the candy," Caroline laughed as she opened the door.

For half an hour she thought the kids were cute and trick-or-treat night a wonderful tradition. During the next half hour she thought the kids were okay and trick-or-treat night a pleasurable event. An hour and forty minutes into her vigil at the door, she thought the kids were a bunch of greedy little brats and trick-or-treat night a mild form of torture for adults. God, what a way to spend an evening, standing in the cold, dumping candy into the gaping sacks of weirdly dressed children who usually didn't even say "Trick or treat," much less "Thank you."

She was snarling to herself after the last child stuck out his tongue at her, when a fresh gaggle of beggars appeared at the door. She emptied her bag of Reese's Pieces and all but three of the children skittered back to the street. "Just a minute—I have to get more candy," she said tiredly, turning to find one last bag of York Peppermint Patties. As she tore it open, a hulking boy wearing a black coat and a Batman mask pushed aside a small child and thrust a grocery bag at her. Stingily she dropped in one piece of candy, staring defiantly into the boy's slitty eyes. He was at least fifteen and as far as she was concerned had no right still to be dressing up. He muttered a curse at her and stalked off. "Cretin," Caroline snapped.

And then a young child, a girl of perhaps six dressed in a clown suit, stepped up to her and sweetly said, "Treats or tickles."

Caroline dropped the bag, sending bright, foil-wrapped treats rolling across the porch and down the steps. The little girl stared, her eyes black diamonds in a dead-white face. "Who are you?" Caroline managed, reaching out for the child. But she moved like quicksilver, whirling and running back to the street, long blond hair creeping out from under her frizzy orange clown's wig. "Trick or treat, dammit." A girl dressed as Madonna stepped in front of Caroline. "And I don't want candy that's been on the ground."

Caroline slammed the door in the girl's face. "David," she whispered. "David!"

He was beside her in an instant. "What is it?"

She gazed at him with wide, terrified eyes. "Hayley was just at the door."

2

Pamela Burke poured a glass of Chardonnay and asked herself for the hundredth time in two days, "Why am I such a bitch?" It was not a question she would ever ask anyone else, but it was a question that had haunted her since she was a child.

She lay down on the flax rug in front of the fire Larry built earlier, before his father called and he'd gone rushing back to the office to check on some mistake he'd made. Which was a frequent occurrence. Larry was not bright. He was handsome and wealthy and stupid. She told Lucille Elder that Larry designed the house, but he was as incapable of such a feat as a child. He was practically incapable even of balancing a checkbook. Still, his father insisted he "manage" the business, even though he bumbled through the work week in agonized confusion and spent most evenings with his father untangling the mess he'd created that day. During the first year of her marriage his constant absences at night had annoyed her; now, two yeas later, Pamela enjoyed being alone in her beautiful house with her ugly thoughts.

Seeing Caroline Corday had really upset her. The woman would always be Caroline Corday to her, even though she was well aware of Caroline's divorce and remarriage, as she was of most things that happened in Caroline's life. She kept a guilty eye on the woman, and it was her distress at actually having

Caroline stop by for a visit that had turned Pamela bitchy, the way she always got when she was upset. "I have a painting by your husband . . . I don't like it, but Lucille says it's tasteful," she mimicked herself aloud. Instead of being flustered, Mrs. Corday had looked at her like she was some pathetic little toad. Her daughter used to look at her the same way.

Pamela had always insisted on going to public schools—they made her feel superior because her family had more money than anyone else's—but she remembered very few of her classmates, even from high school. And why should she, since they were such a boring bunch of braces, pimples, and tacky clothes? But she remembered with searing clarity Hayley Corday from her kindergarten class. She'd hated Hayley. She hated her long blond hair and big blue eyes, the same hair and eyes the princesses in the fairy tales always had. She also hated the way Hayley could draw, making cats and dogs and mommies look like they really looked, not like the unrecognizable blobs that emerged from her own hand. And everyone loved Hayley, even though her clothes were all homemade and she lived in a little log cabin like the one on the maple syrup bottle. The other children were delighted when Hayley's pretty mother and handsome father came to the spring kindergarten picnic, playing ball and hide-and-seek, and then Mr. Corday had given that painting to the teacher. Well, she'd fixed the picture by "tripping" and ramming a knife through it. Mr. Corday had rushed over, more concerned about her than his picture, but Hayley just stared at her, her blue eyes full of knowledge, and Pamela hated her even more.

The fire was dying and Pamela rose, going back to the bar to refill her glass. Then she wandered over to the soaring windows, looking at lights in the distance and the utter darkness hovering over the house like a bat. This was All Hallows' Eve, the night when souls of the dead were supposed to revisit their homes. She shivered, then laughed at herself. Even if she were a superstitious person, which she was not, this was a brand-new house. No one else had ever lived in it, so there was no one to return even in spiritual form. Yet there was something about the house tonight that bothered her, an air of waiting and plotting, as if the house, or something in it, were watching her.

"I'm just spooked because I'm thinking about *her*," Pamela said angrily. "It's just because I'm thinking about that night, that awful night." She stared blindly at her reflection in the window.

It had been the Fourth of July. Annually her parents held a big barbecue on the grounds of their home for the employees of Fitzgerald Electronics, the event being one of her father's few democratic gestures. Both Fitzgeralds had drunk steadily all afternoon, so when night came and it was time for everyone to go to the small park on the riverbank a mile away for the fireworks display, Pamela was sent along with her nanny, Miss Fisher, whom Pamela secretly called Fishface.

About three hundred people had gathered for the event. The night was warm and heavy with the smell of honeysuckle and musty river water slapping against the concrete-reinforced bank. Men sitting out in a boat on the river set off the fireworks. As they burst and twinkled in various shapes across the sky, everybody gasped and laughed and clapped. Everyone except Pamela, who wouldn't wear her glasses and couldn't see anything but bright blurs against the darkness. She was bored stiff and furious with her parents for not attending. They always promised, but they never kept their promises. Not any of them. She viciously dragged the toe of her new pink tennis shoe over the grass, staining it. Not that anyone would mind. They'd just tell her to take better care of her things, then buy her a new pair.

She glanced over at Fishface, a flat-nosed young woman with bulging, red-rimmed eyes who had managed to strike up a conversation with a straggly-looking guy in dirty, patched jeans. Pamela had no use for people who weren't pretty. She made a face at them, but they didn't notice. Stupids. They also didn't notice when she eased away into the crowd and headed for the park entrance. She'd get lost, that's what she'd do. Then Fishface would get in trouble and *everyone* would regret not paying more attention to her. She pictured her mother wringing her hands, her father pacing around shouting that his darling little girl must be found.

She was lost in her fantasy when she reached the sidewalk outside the park gates. As she stepped off the curb, a brown car sped past her. With a tremendous squealing of brakes it slid to a stop inches from the white sawhorses closing off the road construction just beyond. Pamela watched while the driver tried to turn the car around, but the one-way street was narrow with cars parked along either side for the fireworks display, and the driver wasn't very good, because as the car seesawed back and forth trying to make the turn, it crashed into one of the sawhorses. Someone appeared down the street, making purposefully for the car, and squinting mightily, Pamela could see the uniform. A policeman! Before he could get near the car, however, the Person jumped out and ran to him. Pamela always thought of the driver as "the Person" because from what she later calculated to be a distance of about 150 feet, she couldn't tell if the medium-built driver oddly dressed in a hooded raincoat was a woman or a man. Whatever, the Person stopped the policeman and began making gestures, obviously trying to explain things. Pamela inched closer to the car. It was just like her daddy's, which she knew was a Cadillac and expensive. Had someone from the party stolen Daddy's car? She crept closer, feeling very important and top secret. If Daddy's car had been stolen and she found it, she would be a hero. She reached the car and stood on tiptoe, peering into the backseat.

At first all she saw in the glow of a streetlamp was a blanket. Then she gasped as a little girl's face struggled free of the cloth. Her mouth was taped, but Pamela still recognized Hayley Corday, who had been missing for a week. Fishface had read her all the newspaper articles about Hayley's kidnapping and threatened that the same thing would happen to her if she wasn't good. Wow, finding Hayley was even better than finding Daddy's car! Pamela started to call out to the policeman. Then she paused, thinking. If Hayley disappeared for good, Pamela would be the undisputed queen of first grade. There would be no Hayley with long blond hair, no Hayley who could draw perfect dogs and cats, no Hayley with nice parents who came to school and gave the teacher beautiful presents. Hayley's big, terrified eyes begged her to do something—to call out, to open the door, to *help*. But Pamela only gazed back stonily. Then she glanced up to see the policeman walking away and the Person heading toward the car, toward *her*. Her eyes met Hayley's one last time before she skittered back to the park and rejoined Fishface, who hadn't even missed her.

When she learned her father's car had not been stolen, she was disappointed. But three weeks later when Fishface ghoulishly told her Hayley Corday's burned body, missing its head, had been found about ten miles away, she became hysterical for four hours until finally a doctor was called to sedate her. With a child's reasoning, she hadn't considered the consequences of Hayley's being taken away. She had only thought of how much better her life would be if Hayley weren't around anymore. After Hayley's death, though, Pamela became obsessed with both what she had done and fear that the Person would come back for her, thinking she had seen the Person's face. She woke up screaming every night and suffered blackout periods during which she would be found banging her beautiful little head on a wall or a table or the side of the house. For the next eight years she underwent psychiatric treatment, but the doctors were never able to pry her secret out of her. Fear and guilt kept her silent, although she was always afraid that during the nightmares when she talked in her sleep, Fishface had figured it all out. The woman looked at her knowingly sometimes, and for nearly twenty years Pamela had prayed she was only imagining that Fishface knew and would tell.

Something creaked far back in the house, and Pamela jumped, spilling her wine. Just the house settling, of course. She wished she'd made plans to see Rick, the tennis pro at the club she'd been having an affair with since July. If nothing else, she wished Larry would come back. He wasn't entertaining, but he was big and strong, and she felt edgy tonight. She had thought the wine would help, but instead it only seemed to intensify the uneasy feeling that she was being watched. Maybe a tranquilizer . . .

As she started back the long hall to the bedroom, Pamela felt cold air swirling around her ankles. Had she left a window open? Impossible. She hadn't opened a window for weeks, not since the air turned autumn crisp. Stepping into her big bedroom, though, she saw the curtains floating inward. She strode across the room and drew them back to reveal the window pushed high. *Damn Larry!* she thought. He was always doing this. He was such a fresh-air fanatic it didn't matter to him if he gave her pneumonia. She slammed down the window, almost breaking the glass in her fury.

She was tired and nervous and extremely irritable. She ran a hand over her smooth forehead and went into her sea-green bathroom, searching the medicine cabinet for Valium. What would I do without these little blue pills? she wondered, taking one and then another to insure sleep. They were lifesavers. She popped out her contacts and put them in the sterilizing vial, then creamed off her makeup, ran astringent over her face, and followed with eye cream, cell revitalizer, and oil-free moisturizer. Satisfied with her nightly defense against wrinkles, she wandered back to the bedroom.

The room was still cold, and she decided to change into her long fuzzy robe, the one that made her feel cozy, like a little girl. She stripped off slacks and sweater, flinging them on the floor, then stepped into her walk-in closet.

She was flipping through clothes, searching for her robe, when she heard a rustling, like the sound of a breeze whispering through dry leaves. She jerked around calling, "Who's there?" in a high, ragged voice, but of course no one answered. "Who were you expecting? The boogeyman?" she asked herself aloud, trying to laugh off her fear. Really, Caroline Corday's visit had ruined her whole week. Any minute, though, the Valium would take effect, washing through her like a warm, tranquil wave. Then she'd have another glass of wine, maybe watch *The Tonight Show*. But in the meantime, where the hell was her robe?

Hangers grated against the metal rod as she thrust a mass of clothing to one side, furious she couldn't find the robe that always got in her way when she was looking for something else. Then she heard the rustling sound again, only this time it was much closer. Something is in this closet with me, she thought in one frozen instant before her hair was grabbed and her head snapped back with brutal force. Her scream was cut off as a knife sliced smoothly across her throat from ear to ear. Blood spurted forward onto her beautiful clothes. She gazed at the huge red splotches, horrified. Suddenly her hair was released and she fell forward, a puppet without strings. She tried to scream again, but nothing came out. Nothing but blood, gushing all over her hands. Instinctively she struggled to her knees, fighting to escape. She was surprised there was no pain, only shock. Swaying, she slowly turned around, facing the bedroom. She could feel something behind her, waiting to strike again if necessary. Her legs pumped weakly as she crawled while the attacker watched. She toppled sideways, her face scraping against the carpet. God, the blood! It was splashing all around her, and she was getting dizzy.

Ironically, the phone began to ring. She rolled and clambered back up on one knee. Lifting her head slightly she could hazily see the brown phone on the nightstand, shrilling urgently. She dragged herself forward, willing herself across the Bahama Tan carpeted floor that now looked as vast and shimmering as the desert. Maybe by some miracle the receiver would fall off and someone could hear her gurgling through the blood. But of course miracles never happened to her. She didn't deserve them.

At last the phone stopped ringing, but she was hardly aware of it. Her fingers tore into the carpet as very slowly her mind dimmed, finally blocking out the vision of Hayley Corday bound and gagged in the backseat of a maniac's car.

4

"MOMMY, ARE YOU awake?" Melinda whispered in her ear.

Caroline opened swollen eyes to see the little girl holding a tray bearing a cinnamon roll, a thermos, and a yellow chrysanthemum stuck in a clean jelly jar. "Breakfast in bed?"

"That's right. Daddy said you didn't feel so good."

Caroline sat up, taking the dangerously slanting tray from Melinda. "This looks yummy. What's in the thermos?"

"Coffee. Daddy made it. I knew I'd spill it if I didn't put it in a thermos."

"That was very smart of you."

Melinda beamed and circuited the bed to crawl in beside her. "Doesn't that cinnamon roll look *good?*"

"It sure does." Caroline glanced at the child's dark green eyes fastened longingly on the roll. "Why don't you share it with me? I can't eat all of it."

"Well, okay, if you're sure," Melinda said graciously.

Caroline poured coffee from the thermos into the plastic cup. "Where's Daddy?"

"Gone to give someone a baby." Melinda always used this phrase, and Caroline smiled, thinking it sounded as if David went around town fathering children. "He said to tell you to take it easy and he loves you."

"That's nice." She sipped the coffee, which had obviously been made a couple of hours ago. Then she glanced at the bedside clock. 9:30. She hadn't slept this late in-years. "Why aren't you in school?"

"Last night someone broke out all the windows in my classroom. It's *cold* in there." Melinda hugged her arms to her chest and shivered dramatically. "Brrrr!"

"I get the idea. Too bad." Caroline paused. "Was it only the windows in *your* classroom?"

"Yep." This time it was Caroline who shivered, remembering cold air blowing through a broken window and ruffling Twinkle's dirty orange hair. Melinda's bedroom, Melinda's classroom.

Melinda's forehead was puckering. "Do you think the person that broke the school windows is the same one that broke my window?"

"I'm sure it was someone else," Caroline said firmly, hearing the edge of fright in Melinda's voice.

"Maybe it was a poultrygust."

"A what?"

"You know, a ghost."

"Oh, a poltergeist." Caroline frowned. "Melinda, do you believe in ghosts?"

Melinda's eyes widened. "Well, of *course*," she said, as if Caroline had asked if she lived in this house. "Don't you?"

"I'm not sure."

"There were lots of ghosts out last night."

No kidding, Caroline thought. "But not real ones."

"No, but there are real ones, Mommy. It's a true fact." Melinda smiled. "Aurora's downstairs."

"Aurora?"

"My *bean* sprout. Why can't anybody remember? When Daddy drove me to school this morning and someone told us about the windows, he started to come straight home, but I made him wait till I went in to get Aurora. She's in the kitchen keeping warm."

"You've had an awful time keeping your possessions from catching cold lately, haven't you?"

"Well, if somebody would just stop breaking windows!"

"When Aurora realizes how much you love her, she's sure to grow."

"I hope." Melinda licked the cinnamon off her fingers and pointed at the chrysanthemum. "Isn't that pretty?"

"Sure is. Are you going to eat it, too?"

Melinda giggled. "Nope. I'm too full." She looked at her mother. "When Greg and me got home last night you were crying. I heard you. And your eyes are all funny today. What was wrong?"

Caroline's mind flew, searching for an answer. She couldn't tell Melinda she thought she had seen Hayley because Melinda had no idea who Hayley was. Greg knew the story, but she and David had decided it was wise to wait until Melinda was older before they told her about the little girl who had been kidnapped and murdered. She might become fearful of suffering the same fate, and Caroline didn't want her childhood blighted by anxiety.

She was saved from inventing an answer by the ringing of the telephone next to the bed. "Probably Daddy," she said to Melinda. But it was Lucy.

"Caroline, have you heard about Pamela Burke?"

Lucy's voice was too loud and Caroline heard the tremor in it. "No. Has she been in an accident?"

"There was a fire at the house and she's dead."

"Oh, no!" Caroline drew in her breath, thinking. "How did the fire start?"

"Arson. They're sure of it. You see, the automatic sprinkler system kicked on and put out the fire before it really got going. But Caro, that's not the worst of it. Tom was called in on the case," Lucy went on, referring to her lover of two years, homicide detective Tom Jerome. "Pamela was found in the bedroom with her throat slit."

"Good lord! Then she was murdered!" Caroline exclaimed and could have bitten her tongue when Melinda squealed and began tugging at her arm.

"Who got murdered? What's going on?"

Caroline put her hand over the receiver. "No one you know was hurt. I'll explain it all in a few minutes." Then to Lucy. "Do they have any idea who might be responsible?"

"Not yet. Larry was down at the construction company office with his father. He got home to find the house smoldering. He called the fire department from his car phone, but by the time they got there, the fire was mostly out. It didn't take them long to find Pamela."

"What an awful way to die."

"Yeah. But at least she died quickly."

"I'm sure that's not much consolation to Larry."

"I know. I didn't mean to sound flippant." Lucy sighed. "Well, I'd better go. I knew you'd want to hear about this, and I was feeling so guilty I had to talk to someone."

"Guilty about what?"

"About not liking her."

"Just because she's dead doesn't mean she was a wonderful person. Listen, why don't you come over for lunch? Melinda's home—all the windows were broken out of her classroom by some Halloween prankster—and the three of us could have grilled-cheese sandwiches and soup."

"Please come, Aunt Lucy," Melinda chimed in the background.

"Okay. See you around twelve-thirty, if that's all right."

"Great. We'll look forward to it, Lucy."

As soon as Caroline hung up, Melinda's huge eyes grew even rounder. "Tell me, tell me!"

"A young woman of around twenty-five, a woman I used to know when she was a child, was killed last night."

"And it was murder," Melinda breathed.

"Looks like it."

"How?"

Caroline hesitated. She knew children saw so much violence on TV, but having it happen in your hometown was different. Still, Melinda would hear about it on the news. "Her throat was cut. Then her house was set on fire."

"Wow," Melinda murmured. "Has Tom found the killer?"

Melinda stubbornly believed Tom Jerome was the only real policeman in the city and handled all important cases, no matter what their nature. "Actually, Tom *is* working on Pamela's murder. But he hasn't had any luck yet."

"I bet he could use some help. I always figure out the Nancy Drew stories before the end, and I watch *Murder, She Wrote* reruns all the time."

Caroline looked at her gravely. "I'll pass that information along to him. Meanwhile, you can get your magnifying glass all polished up for detecting clues."

Melinda looked stricken. "I don't *have* one!"

"Then we'll go out shopping for one this afternoon. Would you like that?"

"Fabulous." Melinda often imitated Lucy. "But now you'd better take a shower and put on your makeup. You don't look so good."

"Thank you, darling," Caroline said dryly.

When she looked at herself in the mirror, though, she had to agree with Melinda. Her eyes were still red and slightly swollen from crying, and she was unusually pale. Well, that was what makeup was for— for bringing color to white cheeks—cheeks almost as white as Hayley's had been last night.

She closed her eyes. Of course Hayley had not been at the door. Was she losing her mind to have thought so for even an instant? But there was the child, and the doll, and the voice in the storeroom. Hayley's voice. She shook her head and opened her eyes. "You've already had one nervous breakdown, and you're not going to have another one," she said sternly to her reflection. "Hayley was *not* in that storeroom, but something's going on—something I have to find the answer to."

When Lucy arrived a few minutes later, Caroline was already grilling the sandwiches while Melinda stood on a chair to stir the vegetable soup Caroline had made the day before. "This smells extra, extra good," Melinda told her. The child had been knocking herself out all morning to cheer her up, and Caroline felt a violent rush of love for her. What would I do if I ever lost her, too? she wondered, then shook off the morbid thought.

"I could eat a horse!" Lucy announced, hanging over the soup pan. "I was so upset about Pamela I didn't eat any breakfast."

"Pamela is the girl that got murdered," Melinda

said. "Mommy told me and I want you to tell Tom I'm real good at figuring out mysteries."

"I didn't know that." Lucy's voice never held the slightest trace of condescension when she talked to Melinda. "I *will* tell Tom."

"We're going shopping for a magnifying glass this afternoon," Caroline told her, "just in case Tom needs her services. All good detectives need a magnifying glass."

"They certainly do," Lucy agreed. "I know Tom has one."

"Why don't you go with us, Aunt Lucy?"

Lucy frowned. "Well, I left the store one other afternoon this week. I'm not sure I ought to push all the work off on Tina."

Caroline scooped up the first batch of cheese sandwiches. "We don't plan to make it an all-afternoon affair. I just need to get out for a while, and you look like you could use some entertainment, too. Do you think Tina would mind looking after things for a couple of hours?"

Lucy laughed. "She'd probably prefer being alone. I think she finds my methods a bit haphazard. She's a very buttoned-up person."

"She can't be all that buttoned-up if what you told me about her love life is true."

"What about Tina's love life?" Melinda demanded. She had become both curious and proprietary about her idol. "Doesn't she have a nice boyfriend?"

Lucy tried to look innocent. "She has a very nice boyfriend. It's just that she wants to keep him a secret."

"Oh, he's married," Melinda said nonchalantly and turned back to the soup.

Lucy gaped. "Soap operas," Caroline told her. "She knows more about life than I do."

After they ate, Lucy called the store, telling Tina she would be back around three o'clock. "I'm going shopping with Caroline and Melinda. We don't have any appointments this afternoon, so I hope my being gone won't be a problem." Tina was obviously reassuring her because Lucy smiled. "The smartest move I ever made besides starting Elder's Interiors was hiring you. You're not only a genius, but also a sweetie pie." Caroline could just see Tina pulling a droll face over Lucy's effusiveness. "See you later, Ms. Morgan."

Caroline didn't feel like fighting downtown traffic, so they went to a mall about five miles away. The first thing they did was buy Melinda's magnifying glass, which had been Caroline's excuse for getting away from the house. Next they went to an expensive dress shop where Lucy tried on a black-sequined evening jacket ("Wouldn't this look great with jeans?" she asked) and finally settled on a wide-brimmed red hat sporting a feather. Caroline chose a white angora sweater that Lucy pronounced "conservative, but striking," and at last, after much deliberation, Melinda decided on a pink ski jacket and matching mittens.

Not until they stopped for Cokes and Melinda ran over to look at the video games did Caroline tell Lucy about the child who had appeared at the door the night before. "Lucy, she was wearing a costume identical to the one I made for Hayley, and she said 'Treats or tickles' just the way Hayley did."

Lucy looked at her queerly. "I taught Hayley that phrase. It's what my father taught me."

"Chris and I figured it was you. Have you ever heard anyone else use it?"

"Never."

"Neither have I. Anyway, the combination of the phrase and the costume was just too much, don't you think?"

"Well, it *is* pretty coincidental," Lucy said slowly, "but coincidences do happen."

"Not one right on top of another. Monday night after I came home from the movie, I found Twinkle on Melinda's bed."

"Twinkle?"

"Hayley's clown doll."

Light dawned in Lucy's eyes. "Of course! I remember now. She adored that doll and took it everywhere with her."

"That's right. She had it when she was kidnapped. It was never found."

Lucy shook her head. "Caroline, it couldn't be the same doll."

"That's what David said, but it *is*. I just don't understand how it got there."

"Wasn't Fidelia cleaning for you that day?"

"Yes." Caroline saw Lucy's eyes narrow slightly. "Fidelia wouldn't do something like that."

"Were any locks jimmied or windows open?"

"The window in Melinda's room had been broken. I thought someone could have reached through, unlocked the window, and raised it, but the policeman who came out said there were no ladder marks in the ground beneath the window."

"We haven't had much rain. The ground is hard."

Caroline smiled. "Living with a detective is rubbing off. That's what the policeman said. But there's an aster garden beneath the window, and not one flower had been crushed or broken off."

"And there's no other way to reach the window from outside?"

"None."

"Then the only answer is Fidelia. She was in the house, and after all, Caroline, you don't know her very well."

"I think I do. And what on earth could she have to gain by frightening me? But even if she were capable of such nastiness, where would she have gotten Twinkle?"

Lucy jabbed absently with her straw at the crushed ice in her cup. "You're sure it was Hayley's doll?"

"I'm sure. I'll show it to you when we get home."

Lucy was unusually subdued on the ride back. Caroline knew she had upset her even more, but she couldn't help herself. Aside from David, Lucy was the only person she could really talk to about Hayley. Any mention of the adored, murdered child sent Caroline's aging parents off on a tirade ("An *artist!* What self-respecting man lets his wife work while he daubs paint on a canvas? We told you he was shiftless, irresponsible. If he'd been looking after the child properly, this would never have happened"), and she hadn't seen Chris since she ran into him three years earlier at Hayley's grave. And she had to admit she was disappointed in David's reaction. Although he had been gentle and comforting Halloween night when she saw the child, she could tell he thought her imagination was out of control, spurred by grief and the break-in. So she needed someone to listen to her, someone who would take her seriously.

When they got home, Melinda immediately went into the backyard with her magnifying glass to look for clues. "I'm going to find out who broke my window," she told Caroline. "They probably left footprints all over."

As soon as she was safely engrossed in her investigation, guarded by the faithful George, Caroline took Lucy upstairs. "When you see the doll," she told Lucy, "you'll recognize it. You'll *know* it's Twinkle."

Before going to bed the night she found it, Caroline stashed the doll in an old hatbox on the shelf in her closet. When she pulled it down, Lucy smiled. "Caroline, you've had that box ever since I've known you. You used to hide presents for Hayley in there."

"Well, there's no present in there now. There's only—"

The box was empty.

Caroline felt like crying in frustration. "I don't understand. I put Twinkle in here just two days ago. I didn't want Melinda to see it."

Lucy gave her a sympathetic look. "Could David have taken it?"

"I don't think so."

"How about Melinda?"

"If she'd come across the ratty old thing, she would have brought it to me. Besides, she never pillages through my closet."

"Fidelia?"

"How would she know where I hid it?"

"Could someone have gotten in?"

"The locks were changed the day after the break-in, and there haven't been any more broken windows." Caroline sank down on the bed beside Lucy. "I so wanted you to see it so you could verify that it was Twinkle."

"Couldn't David do that? He was around during Hayley's childhood."

"He was around me, not Hayley. He'd only seen her and Chris a few times."

Lucy patted Caroline's leg. "Look, honey, I don't know what's going on, but you'll have to let it go for now. It's making you crazy."

"Thanks."

"You know what I mean. You're wire-tight."

Caroline folded her arms across her chest. "I know I sound nuts, but how can I forget that child Halloween night, finding Twinkle, discovering that Hayley's angel had been destroyed?"

Lucy's eyes widened. "The angel on her tombstone?"

"Yes. I found it on her birthday."

"It was all right that morning when I took my flowers."

"That's what I figured, but by five o'clock the damage had been done." She looked into Lucy's eyes. "Its head had been hacked off."

Lucy winced. "God."

"And that's not all. There was a bouquet of black silk orchids on the grave with a card inscribed in childish printing reading, 'To Hayley, Black for remembrance.' "

Lucy stared at her. "Are you sure about all this?"

"Why do you keep asking me that? Of course I'm sure."

"Do you have the bouquet?"

"Well . . . no. It frightened me so much I bolted away from the cemetery. I went back the next day, but the bouquet was gone."

"No doll, no bouquet."

Caroline bristled. "Maybe the doll isn't here now, but David saw it, too."

"He just couldn't identify it."

"What about the tombstone?"

"Look, Caro, I hate to sound harsh, but Hayley's murder was one of the most sensational news events in this town for the past twenty years. A lot of creeps are wandering around out there. One of them could have torn up the tombstone and put the bouquet on the grave."

"I guess so. But I really don't think—"

Lucy looked away, raking her hand through her shaggy hair the way she always did when she was upset. "Caroline, you've got to get this business off your mind. Let it rest for a while. Let *Hayley* rest."

Caroline was stung. "Don't you think I want to let her rest?"

"Frankly, no. You haven't let go of this thing for nineteen years. You even hired private investigators to look for her *after* her body was identified."

Caroline's eyes dropped. "I couldn't believe she was dead."

"Because you didn't want her to be. But she is. That's the cold, ugly truth. She's *dead.*"

For an instant Caroline felt like slapping her best friend of nearly twenty-three years. Then she felt her anger ebb away. "You're right, of course. She's dead. But there was a doll, and a bouquet, and a little girl at the door looking exactly like Hayley on her last Halloween. I'm scared."

"Then we'll talk to Tom. Maybe he can help you."

"Oh, Lucy, you don't know how much better that would make me feel."

Suddenly Caroline noticed that Lucy looked unnaturally pale and she was distant, frozen-faced. Maybe hearing all this on top of finding out about Pamela's gruesome murder was too much for her. Lucy liked to appear much tougher than she really was. Only

Caroline, and possibly Tom, seemed to realize that beneath the flashy exterior was a fragile being.

"Why don't you come downstairs and have a cup of coffee before you go back to the store?"

Lucy smiled faintly. "Thanks, but I really should be going. I've already been longer than I told Tina I would be."

After she left, Caroline went into the kitchen to make coffee. Melinda had come inside and was in earnest conversation with Aurora when she returned to the kitchen. Telling her mother that plants liked to have people talk to them, she went on unself-consciously explaining to the pot of dirt about magnifying glasses and footprints and Nancy Drew as Caroline sat at the table, staring out over the brilliant chrysanthemum bed. When the phone rang, Melinda ran to answer it.

"It's for *me*," she said importantly as Caroline automatically reached for the receiver. "A friend."

"Oh, pardon me," Caroline laughed. While she drank a cup of strong, black coffee and idly sketched a flower design for the elaborate tablecloth and napkins Lucy had commissioned, Melinda giggled and chattered delightedly on the phone for twenty minutes. When she hung up, she announced, "That was my new best friend."

"Your *new* best friend," Caroline said. "What about Jenny?"

"She's okay, but yesterday she made fun of Aurora, and it hurt her feelings. I don't want a best friend who's mean to plants."

"I wouldn't either. Is your new best friend in your class?"

"No, she's younger than me. I met her last night when I was out trick-or-treating. She came up right after Greg and me left the house and told me how much she liked my costume. She stayed with us for a little while, then she went off by herself. She had on a really neat costume, too. She was dressed like a clown."

Caroline sloshed hot coffee on her hand but ignored it. Slowly she asked, "What is this little girl's name?"

"Hayley."

5

CAROLINE JUMPED UP from the table. "Hayley? Hayley *who?*"

Melinda looked at her with big green eyes. "I don't remember her last name."

"Corday?"

"Maybe. I'm not sure."

"Well, *think!*"

Melinda's face puckered and she realized she was scaring the child. Caroline stooped to enfold her in her arms. "I'm sorry, honey. It's just important that you remember everything you can about your new friend."

"Why? She's just a kid, like me, only littler."

Caroline sat back on her heels and tried to smile. "I saw a child last night who looked like a little girl I knew a long time ago named Hayley. It must be the girl you met last night."

Melinda looked confused. "But Mommy, she couldn't be the little girl you knew a long time ago."

"Why not?"

"Because she wouldn't be a little girl anymore."

"Well, you've got me there, kid. Okay, it couldn't be the same little girl. But I'd like to meet your friend anyway."

Melinda brightened. "Then I'll ask if she can come over and play sometime."

"Good. Do you know where she lives or her phone number?"

"Nope. All I know is that she lives somewhere in the woods in a log cabin."

Caroline tensed but tried to keep her voice casual. "Did Hayley tell you anything about her parents?"

Melinda's eyes wandered around the room as she thought. "She said her daddy paints pictures. I guess she meant he was an artist," she explained with a forbearing smile at her young friend's limited vocabulary.

"An artist." Caroline's heart hammered. "What about her mommy?"

Melinda tugged on a long chestnut curl, furrowing her brow. "I don't think she said anything about her mommy. No, I'm sure she didn't. But I told her about you."

"What did you say?"

Melinda smiled sweetly. "That you're real pretty and sew a lot. She said you sounded nice."

"That's all?"

"Yep. Can I go watch *Guiding Light* now?"

Caroline longed to question the child further, but she didn't want to frighten her. She smiled. "Sure, baby. Later you can tell me everything that happened on the show."

Caroline sat down heavily on one of the kitchen chairs. Could all this be some kind of horrible joke?

Mommy, I need you. Caroline could hear the voice in Lucy's storeroom. Hayley's voice. She put her head in her hands, remembering the months after Hayley died when shock and denial made her think she saw Hayley everywhere. Heard her voice. *Knew* she was alive.

"But this is different," she said aloud. "Before I never found Hayley's doll. My little girl never received a call from a child named Hayley who lives in a log cabin and has an artist father." She sighed. "Or rather *claims* to be named Hayley and live in a cabin. I have to be rational about this. But why would anyone put up a child to doing that?"

When Greg got in from school half an hour later, Caroline pounced. "Did you meet a little girl in a clown suit last night?"

He went like a heat-seeking missile for a platter of grapes, firing about five into his mouth while looking puzzled. Finally he nodded. "Oh, yeah, there was a kid. Well, I didn't really meet her. She came up and started talking to Lin."

"What did she look like?"

"I don't know. She had on a costume and makeup. She was shorter than Lin, so I guess she was younger. They chattered like crazy, but I wasn't listening." He consumed more grapes, gazing at her quizzically. "What's the deal?"

Caroline hesitated, not knowing how he would react if she told him the truth. Unlike his father, he had a tendency to be hotheaded. If he took her seriously, he might go storming off in search of the little girl. No, she would downplay the problem for now. If it persisted, she would tell him the truth.

"It's just that Melinda seemed so taken with this little girl and wanted to invite her over, but she doesn't have any information about her. I thought you might know something."

Greg's dark eyes regarded her skeptically. "Mom,

you're terrible at lying. Want to tell me what's really going on?"

"No. Not now."

"Okay." He pitched the naked grape stem all the way across the kitchen and hit the wastebasket. "I'm ready to listen when you're ready to talk."

Caroline was still smiling as he ambled out of the room and the phone rang. Abruptly her smile faded. Could it be the little girl again? Would she speak if Caroline answered the phone?

Her hand shook slightly as she picked up the receiver. She paused before saying hello, and David snapped, "Melinda, are you playing with the phone?"

"No, David, it's me," Caroline said, letting out her breath.

"Why didn't you say anything?"

"I was—" I was what? she thought. Afraid you were Hayley? "What's wrong?" she asked quickly, hoping she didn't sound as nervous as she felt. "Why are you calling?"

David seemed too distracted to notice she hadn't answered his question. "I've had a hell of a day, and I'm going to be late. Don't expect me before six-thirty."

Caroline glanced at the big kitchen clock above the counter. 3:50. That would give her plenty of time to fix a special dinner to put him in a better mood. "We'll see you then. If you're going to be later, will you call?"

"If I can." His voice softened slightly. "How're you feeling today? Still upset?"

"We'll talk about it this evening. See you later."

She went into the family room where Greg was surreptitiously watching *Guiding Light* with Melinda while pretending to read *Omni*. "Kids, your dad's going to be late. Do you want to eat at the regular time or wait and eat with him?"

"Wait for Daddy!" Melinda piped, too engrossed to look at her.

Greg made a great show of glancing up from his magazine. "Yeah, we'll wait."

But by 7:15 when the stuffed pork chops were turning hard, the baked apples mushy, and the green beans flabby while the kids prowled around the kitchen like starving wolves circling a campfire, they decided to go ahead without David.

"I've probably never been this hungry for five years," Melinda announced, drowning her tossed salad in French dressing. "How about you, Greg?"

"It's been six or seven for me." He smothered a grin. "Mom, you ever been this hungry?"

"I believe one day when I was a senior in high school I was just about this hungry."

Melinda looked interested. "Did you forget your lunch?"

"No, I was on a diet. I believed what the Duchess of Windsor said—that you can never be too rich or too thin."

Greg dug into his apples. "Who's the Duchess of Windsor?"

"Princess Di's sister," Melinda said witheringly. "Don't you know anything?"

Caroline smiled. "No, honey, she was married to the Duke of Windsor, who used to be King of England. He gave up the throne so he could marry her."

"Wow." Melinda was impressed. "Why couldn't he be king anymore?"

"Because Wallis Simpson—the Duchess of Windsor—was a commoner."

"You mean like a pheasant?"

Greg roared with laughter. "That's *peasant,* squirt."

Melinda glared at him, then turned back to Caroline. "Sleeping Beauty was a *peasant,* and she got to marry the prince."

"Well, that's just a story, punkin. Life isn't always like the fairy tales."

"Hayley likes fairy tales," Melinda volunteered, pushing green beans under her pork chop bone where she thought Caroline wouldn't see them.

Greg's eating slowed when Melinda said "Hayley," and although he didn't look up, Caroline could tell he was listening intently. After all, there weren't many little girls named Hayley.

"What's her favorite story?" Caroline asked casually.

"Snow White and the Seven Dwarfs. Only she says *warts.*"

Melinda giggled delightedly as Caroline's blood turned to ice. "Daddy, will you read to me about the Seven Warts?" she could hear Hayley asking Chris. "Who's your favorite? Mine's Droopy. He's the sweetest and saddest."

Caroline's fork hovered between her mouth and her plate. "Does Hayley have a favorite dwarf?"

"I don't know. I'll ask her." Melinda looked at her brightly. "I cleaned up my plate. Is there any dessert?"

"Cheesecake. In the refrigerator."

"Oh, goody!" Melinda dashed across the kitchen to fling open the refrigerator door. Finally Greg's eyes met Caroline's. She would have to explain the situation to him after Melinda went to bed. "It's got cherries on top! Want some, Greg?"

"I'll get it, squirt. You'll drop it."

"I will not!" But Melinda stood aside as Greg pulled the dessert from the shelf and began cutting slices. "Three great big ones," Melinda directed.

"Not for me," Caroline said thickly. "I'll have mine later with Daddy." She got up and poured a cup of coffee while the children ate. A child dressed like Twinkle and talking about Snow White and the Seven Warts. Even if someone *were* playing a sick joke, how would they know about Hayley's mispronunciation of *dwarfs?* Her hands had begun to tremble by the time Melinda and Greg had finished their cheesecake, and she let them escape back to the television without even asking if they had homework. For once she was too distracted to care.

By the time David arrived at eight, the food was ruined and nerves had turned her aggressive and peevish. "Why the hell didn't you call? Dinner's a mess."

David threw her a startled glance as he hung his coat on the coat tree. "I ran into problems. Almost lost a mother, in fact."

Chastened, Caroline said, "I'm sorry. I guess I should have put everything away earlier so I could heat it up when you got in.".

David came over and put his arm around her. "I'm not hungry anyway. What I'd really like is a very large Scotch and water."

"There's cheesecake."

"Some of that, too."

"Cheesecake and Scotch? Now there's a combination."

He laughed. "Forget the Scotch. I might get called out again tonight. Make it cheesecake and coffee."

"Coming right up. Have a seat." While she put on

a fresh pot of coffee and sliced cake, she said, "So the mother pulled through all right?"

"Barely. The foolish thing was seven months pregnant and up on a ladder cleaning windows. She toppled off and fell on a shovel standing nearby."

"My God! And the baby?"

David shook his head. "Gone. It was a girl—a perfect little girl."

"Oh, David, I'm so sorry." Caroline set the cake in front of him, noticing that he looked tired enough to fall down. "By the way," he said, lifting a cherry onto his fork, "wasn't it Pamela Burke you and Lucy went up to see the other day?"

"Yes. I suppose you heard about her death."

"This is great, honey. Yeah, I heard some bizarre story about Pamela being found in a burning house with her throat cut."

"It's true. Tom's on the case. She was murdered."

"Horrible."

"Something else horrible happened today. Melinda got a call from a little girl she met last night, a little girl who was dressed for Halloween in a clown suit."

David raised his eyebrows. "You think it was the kid who was here?"

"I'm sure of it. David, she told Melinda her name is Hayley, she lives in a log cabin, and her father is an artist."

David laid down his fork. "What the hell?"

"*And* she said her favorite fairy tale is Snow White and the Seven Warts. That's what Hayley always said—warts instead of dwarfs."

David took a deep breath. "This is getting very strange."

"I know. David, I'm scared, especially since Twinkle is gone from my closet."

David looked uncomfortable. "Caroline, that's my fault. I threw it away."

"*Why?*"

"It's impossible that the doll was Hayley's. I thought it was some stupid trick of Fidelia's."

"But why throw it away?"

"I don't know. You kept clutching at it. You seemed terrified of it and possessive of it at the same time. I was worried about you."

Caroline sat back in her chair. "You thought I was going off the deep end again, right?"

David laid down his fork. "You've been going on and on about Hayley for days."

"I haven't been going on and on about *Hayley*. I've been telling you what's been happening. You can't deny someone broke in here and put Twinkle on Melinda's bed."

"I saw a broken window and a clown doll, yes."

Caroline stared at him. "That was very carefully worded. What are you suggesting—that *I* broke the window and put a clown doll on Melinda's bed?"

"I didn't say anything like that."

"But you implied it."

"No, I didn't. What's gotten into you?"

"I want to know where you think that doll came from. And don't say Fidelia."

"How can I give you an honest answer if you tell me what I'm allowed to say?" David sighed in irritation. "I don't want to argue with you."

"Well, I want to argue with you." Caroline could feel her cheeks getting hot with her anger. "I suppose Fidelia hired a child to come up and talk to Melinda about living in a log cabin and having an artist for a father, too. Or maybe you think I made that up."

"I think I'd like that Scotch after all," David said,

getting up and going to the kitchen cabinet where they kept the liquor.

"What did you do with Twinkle? Excuse me, I mean the anonymous clown doll."

"The trash was being collected the next morning." David rattled ice into a glass. "After you went to sleep I got the doll out of the hatbox and put it out on the street with the rest of the garbage."

"Great."

"I'm sorry. If I'd known you were going to get this worked up, I'd never have touched it." David sat down at the table again, his expression grave. "Caroline, I'm not saying you're making things up, or that there's nothing going on. There is. But you have to remember how many people thought either you or Chris had murdered Hayley. Even the police were suspicious at first. Of course, they always look to the parents first when a child disappears. They soon realized they were wrong. But probably a lot of cranks out there never stopped believing it."

I know you killed your little girl. Caroline could still hear the hateful voices of women who approached her in the grocery store, a filling station attendant, an old man who had come to their door. There had been letters. *Why did you do it? What did it feel like to cut off a child's head? And by the way, where is her head?* But the phone calls had been the worst. Dozens of them until at last Chris had the phone removed. Lucy told her that to this day he still wouldn't have a phone in his house.

Caroline clasped her hands on the table. "David, it was so long ago. Why, after nineteen years, would all this start out of the blue? And who could know so much about Hayley? Certainly not Fidelia."

"Fidelia knows people who knew you and Chris,

and I think she's a kook not one bit above stirring up trouble just to see what happens."

"I don't know what she's ever done to make you think that."

"I don't know what she's ever done to make you believe in her so much. I'd think after your past experiences with people, you'd be a little less trusting."

Caroline looked at him. He was right, of course. Many years ago the dark side of human nature had shattered her world. She had no reason to trust anyone, especially a woman she'd known for only a year.

David reached over to cover Caroline's hands with one of his own. "We'll get to the bottom of this, honey. I promise."

Caroline tried to smile back, wondering why for once David's calm reassurances didn't make her feel any better.

6

1

THE NEXT MORNING David got an early call and after downing a quick cup of coffee was gone by 7:30. Caroline fixed the kids French toast and sausage for breakfast, then drove Melinda to school. When the child climbed from the car, Caroline impulsively said, "Honey, if you see Hayley today, get her full name and address, but don't go anywhere with her."

Melinda's eyes widened in mild surprise. "I've never seen Hayley here at school."

"How would you know? She was wearing her clown makeup the night you met her."

"Oh, yeah, I forgot. But she's never come up to talk to me. She was only a *little* girl, Mommy. Maybe she doesn't go to school yet."

"I certainly hope not," Caroline said under her breath, then with a bright smile, "If she does approach you, remember what I said. Don't go anywhere with her. Don't go anywhere with *anyone.*"

"Mommy, you've told me that a hundred and ten times. I *won't.*"

"And if anything unusual happens, you run and tell your teacher."

78

"Unusual like what?"

"Oh, I don't know. Just stick close to Miss Cummings."

Melinda was looking at her as if she were crazy. "Okay," she said impatiently. "Whatever you say. See ya later, alligator."

If only I could stay with you, Caroline thought as Melinda turned to blow her a kiss, then skipped through the school doors. If only I could protect you twenty-four hours a day. But protect you from what? I have no idea what is threatening us, much less how to ward it off.

So far she had done the only thing she could at this point by talking to the principal of Melinda's school and asking him to make sure someone kept an eye on the child at all times. "Well now, Mrs. Webb, we always try to do that," he said with an absent, patronizing tone that had abruptly changed when she told him she'd already had one child kidnapped and murdered, and now Melinda seemed to be the focus of another pervert's attentions. "The police are already conducting an investigation," she lied blithely. "I'm sure they'll be concerned with how the school is assisting in this matter."

"Yes, indeed," he'd said, suddenly earnest. "You can count on us, Mrs. Webb."

I'm sure I can, she thought. Otherwise you know you can count on some very bad PR.

After dropping off Melinda she had intended to go straight home, but as she pulled away from the school, she headed south. I'll just drive around for a while to calm my nerves. She told herself this all the way to Longworth Hill, atop which sat Chris Corday's cabin.

She had returned to the cabin only once since eigh-

teen years earlier Chris had taken off for a week with
a young art major from the university. There had
been others in the year before her, and although Caroline cried and railed, she was determined to stick by
the man she loved, a man driven half insane by grief
and guilt over Hayley. But her own emotional state
was precarious, and when after a six-day absence
Chris returned to the cabin, reeking of alcohol with a
stoned nineteen-year-old clinging to his arm, she had
simply walked out, climbed in her ancient Fiat, and
driven to Lucy's. Later that day, deadly calm although her eyes burned and her head pounded, she
had seen a lawyer and started divorce proceedings.
Two days later she returned for her things. Chris had
not tried to stop her. In fact, as he sat on their old
Boston rocker watching her pack, he seemed relieved, and she knew that for some reason she didn't
understand, he had been trying to force her to leave
ever since the body of their child was found.

But now as her red Thunderbird smoothly climbed
the gravel road her Fiat once found almost impossible, those months after Hayley's death receded in her
mind, and she remembered most vividly coming here
after her wedding in the park. A product of the sixties, she had worn a long, old-fashioned dress of eye-
let lace and daisies in her hair. She rolled her eyes at
the memory. But Chris had told her she was the most
beautiful woman he had ever seen, and her happiness
that day was so great she almost didn't mind that her
parents had refused to attend the ceremony, had in
fact cut her off for marrying an unemployed artist. Of
course, this banishment ended five months later when
Caroline discovered she was pregnant. Then they descended with offers for a house in a nice develop-
ment and a job for Chris in her father's real estate

firm. Both had been declined. Chris continued to paint while Caroline worked as a medical secretary for David Webb, who allowed her to stay on the job until two weeks before Hayley's birth, delivered the baby for free, and also continued her salary during her six-week maternity leave. "You know he's in love with you," Chris always told Caroline. "He's steady, affluent—probably the kind of guy you should have married instead of me. He's even single, and there aren't any former Mrs. Webbs to clutter things up." When Hayley disappeared, David offered a ten-thousand-dollar reward for her return and two weeks later doubled it to twenty. It was then people said they'd been having an affair, but Chris had never suffered a moment's jealousy. He had always known she was wildly in love with him, that other men really didn't exist for her. And for a while, he had felt the same about her.

Her throat tightened when the cabin came into view. There it sat, tiny and weathered and unbelievably beautiful. When she shared it with Chris she had kept flowers blooming all around the porch, and it now looked rather forlorn with not even a shrub to soften its crude lines. Still, the lawn was fairly well tended, and wind chimes dangled from the porch roof. New wind chimes, the delicate painted-glass kind she had always hung on the porch. Did Chris replace them every year?

She pulled up in front of the cabin and shut off the engine, climbing out before she could give herself time to think. If she thought, she might turn around and leave. Before approaching the door, though, she did pause long enough to look up the hill to the very top where the Longworth mansion hulked, rambling and ivy-covered, like an old, furry monster. As usual its lawn was manicured within an inch of its life, and even now Caroline could see the form of a woman wearing a flapping black cape and huge sun hat absorbedly wrapping a wire cage around a rosebush. As if sensing she was being watched, the woman's head jerked up and she looked back at Caroline. Old Millicent Longworth, Caroline thought ruefully. Still fighting the forces of nature as if they were a personal insult. During her younger years she had traveled around Europe and the Orient with her brother, Garrison, visiting museums, becoming a professional collector. She came home the year Caroline and Chris were married, the year her father died and she assumed maintenance of the family home and business while her brother remained in Florence with his new wife. In all the years they had lived side-by-side, though, Caroline had never said more than a few words to Millicent. She had been strange even then.

Caroline pulled her gaze away from Millicent and climbed the porch steps. A ragged, battle-scarred black cat skittered off the narrow windowsill as her shoes clattered on the raw boards of the porch. "Hi, cat," she said softly, but the animal was already streaking up the hill toward the Longworth house. Dr. Doolittle I'm not, she thought wryly, but then that cat looked as if life had given it good reason to be wary.

Her rap on the door sounded like a crash of thunder in the quiet morning air. When there was no immediate response, she glanced at her watch. Nine-twenty. Surely Chris would be up by now.

If he was alone.

Caroline felt herself blushing and like an embarrassed teenager was turning to flee when the door swung open. Brilliant, if slightly bloodshot, blue eyes gazed into hers for a moment before Chris said, "Caro? Is that you, sweetheart?"

Sweetheart? Caroline blushed even more and was furious. Chris called half the women in town sweetheart. It meant nothing. "Of course it's me," she said shortly, annoyed with herself and with him. "I can't have changed all that much since you saw me three years ago."

Chris grinned, deep dimples forming on either side of his mouth. He was forty-nine now, and the years of hard living showed in the lines around his eyes and the faint softening of his jaw. But his ash-blond hair was barely touched by gray, his skin was tanned, his eyes were both devilish and caressing. He was still the most devastatingly sexy man she had ever known.

"Don't bite my head off, Caroline. You're the only person I know who time never seems to touch." How she had always loved the lazy, whiskey-edged timber of his voice. This was a mistake, she thought. It was one thing to tell Lucy Chris meant nothing to her anymore. It was quite another to face him. "I'm just surprised to see you," Chris was going on.

"Yes, well, I'm surprised to be here." She jammed her hands in the pockets of her white knit parka. "I hadn't intended to come, but I need to talk to you." She glanced at his naked, muscular chest above slim jeans and bare feet, and her eyes shifted away. "If it's convenient, that is. I mean as long as—"

"There's not a naked woman panting in my bed?" He smiled, clearly amused by her discomfort. "Well, you're in luck, sweetheart. Even aging studs have to take a night off every now and then."

"Please stop trying to shock me. And don't call me sweetheart. I hate it."

The amusement died in Chris's eyes. "I'm sorry. You're right—you deserve better. Come in and I'll show you I can still act like a gentleman."

Caroline didn't know what she had expected to find in the cabin—lava lamps, glass beads, mirrors, fur throws. Instead she found the room she had walked out of all those years before. The same navy-and-red Oriental rug lay on the scuffed pine floor, the same oak hutch displayed Chris's grandmother's bright-blue country crockery, the same white doilies she had crocheted still decorated the arms of a Victorian settee upholstered in yellow brocade. It was all eighteen years older, faded and frayed, but otherwise exactly like the home of their marriage. She could almost see herself sitting on the rocker holding Hayley on her lap.

"Coffee?"

Caroline jerked back to the present. "Sure, if it's made."

"I'm on my second pot. Despite Lucy's tall tales, I *do* get up early to paint."

Caroline smiled thinly, remembering how he had always gotten up with the sunrise to begin work, sometimes not even taking a break until noon. "I had a brief encounter with a cat on the porch. Is it yours?"

He handed her a mug of coffee, black. At least he remembered that much. "Yeah. One night about a year ago I woke up to hear a hell of a cat fight going on in the front yard. I tried to ignore it, but then one of the cats started really shrieking, so I ran out. The other cat was twice her size and had taken off most of her ear and raked out an eye. It was terrible. I woke up the vet although I thought it was useless, but he saved her. Her name's Hecate."

"Hecate? Isn't that some goddess associated with sorcery?"

Chris smiled, nodding. "I figured she must have some pretty strong magic going for her to pull through the mauling she took. I just wish I'd gotten to her sooner that night. But not being around when I'm needed is my specialty." He took a sip of coffee, then went over to the settee, leaving the rocker for her.

Caroline felt slightly stiff-legged with self-consciousness as she took her accustomed place on the rocker. Sitting together in this room drinking coffee and talking, they could be reenacting a scene from twenty years ago. "I also saw Millicent."

"Gardening. She's been at it since seven this morning. She's obsessed. Garrison doesn't seem to share her passion."

"Garrison? Oh, the brother. He was in Italy when we were married."

"He came back about eight years ago. His wife is dead and his health is bad. Heart, I think. So how's David?"

"Working too hard. As always."

"And the kids?"

"Greg is a sophomore. He's very preoccupied with his friends and basketball, which results in mediocre grades. But he's a wonderful boy. And Melinda— well, she's just the most delightful little girl—"

She broke off, realizing how tactless she was being, for Chris certainly remembered another delightful little girl. She took a deep breath. "Chris, I've come here to talk to you about Hayley."

The look of a dying animal flashed in his eyes. "What's there to say, Caro?"

"I don't want to talk about her kidnapping or her

death. I want to tell you what's been going on for the past few days, ever since her birthday."

A deep crease appeared between Chris's eyebrows as she described everything from the voice in Lucy's storeroom to Melinda's call from her new best friend. "David reminded me of all the people who thought we'd killed Hayley. He thinks maybe it's some nut who's surfaced and decided to harass me because of it. That's why I wondered if you've experienced anything odd."

"Nothing. Absolutely nothing. And Caroline, that angel wasn't broken when I took flowers to the grave the night before Hayley's birthday."

"Lucy said it was okay when she was there early that morning, too. It must have happened in the afternoon. There's hardly ever anyone around. It would be easy for someone to get away with that kind of destruction, even in daylight."

"I know. The place has gone to hell." Chris shook his head. "The angel could have been random violence, but the other stuff? No way. And I'm afraid I have trouble buying the idea that after almost twenty years someone has decided to terrorize you over Hayley."

"That's what I said."

"What do you think *is* going on?"

She lifted her hands. "Oh, Chris, I don't know. Whatever is behind this knows an awful lot about Hayley. Too much."

"What do you mean, *whatever* is behind this? What are you suggesting? A ghost?"

The anger that had throbbed so close to the surface recently flashed through Caroline. She stood up. "Don't make fun of me!"

"I'm not making fun of you." Chris stood also,

putting his hands on her shoulders as he looked down into her eyes. "Do you think I could find amusement in anything having to do with Hayley? I just want to know what you think is happening. An honest answer."

Caroline relaxed. "I shouldn't have flown off the handle because I can't say the idea of the supernatural didn't cross my mind. That voice in the storeroom was Hayley's. I'd swear to it. At least I think I would. And that's what frightens me. I know that's impossible."

"Yes, it is, Caroline. Someone is trying to scare you."

"Who, Chris? Who would do such a thing?"

"And why aren't they doing it to me? I was responsible for what happened to her. If I hadn't gone off and left her alone in the woods . . ."

Bright sunlight played over the lines around Chris's eyes. They used to be laugh lines, Caroline thought with a pang. Now they're crow's feet. "Chris, you were knocked unconscious after you left Hayley. How were you supposed to stop what happened?"

"I shouldn't have left her alone to go in search of some nonexistent animal caught in a trap." He shuddered. "You know, sometimes I can still hear that scream. It didn't sound human, but it must have been."

"Of course it was. Someone wanted to lure you away from the clearing. The police went over all this with you. Hayley's kidnapping was planned. If it hadn't happened that night, it would probably have happened another time."

"Part of me knows that. But a bigger part always

says, 'If you were the kind of father that little girl needed, *deserved*, she'd be alive today.' "

"That's my parents talking."

"It's me too, Caroline. She was taken as punishment."

"Chris, this is silly." But the pain in his voice cut through her, and almost unconsciously she pulled his head down to her shoulder, burying her face in his clean-smelling hair as his body shook with a silent sob. "Chris, don't. Please don't torture yourself any more. It's wrong."

"Not wrong. Just useless." He took a deep, shuddering breath, then gently pushed her away. Just like always, she thought distantly. He always pushed me away when he needed me most.

Then guilt swept over her. Why was she so ready to give comfort and love to Chris when she was married to another man, a man who adored and trusted her, a man who would never put her through what Chris had after Hayley's death? What would David think if he saw her here, clinging to Chris?

Abruptly she stepped backward, forcing herself to look polite, distant, in control. "Well, I just wanted to discuss this with you." She made her voice crisp. "Get your opinion. Keep you apprised."

Chris looked at her quizzically before a tiny smile flickered across his face. He knows what I'm doing, she thought as she quickly turned to gather up her jacket. He knows I still care and he probably finds it hilarious after all these years. But his smile disappeared as he helped her on with her parka. "I'm glad you told me, Caroline. And I hope you'll let me know if anything else happens."

"Yes, I will."

She pulled open the front door and stepped out on

the porch where the wind caught her hair and swept it across her face. She reached up to brush it back, but Chris was ahead of her. "I'm glad you didn't cut your hair," he said softly, tucking it behind her ear.

"I did cut it." Caroline's voice shook slightly. "It used to be down to my waist."

"I know. But you didn't cut it short. It's still beautiful."

Caroline remembered Chris pulling her silver-backed brush through its gleaming length, and her throat tightened. "Thanks. Thanks for the compliment and for listening. Goodbye."

He said something but she didn't hear as she rushed for her car, her vision gone blurry with tears.

2

Millicent Longworth whacked off a stray piece of wire with her cutters and smiled as she looked at the neat cage she had just constructed. Yes, a job worth doing was worth doing well, she always said. That cage could stand up to anything but a tornado, protecting the rosebush from the brisk winter winds that swept over the hill. Now, she had only fourteen more to build to protect the rest. . . .

Suddenly she caught a blur of movement to her right, and her sharp eyes fastened on the black cat peering at her from behind one of her rosebushes. She hated that thing with its missing ear and one accusing green eye. It reminded her of something out of a Poe story her mother had read to her when she was a child.

She rose and flapped her cape at it, shrilling, "Get away! Get away!" until the cat fled back toward its home. How fitting, she thought. A maimed cat for a sinful man.

"Millicent!" Garrison Longworth walked slowly across the lawn, slight and stoop-shouldered, wearing brown flannel slacks that hung on him, as if he had recently lost around twenty pounds. Thick, white hair rimmed a shining bald pate, and his periwinkle-blue sweater exactly matched the benign eyes regarding his sister from behind gold-rimmed glasses. "Millicent, who are you talking to?"

Millicent sighed. She'd thought he was safely occupied with his art books for the entire morning and she could finish her work. "That cat of Corday's. I hate it up here messing around my roses."

"You always did hate cats. I don't understand it. They were sacred to the Egyptians."

"In case you hadn't noticed, I'm not Egyptian." Garrison laughed, as usual enjoying her sarcasm, and she looked at him with a mixture of exasperation and concern. "Where is your jacket? It's cold out here."

"Yes, it is. I heard you shouting and just dashed out to see if I could help."

"Well, go back inside now."

"It's time for you to take a break. You've been at this all morning. How about some tea?"

Millicent pushed her sun hat back on her head, knowing it was useless to argue with Garrison. He would stand and nag her until she did what he thought best. "I suppose I have earned a breather," she said in resignation. "Tea sounds good."

Garrison took Millicent's arm as they walked back to the house and through the double front doors. "I'll get the tea, dear," Garrison said. "The kettle is already on. You just relax in the drawing room."–

She laid her hat and wire cutters on a Regency

console table and gazed at her face in the mirror above. Ravaged, she thought. Dry hair, dry skin, sagging eyelids, a pinched nose. Why couldn't I have aged with a little style? Why couldn't I have remained dignified at the very least instead of looking like I clean toilets for a living?

She shrugged out of her cape, letting it fall to the floor, and wandered into the faded splendor of the drawing room. Her mother had decorated it, her mother who hanged herself when Millicent was fifteen and Garrison twelve. Her name had not been spoken in the house again, Father's orders. But Millicent thought of her often, with her heavy dark hair in its sleek chignon, her sad blue eyes, her beautiful voice that had always hummed "Für Elise" so softly you could barely hear it.

"Here's the tea," Garrison said, carrying in a Lowestoft tea service they had bought in England many years before. He poured with the grace of a woman, the same grace he brought to all his gestures. He was the fine-boned, elegant one. She had always looked like a field hand.

"Gar, do you ever think about Mother?" she asked, taking a cup.

He looked up in surprise. "Certainly. Sometimes. More since I've come home. Why do you ask?"

"She's been on my mind this morning." She gazed into her teacup, her heart pounding with the mention of the forbidden subject, almost as if her father might walk in and punish her. But this morning she felt compelled to go on. "Why do you suppose she did it?"

"A lover."

"Gar! You spent too many years with the sophisticated Europeans. Of course Mother didn't have a lover."

"Oh, yes. She was pregnant. Father told me."

Millicent was astounded. "He *told* you! He never told me."

Garrison smiled dryly. "You were a lady. Such matters are not for a lady's ears, or so he thought."

"So mother was caught between him and a lover."

"No, she was caught *by* him *with* a lover, and the paternity of the child was in question. He said he was going to divorce her. Of course he wouldn't have."

"No," Millicent said thoughtfully. "That would have meant family disgrace." She set down her cup and looked at her brother. "Isn't it silly that after all these years we never talk about Mother's suicide? Here you've had the answer all along, and I never knew it."

"It's a subject best forgotten." He held out a plate of cookies to her. "Lido, your favorite."

Millicent absently reached for a cookie, still rocked by what Garrison had just revealed. "Speaking of sex and infidelities," she said, "that so-called artist had a very interesting visitor a few minutes ago."

"Christopher?"

She nodded. "Caroline was there."

"Caroline?" Garrison's broad forehead creased. "A new girlfriend?"

"Do you think I'd make note of a new one considering the string of women he parades in and out of there? No, Caroline was his wife."

"Oh, yes." Garrison dropped a sugar cube in his tea and stirred with a highly polished sterling silver spoon. He had thin white hands covered with liver spots. "I never met the woman."

"She was the mother of the little girl, you know."

"Ummm."

"The little girl who was kidnapped and murdered."

"I know who you mean, Millie. Let's talk about something else."

Millicent shifted in her seat, looking troubled. "I will never forget when that child vanished."

"Dear, if you don't mind my saying so, you're being a tad morbid this morning. Let's not go over all this again. Just drink your tea."

Millicent jiggled her foot. "The little girl wandered up here a few times. But I didn't encourage it."

"I know that."

"I don't even like children."

"I know that, too. Another cookie?"

"But they blamed me. I was hauled in and given a lie detector test." Her voice rose. *"Me,* Millicent Longworth, in a police station being given a lie detector test for something I didn't do."

Garrison was starting to look alarmed. He leaned toward his sister. "It was very unfair. Very embarrassing. But you were completely cleared."

"Not without doubts. I didn't do well on the lie detector test. A shadow has followed my name ever since."

"My dear, you sound like a bad novel. You're also exaggerating. In a situation like that, everyone who knows the child or has come in contact with it is questioned unmercifully. I've read that. I've also read that lie detector tests are notoriously unreliable."

"But I'll never forget it, Gar. I'll never forget the humiliation." Millicent banged down her cup on the table, her hand trembling. "What on earth would Father have said?"

"Father was long gone."

"But the family name was so important to him, and my public humiliation tarnished it."

"Father was a fanatic whose ideas are best forgotten. Don't trouble yourself about what he would have thought. He did drive our mother to suicide, you know."

"He simply threatened divorce. You said he wouldn't have gone through with it. Any man would have done the same."

"I wouldn't have, not with someone as fragile as Mother. If he hadn't treated her so abominably all those years, she would never have taken a lover to begin with."

"She was very unhappy, wasn't she?"

"Yes. We all were."

"That little girl had eyes just like Mother's. Beautiful blue eyes."

Garrison drew a deep breath. "Millicent, I want you to take one of your pills. They'll calm you. Then let's not talk anymore about Father. Or Mother. Or that child. Especially that child."

"Why especially the child?"

"Because old memories are too painful for you. The past is dead, thank God. And you're just getting upset again for nothing." He smiled. "Now drink up. Then you can go back and finish with your roses."

7

1

PAMELA FITZGERALD BURKE's funeral was held Sunday afternoon. Caroline had not even considered attending, but Lucy felt she should be present and Tom wasn't free to go with her. "I know I'm asking a lot," she told Caroline that morning on the phone. "It'll be depressing as hell, of course. And I'll feel like a hypocrite because I thought Pamela was a louse, but I do like Larry, poor dumb sweetie that he is, and I did make a lot of money from them decorating that house. I guess it's only right that I go."

"I agree," Caroline said, dreading the funeral but feeling she shouldn't let Lucy down. "Of course I'll go with you."

So she put on her navy wool suit, warm enough without a coat for the still mild early November weather, and drove to the plush condominium where Lucy had lived for nearly ten years. "People see me and they think of candles stuck in Chianti bottles," Lucy once joked. "But I like luxury. I always have. That's why I stopped painting except for fun. I'm no Chris Corday, and I knew I would never make anything as an artist, not really, and I want to live well." She was living well now, Caroline thought as she stepped into the black-and-white foyer with its dramatic row of stage lights around the ceiling. Lucy had paid as much for her two-bedroom, tenth-floor condo with postage-stamp terrace as she and David had for their four-bedroom house with three-acre lawn. Caroline knew she could never be happy in this elegant birdcage of a home, but Lucy loved its overpriced splendor as a symbol of all she had attained.

"God, I don't want to go to this thing," Lucy moaned, looking unlike herself in an unflattering somber brown suit, her hair smoothed into the semblance of a beauty salon set. Caroline never understood why Lucy, when trying to look conservative, always went the limit to dowdy. "You're an angel to go with me."

"I wish I could say it's my pleasure." Caroline followed Lucy's tall figure down the carpeted hallway to the elevator. "Why don't you slow down? The funeral doesn't start for forty-five minutes."

"But considering all the publicity Pamela's death got, people will be everywhere."

Lucy had figured right. Although they were half an hour early, the funeral home parking lot was already full. They parked far down the street and walked back, scuffling through leaves the strong breeze was lifting from the trees. When they neared the door, Caroline spotted the state attorney general and the president of the city's largest bank going in. How Pamela would have loved the attention, she couldn't help thinking.

People were still milling around the "slumber room" where Pamela lay while attendants brought in more gilt-and-maroon chairs. Pamela's mother, massive in yards of black silk and ropes of pearls, looked more like a Czarina of Russia than a grieving Ohio

mother. Pamela's father stood like a soldier at the
head of Pamela's open casket. Larry hovered at the
casket's foot looking tragically bereft and comically
awkward at the same time.

Lucy and Caroline made their way toward him.
"Larry, I'm so sorry," Lucy said, taking his hand.

Larry nodded, his big spaniel eyes filling with
tears. "Is your boyfriend going to find out who did
this?"

He sounds like a child, Caroline thought briefly.
He was clutching at Lucy's hand beseechingly as if
she had the power to decree Tom's success or failure.
"Tom isn't here because he's working on the case
right now," she said sympathetically. "If it's any
comfort, you can be assured that he won't leave a
stone unturned."

Larry sniffed. "I just can't understand who'd want
to do such a terrible thing to Pamela. She was so
sweet."

Lucy smiled uncomfortably. Then she turned to
Caroline. "This is Caroline Webb. She knew Pamela
when she was a child."

Larry brightened. "You did?"

"Yes, when she was in kindergarten. She was very
beautiful, even then."

"Very diplomatically done," Lucy murmured as
they moved away from Larry.

"I had to say something, and I couldn't very well
verify her sweetness."

"Neither could I. That's why I threw the ball to
your court. But listen, Mr. and Mrs. Fitzgerald are as
hard to talk to as Pamela, and you don't even know
them. Why don't you get a seat and I'll handle
them?"

"Okay," Caroline said. Although she felt sorry for

the parents of any murdered child, she really had no idea what she could say to people she had never met about a woman she didn't like. "I'll look at the flowers first. All the seats seem to be taken."

Although Pamela rested in the largest room of the largest funeral home in the city, every wall was lined with baskets—huge, expensive baskets filled with colorful offerings for the young woman with no friends. Yellow roses, pink glads, red carnations, white lilies. They were beautiful and endless, soaring to the ceiling on racks, filling the room with their heady scents. Feeling a little dizzy from the perfumy air, Caroline walked toward the back of the room where a window was raised about three inches to let in the sharp autumn breeze. A young man was just setting down a chair and Caroline sank onto it, taking a deep breath.

She closed her eyes, listening to the women sitting in front of her. "Well, you know, Edith, her marriage was in trouble," the older one was saying with great authority. "Everyone was aware of her carrying on with the tennis pro at the club."

"I heard it was Larry who was involved with someone else."

A muffled scoff. "Larry? Certainly not. He worshipped that little snippit. Too stupid to know better."

"So you think Larry murdered Pamela when he found out?"

"Possibly. Or maybe the pro killed Pamela when she wouldn't leave Larry. I haven't quite worked out all the details. But in either case, it's a *crime passionelle*. Crime of passion. In France they can get away with that kind of thing."

"Really?" Edith sounded impressed.

"Oh, yes. Even here the killer won't get more than

ten years for it. Of course, someone with the Burke name probably wouldn't get five."

Oh, for Pete's sake, Caroline thought. Can't they wait until after the funeral to sentence the widower? Annoyed, she stood up, intending to go in search of Lucy. Then she saw them nestled at the bottom of the flower rack.

A rich cluster of black silk orchids.

Slowly Caroline knelt, bending close to read the small white card inscribed with round, childish printing:

To Pamela

Black for Remembrance

"My God," Caroline gasped. "Oh, my God."

"Mrs. Webb, are you all right?"

Caroline's gaze jerked away from the flowers to find Tina Morgan standing over her, her lovely face concerned. "No, I'm not all right. I feel . . ."

I feel like I might scream.

Although she didn't say the words, she felt as if Tina heard them just the same. She extended her hand. "Would you like to go outside for some air? It's really stuffy in here."

Wordlessly Caroline took her hand. She pulled up Caroline sharply, and when she blinked at her in surprise, Tina smiled. "It makes me nervous to have anyone kneeling at my feet unless they're proposing." Caroline managed to smile before she let Tina lead her from the crowded room.

The sky that had been clear only an hour ago was

now drifted with dirty-looking clouds, and light had faded from the day.

"Would you like to find somewhere to sit down?" Tina asked.

"I'm afraid there isn't anyplace." She glanced at Tina, who wore no coat over her slim charcoal-gray suit with a bright scarlet scarf tied like a cravat at the throat. She looked sleek and jaunty and breathtakingly lovely. "I'm all right now, Tina. You don't have to stay with me. Go back inside where it's warm."

Tina shook her head. "I don't want to go back in there. I only came because I felt an obligation to Larry. But maybe I'm speaking out of turn. Maybe you liked Pamela."

"Actually, I didn't. Not even when she was a little girl."

Tina turned to her with interest. "You knew her then?"

"She was a friend of my daughter. Well, not really a friend. Just someone she went to kindergarten with."

Tina frowned. "You have a grown daughter?"

Caroline swallowed hard. "No. She died two months before her sixth birthday."

"Oh." Tina glanced at the darkening sky, her black bangs ruffling across her unlined forehead. "My car is in the parking lot—I got here early. Why don't we get some coffee to go and take a drive?"

"I'd like that very much," Caroline said gratefully, not wanting to be alone even though she felt a little embarrassed at showing her distress around this self-possessed young woman.

They climbed into Tina's old Volkswagen, which she drove with astonishing carelessness. As Caroline cringed when they pulled into McDonald's drive-thru and came within an inch of hitting the building, Tina grinned apologetically. "I've always been a godawful driver. If I make you nervous, I'll take you home."

"I trust you enough to go for a drive," Caroline said, wondering if she might not regret her good manners later when Tina piled into a telephone pole.

They pulled away from the window, and Caroline fought desperately to keep her coffee from spilling as they slammed and jerked back to the highway. She had just taken a huge scalding sip, trying to lower the coffee level in the cup, when Tina asked suddenly, "Have you heard about my affair with Lowell Warren?"

Coffee went the wrong way down Caroline's throat. She coughed and looked at Tina's placid profile through her resulting tears. "Affair? Well . . . I . . ."

"You have. I hope you don't think I'm awful."

Caroline's voice emerged stiffly. "I believe everyone's life is his own business."

Tina smiled slightly. "But that doesn't keep you from making judgments."

Recovering from her initial surprise, Caroline spoke more normally. "No, I guess it doesn't." She sipped coffee. "Theoretically I find the idea of adultery wrong. But there are circumstances . . ."

She trailed off, picturing the hard, self-satisfied face of Claire Warren as she'd appeared on local talk shows and news spots, always holding some hapless animal and talking brightly about how animal rights mean so *very* much to her. "I don't think you're awful at all."

"Lowell is a wonderful man. That sounds so trite, but he is. Of course he promises marriage, but they all do."

"Then you'd marry him if he were free?"

"Oh, yes. But he's been married to Claire for a long time. If he hasn't left by now, I doubt if he will at all." There was a trace of melancholy in Tina's voice, and Caroline realized how desperately she wanted to marry Lowell. As if knowing she had betrayed herself, Tina began fishing around in her big purse and withdrew a package of Salems. She shook the pack, caught a cigarette between rose-tinted lips, dug in her purse again until she came up with a silver lighter, and touched flame to the cigarette tip. "Do you still miss your little girl a lot? The one that died, I mean?"

Incredulity and anger rose in Caroline at the heartlessness of the question until she looked into Tina's innocent ebony eyes and realized she was simply blunt, not cruel.

"Yes, Tina. I miss her every day. I always will."

Tina blew out cigarette smoke in a thin stream. "You must wonder why I asked such a stupid question. It's because I lost a child in March."

"Oh, Tina, I didn't know that!"

"No one does except Lucy. I'd rather Lowell didn't know at this point."

"I've only met Lowell a couple of times at parties, and I certainly won't tell anyone else, not even my husband."

"I wasn't married. I had a hell of a time taking care of Valerie, trying to work and be a full-time parent. But we were doing okay. Then she got leukemia." Tina's face was bleak and hard as a stone. "Can you believe it? Four years old and she gets leukemia."

Caroline wished she'd brought a coat. She suddenly felt chilled to the bone. "Why haven't you talked to Lowell about your child?"

"I've lost everything I ever loved in my life. Lowell can be a little old-fashioned, in spite of our affair. This is his first, you know. He might think my being an unwed mother is just too much, and I don't want to lose him, too." Her hand shook as she brought the cigarette to her lips and drew deeply. "Besides, Lowell could sympathize, but he wouldn't understand. He's never lost anyone. He couldn't tell me if you ever get over the pain."

"I wish I could be more encouraging, but you never do get over it. Having someone you can talk with about it helps, though."

Tina rolled down her window and flipped out the cigarette. "I told Lucy, but I don't want to talk about it with her. She's my employer. It just doesn't seem appropriate. After you told me about your daughter, though, I wanted you to know. We share a bond."

"An unhappy one. But I'm glad you told me, although you *could* talk to Lucy, even if she is your employer. I know how much she cares about you."

"She's a very kind person. She took me on faith, you know. After Valerie died I simply walked away from my job in New York City. They refused to give me a reference. That's why I had to tell Lucy about Valerie—to explain the lack of references."

"How did you end up here?"

"I'm from the Midwest. Indianapolis. I had no desire to go back—all I have left there is a stepfather—but at the same time, I didn't want to stay in New York, either, so I picked someplace not too different from home." She reached up and pulled off her right earring of jet and gold, massaged the lobe, and asked abruptly, "What scared you so much at the funeral home?"

Black silk flowers. A note in a childish hand.

"Tina, did you see a bouquet of black silk orchids mixed in with the other flowers?"

"I didn't look at the flowers at all. I just looked at Pamela. She was beautiful. She looked like a much nicer person than she really was. But anyway, you say there was a black bouquet?"

"Yes. It seemed so strange. *Black* flowers. A note reading, 'To Pamela, Black for remembrance.' "

Tina's brows drew together. "That's an odd phrase. It's also pretty sick. But then Pamela wouldn't have won any popularity contests. Lucy couldn't stand her, and you know how forgiving *she* is."

"I know. I don't remember Lucy ever taking such a dislike to a customer. But that bouquet, Tina. I wonder if it came from her murderer."

"If he sent it, he's got a hell of a lot of nerve. That kind of thing can be traced."

Caroline bit her lip. "Maybe. But what really frightened me is that I saw a similar bouquet on my little girl's grave Monday. Same kind of flowers, same message written in the same printing."

Tina drew in her breath. "Good lord. Then you think the person who put the flowers on your child's grave had something to do with Pamela's death?"

"*And* Hayley's. She was murdered, too."

"God, Caroline!" Tina slowed the car and looked at her. "Your daughter was *murdered?*"

"Yes. She was kidnapped. Her body was found a month later, decapitated, burned."

Tina's hand touched her stomach as if she felt ill. "That's horrible. I'm so *sorry.* I can't believe Lucy never mentioned it." She looked back at the road. "Who did it?"

"Her murderer was never found."

This time Tina looked at her in disbelief. "You never had a clue as to who it was?"

"Not really. The police suspected a weird old woman who lived near us, but she had an alibi."

"Then the person who murdered your daughter could still be around," Tina said slowly.

"Yes. This week someone broke into our house and left the clown doll Hayley had with her when she was kidnapped."

"Caroline, I hope you've gone to the police."

"I just found the second bouquet today, and no one believes the clown doll was Hayley's Twinkle, especially since I don't have it anymore. They think it was a similar doll I made twenty years ago."

"You have to go to the police, though. Right away. After all, you have another little girl."

Caroline stiffened. "Yes, I have another little girl," she murmured. She gazed miserably out the window, only slowly becoming aware that Tina had turned off the highway onto a narrow asphalt road leading through a wooded area. "Tina, where are we?"

"The wildlife preserve. Haven't you ever been here before?"

"Sure," she said, glad to turn her attention away from the significance of the bouquets, if only temporarily. "Hard to think that in World War II the whole area was devoted to munitions manufacture."

"I know. At the end of the war they just walked off and left all the buildings to crumble."

Caroline looked at the brooding old boiler house with its leathery ivy crawling up the chimney and broken windows opening to musky darkness. "I wonder if Claire has ever been out here, considering her great love of animals," Caroline couldn't help saying.

Tina giggled. "Funny you should mention that. Lowell was telling me she won't set foot here, even though the local PBS station wanted to do a segment on the place. It's not the most appealing setting in the world and doesn't lend itself to those designer jumpsuits she wears when she's 'communing' with the animals. She insisted on the zoo instead."

"Well, I can't say I blame her. This area has always given me the creeps."

Tina looked abashed. "I'm sorry. I shouldn't have driven clear out here. I'll get you back now. The service is probably over and Lucille will be wondering what happened to you."

Twenty minutes later, when they reached the funeral home, Caroline spotted Lucy sitting in her car. Tina jolted up, and after thanking her for the ride, Caroline rushed over to Lucy's Corvette.

Lucy looked both annoyed and alarmed. "Caroline, where have you been? I was just about to go to a pay phone to call David."

"I'm sorry. I know I shouldn't have deserted you, but something happened."

"What?"

"Remember my telling you about the bouquet of black silk orchids on Hayley's grave? Well, there was a bouquet just like it at Pamela's funeral. And the message said, 'To Pamela, Black for Remembrance.' "

Lucy stared at her. "Caroline, are you sure?"

"Yes, I'm sure. I want to see Tom. Can you take me to the police station?"

Lucy lifted a quieting hand. "Caro, don't get all haughty with me because I asked a perfectly natural question. Of course you don't have to go to the police station to see Tom. He'll be home in about an hour. You can talk to him there."

2

Lucy and Tom had been living together for nearly two years. Although seven years her junior, Tom was anxious to get married. It was Lucy who dragged her feet. "I'm forty-eight, Caro," she always said. "I can't give him children."

"Lucy, he *has* children. And a very nasty ex-wife. Is that what's bothering you?"

"Marian? Heavens no. The woman lives in Chicago and he never even sees her—why should I worry about her?"

"Well, something's holding you back. And one of these days, I'm going to get you to tell me what it is."

One of these days had never come, but Tom and Lucy lived on quite happily, although he fussed about her elaborate apartment. "I'm a detective on the police force, for God's sake," he would laugh, "and I live in a place that looks like a sex goddess's dream."

But Lucy ignored him, knowing he admired her taste and got a kick out of the apartment with its movie-land glamour. Long black couches and ebony tables were reflected over and over in soaring mirrors, and even if the snow-white carpet was a pain to keep clean, it was unbelievably sumptuous, exquisite under bare feet. A black-and-gold-lacquer Chinese screen hid a bar, at which Lucy now stood pouring three brandies while Tom talked quietly with Caroline.

"I read the report on your breaking and entering. It

said that aside from the broken window, the intruder left no traces."

"Except for the doll." Caroline looked into Tom's long face with its narrow, high-bridged nose and stone-gray eyes. Those eyes had put her off when she first met him—they looked frighteningly cold and analytical. They could still look that way to her, especially when he was concentrating or thinking about a case, but she now knew there were other times when they softened and darkened with kindness, concern, or even love, as they did when focused on Lucy. She liked Tom and she knew he was an excellent policeman, and in fact had been something of a whiz kid who would go to the top fast. She felt calmer just telling him about the events of the past few days, sensing she had his complete attention. There was nothing patronizing or dismissive in his manner. "I just don't know how someone could have propped a ladder against the house and climbed in that second-floor window without the neighbors seeing him," Caroline went on.

"You have neighbors on all four sides?"

"No. The house across the street has been vacant for about five months."

"How about the other three?"

"All occupied, but the next-door neighbors on the right both work. Neither one was home. The wife in the house on the left was around, though. She didn't see anything. Neither did the old couple who live in the house on the next street. Their backyard adjoins ours, and the man was outside raking leaves most of the afternoon. I don't know how he could have missed someone climbing in the back window."

"Is it possible someone had a key to your house? How about your cleaning lady—what's her name?"

"Fidelia Barnabas."

"Lucy says she's pretty strange."

"But she isn't. Oh, she reads Tarot cards and knows a lot about the occult, but I think it's all for fun. Besides, she didn't have a key to the house, and even if she did, she wouldn't have needed it if she was already alone there. And where would she have gotten Twinkle? That's the part everyone seems to ignore. It was Hayley's doll on the bed."

Tom took the brandy glass Lucy silently offered and swirled the liquid around the sides for a moment. "Lucy tells me you made the doll for Hayley."

"Yes."

"But you also made other ones."

"Similar, but not exactly like Twinkle. The hair was a different color. And Twinkle's smile was bigger."

"Are you sure about Twinkle's smile after all these years?"

"Yes, I am. Now who could have had that doll except Hayley's murderer?"

Tom looked sympathetic. "Supposing that it *is* Twinkle and not one of the others you made, a lot of people could have it. It could have been lost before the kidnapper got out of town with Hayley. It might have been floating around the area for years."

"I never thought of that." Caroline frowned. "But why would someone keep the doll for so long before putting it in my house?"

"Crazies have a logic of their own, Caroline."

"I guess so." Caroline sighed. "Do you have any leads on who murdered Pamela?"

Tom shook his head, his high cheekbones catching the light from a hanging crystal globe above an end table. "Nothing, Caroline. We do know the fire was started with kerosene and that Pamela's throat was cut with a four- to five-inch serrated blade. Probably a kitchen knife, which makes it practically impossible to find. The throat was cut from left to right, meaning the murderer was right-handed. Both the carotid artery and the jugular vein were cut as well as the vocal cords. It shouldn't have taken her long to bleed to death—maybe a couple of minutes tops. We found blood all over the clothes in her closet and several hairs—all Pamela's—so I'd say she was grabbed by the hair from behind in there."

"Good heavens," Caroline breathed. "Someone waiting in the closet for her. It's like a horror movie."

"Very theatrical, especially considering that the killer sprinkled kerosene all over the bedroom, then started the fire with kerosene in the living room, which is at least a hundred feet away from where her body lay."

"Maybe the killer wanted you to discover that Pamela's throat had been cut," Lucy volunteered, sitting cross-legged on the floor, her high heels discarded beside her.

"Then why start the fire at all? Especially when the automatic sprinkler system must have gone off as soon as the smoke started?"

Lucy smiled. "My point exactly. The killer didn't want Pamela's body destroyed. The fire was a symbolic act."

Tom looked at her admiringly. "Lucy, you're great. Would you like to work with me?"

"Yes, but I know you're just buttering me up. You can't tell me you hadn't already figured that out." She looked at Caroline. "He does this to me all the time. He wants to make sure I'm as smart as I should be."

Tom grinned. "You are, don't worry."

Caroline smiled absently at their teasing, but she couldn't throw off her own anxiety. "Tom, do you think the flowers prove there's a connection between what's been going on with me and Pamela's murder?"

"You have to keep in mind that Pamela was almost universally disliked, and apparently she was involved with someone else. Neither Larry nor Rick Loomis— the guy she was involved with, who by the way has an assault record—are out of the picture as suspects. Still, I wish we had both bouquets so we could compare the handwriting."

"I went back to Hayley's grave the next day, but the flowers were gone."

"All of them," Lucy asked, "or just the orchids?"

"Just the orchids."

"That's pretty suspicious in itself," Tom said. "Tell you what—I'll go out to Pamela's grave tomorrow and see if I can find the second bouquet. At least that way we'll have a sample of the handwriting. Then all we have to do is find the florist the flowers came from and we'll be able to find out who sent them."

"If they were artificial flowers, they might not have come from a florist," Lucy pointed out.

Caroline nodded. "She's right, Tom. There was nothing professional about the flower arrangement. It was just a bunch of silk orchids tied with a black velvet ribbon. A child could have done it."

"Well, you can bet a child didn't do it," Tom said grimly. "Just think about the message: *Black for remembrance*. That's not a child's phrase."

"No, definitely not," Lucy said, then she looked at Caroline. "What is it? What's wrong?"

"I just thought of something." Caroline's face felt stiff with shock. "The phrase. It's wrong. The color is wrong."

Tom leaned forward. "Tell us what you mean."

"For Hayley's fifth birthday we got her a kitten. Shadow. It died. She was broken-hearted and Chris gave it a real funeral. He even put a bunch of violets on the grave. 'Violet represents nostalgia and memories,' he told Hayley. 'It's the color for remembrance. So every year we'll put violets on Shadow's grave to let him know we remember him.' "

"So that's why Chris puts violets on Hayley's grave," Lucy said slowly.

"Oh, my lord," Caroline murmured.

Tom looked at Caroline intently. "I know where you're going with this, but forget it. Hayley was five years old when Chris told her that. Five-year-olds don't understand concepts like nostalgia."

"But they understand remembering."

"Okay, maybe. But so do a lot of people. They also know elementary color symbolism like black for death, and black is the color mentioned in the phrase, not violet."

Later, as night shut out the gray dreariness of the day, Lucy curled her naked body closer to Tom's in the king-sized bed. "I didn't have your full attention a few minutes ago."

Tom stroked her disheveled hair. "Sorry."

"Something on your mind."

"Caroline."

"Wonderful."

Tom laughed the deep, joyous laugh that first attracted her to him. "I didn't think I could make you jealous anymore. But there's nothing to worry about. My thoughts were strictly those of a policeman."

"Do you think something serious is going on?"

"Don't you?"

"I'm not sure. There was a time after Hayley's murder when she wouldn't believe Hayley was really dead."

"Well, I can understand that reaction. If you had children, you might know—" Lucy stiffened and Tom said quickly, "Sorry, honey."

"It's all right." Lucy's voice sounded small and far away.

"I'm an insensitive jerk."

"I know," Lucy said with a hint of laughter. "It's not your fault. You can't watch every word you say. I wouldn't be so touchy if I hadn't almost had a child of my own."

"Don't think about it."

"One foolish decision. One hour in a quack's office and I'm maimed for life."

"You were in an impossible situation. You did the noble thing."

"Noble? How can you call an abortion noble?"

"Sometimes I think it is. In your case it was. How could you have known how it would turn out?"

Tears dragged mascara down Lucy's face, and she wiped them impatiently away. "Oh, well, water over the dam or under the bridge or wherever bad water goes." She laughed shakily. "So what about Caroline?"

Tom was silent for a moment. "I'm not convinced all she's telling us is accurate. No one else has seen any black bouquets, and only she insists the clown doll was Twinkle. Still, we can't forget what happened to her first daughter. Since the killer was never found, he might have been waiting for a second opportunity."

"A second opportunity?"

"I didn't want to say this to Caroline, but it's highly unlikely that some person not connected with Hayley's kidnapping found the doll and is now using it to frighten her. If it really was Twinkle Caroline found on the bed, it's probably been in the hands of the murderer all along."

"So why would he surface now?"

"Who knows how his mind might work? Maybe it has something to do with Melinda being only two years older than Hayley when she was killed."

Lucy raised up on one elbow. "Tom, you don't really think someone is after Melinda, do you?"

"I don't know. But it's better to be safe than sorry. I'm going to assume that Caroline isn't imagining anything and look into it."

"Why you?"

"I can't take it to someone else because we don't have one shred of concrete evidence to link what's been happening to Caroline with Pamela's murder. Hell, we don't even have any concrete evidence of what's been happening to Caroline except for a broken window."

"So where will you start?"

Tom went silent again and Lucy could almost feel his brain racing the way it always did when grappling with the intricacies of a case. "I'm going to start at the beginning—with Hayley Corday's kidnapping."

3

I wish we had both bouquets so we could compare the handwriting.

Tom's words played over and over in Caroline's mind as she tossed in bed, struggling for sleep. She couldn't stop thinking about the flowers. So far she had no proof of anything that had been happening—no Twinkle, no flowers. She needed the black bouquet, and although Tom said he would stop by the cemetery tomorrow and look for it, she wondered if it would still be there. After all, the flowers on Hayley's grave had disappeared by the next day.

She could get them herself. She glanced at the clock: 12:20. So late to go to a cemetery. Still, if this bouquet vanished, she might lose credibility in Tom's eyes.

David was sleeping deeply. Quietly she slipped from bed and put on jeans, a heavy cable-knit sweater, and Reeboks. As she went down the hall she looked in on Greg and Melinda, both of whom were sleeping soundly, Greg sprawled over three-fourths of his double bed, Melinda rolled into a tight ball by George's side. The dog raised his head as Caroline opened the door, and when she motioned to him, he got up and jumped from the bed light as a cat. Once in the hall, Caroline turned to him. "You know you aren't supposed to sleep on the bed," she whispered. "But we'll talk about that later. Right now I need for you to go with me."

Down in the kitchen she found the flashlight, zipped up her parka, attached George's leash, and locked the door behind her. She didn't leave a note for David. The cemetery was not far away, and with any luck, she would be back before he noticed she was gone.

George happily took his place on the bucket seat beside her, clearly thrilled at the prospect of a trip. His tongue lolled and he peered curiously out the window, his nose leaving smears, as they drove along deserted streets. When they reached the cemetery, Caroline saw the big wrought-iron gates standing open and realized she hadn't even considered the prospect of being locked out, although Rosemont was the most expensive and well-protected cemetery in the city—a far cry from the shabby place where Hayley rested. She drove slowly through the gates, unhappily spotting the small brick guard booth to her right. A light glowed inside, but no uniformed man stepped out to ask what business she had in the cemetery at this hour. Well, maybe he was making rounds or something, if cemetery guards actually did that kind of thing. Or maybe he had a television inside that had captured his attention. Whatever the case, she was glad she could slip past and quickly lose herself in the cemetery's rambling, hilly acres.

Because she and Lucy had not come to the gravesite earlier in the day, she wasn't sure where Pamela was located, although she had a feeling it would be in the "new" section since both the Fitzgeralds and the Burkes had come to the city within the last forty years. She drove around the maze of asphalt streets, looking for the masses of flowers that always indicated a fresh grave. When she finally spotted one, she got out, George by her side, and by the glow of the flashlight wended her way through the carefully tended grass only to find the new grave belonged to a member of the Mathis family. "Wrong place," she muttered to George. "Back to the car, boy."

Worrying about running into the cemetery guard,

still she drove around for ten more minutes before she located another possibility on a slope near the back of the cemetery. She could not park near it and momentarily lost sight of it when she turned off the lights and got out of the car. The flashlight had not really been necessary earlier, but black gauze clouds had edged across the moon, and she was in almost total darkness. Even the flashlight beam seemed feeble, and she wondered if the batteries were about to go dead. They couldn't have chosen a more suitable place, she thought as she started up the hill, trying not to step on graves. George trotted beside her, her guardian against the night, and she couldn't help talking to him just to shake off the sudden uneasiness she felt.

"This isn't the way I'd planned to spend my evening," she informed him. "I feel like a grave robber." His ears went up and down as she talked, and he raised his head to lick her hand. "Just a couple of ghouls, that's us, George. Well, let's see. I think the grave was up here to the right."

She flashed the beam around and found a mountain of fresh flowers. "Now if this isn't it, I'm going to give up. I don't like it here. I feel like someone's watching us. But that's silly. There's no one else around. Cemeteries usually don't draw midnight crowds."

Her voice sounded thin and frightened, and she was disgusted with herself. There was nothing scary about the darkness. There was nothing scary about the cemetery. It was a beautiful place, calm and quiet.

And full of dead people.

"Caroline, you are an idiot," she told herself sternly as she picked out the name on the towering

headstone rearing over the grave. *Fitzgerald.* So
Pamela had been buried with her family, not Larry's.
Well, she wasn't surprised. From everything she'd
heard, Pamela had not truly been committed to Larry
or anything connected with the Burke family except
its money.

"Okay, George, we've found the spot. Now all we
have to do is find the black orchids."

Hundreds of flowers. Thousands of flowers. Had
anyone except a national figure commanded such a
tribute of flowers? Caroline wondered. She knelt,
shining the flashlight over the baskets heaped on
the grave. Flowers on top of flowers shriveling in the
sharp night air. Leaning forward onto her knees, she
sorted through them, starting at the head of the grave
and working toward the foot, trying to be methodical.
Glads and lilies and roses. Carnations and tons of
baby's breath. Even white and purple orchids. But no
black silk ones.

"Damn," Caroline muttered, sitting back on her
heels, her hands reeking of floral scent. Could the
bouquet have been left behind at the funeral home,
discarded as inappropriate? But if that were the case,
why had they been displayed at the funeral home?
She crawled forward, determined to rummage
through the pile one more time.

And then George began to growl.

The sound started deep in this throat as his ears
perked to attention. "What is it, boy?" Caroline
asked shakily, following his gaze to the top of the
slope where a huge oak reared against the black sky.
"Is someone up there?" Maybe the guard, she
thought nervously. George's eyes narrowed and the
hair on his back raised. Caroline grabbed his leash

and stood. "Come on, George, back to the car," she ordered.

The dog remained at rigid attention, the growl deepening until it seemed to shake the ground. If it were the guard, Caroline reasoned, he would certainly have shown himself by now. The dog tensed. "George, *please,*" Caroline wailed with an abrupt, blinding fear.

Suddenly he jerked away from her and ran up the hill. She could barely see his shape pausing by the tree. Then he sat down, threw back his head, and howled. It was a chillingly mournful sound that cut the night like a death cry.

"My God, George," Caroline gasped. "George, come! Come right this instant!" The dog bayed on, ignoring her. Caroline was beginning to feel as if she couldn't get her breath. "George, I'm leaving." She backed away. "I'm going now. Go *home.* I'm going *home.*"

George knew the word *home.* He stopped in midhowl, hesitated, then bounded down the hill and jumped up, planting his big paws on her shoulders. "Good boy!"

She grasped his leash and slipped the loop around her wrist, determined not to let him get away again. "C'mon. We've got to get back to the—"

As the dog dropped down, Caroline looked with horror at the smears on her pale jacket. In the moonlight they looked inky, but she knew they were blood.

She went limp with shock, and George took advantage of her momentary weakness to drag her up the hill. Her wrist was trapped by the leash and she couldn't get free. She stumbled once on the damp grass and heard herself sob as she clambered back to her feet, but George was eighty pounds of relentless will and muscle. He didn't stop until he had deposited her at the base of the tree.

So it was the cemetery guard after all, she thought distantly. He lay across the gnarled roots, the front of his uniform shirt soaked with blood.

8

~

1

LATER CAROLINE WAS amazed at how calmly she knelt and took the man's wrist, feeling the faint pulse. By now George was quiet, and she left him, alert and protective, while she ran down the hill to the car and drove to the guard booth.

Lights blazed inside. A small color television blared and she turned it off, reaching for the black phone on the long, cluttered metal table. As soon as Tom said hello, she realized she should have called 911 instead. But calling Tom had been instinctive.

"Tom, it's Caroline." Her voice was friendly and controlled. "I'm sorry to wake you and Lucy."

"Lucy's at her mother's. What's wrong?"

"I'm at Rosemont Cemetery, and I found the guard up on the hill where Pamela Burke was buried. He's either been shot or stabbed in the chest, I can't tell which."

After a beat of silence, Tom asked, "Is he dead?"

"No, but he's unconscious, and there's a lot of blood."

"You're in the guardhouse?" Caroline nodded. "Are you in the guardhouse?"

"Oh, yes."

121

"Don't go back to him. Stay where you are. I'll be right there."

Caroline suddenly felt her knees weakening. She sat down on the padded metal chair, absently noting the pornographic magazine spread on the table, the half-empty bag of Oreo cookies, the drip coffee maker with murky, strong-smelling dregs sizzling in the pot. She turned it off and closed the magazine, then wondered if she should have touched anything. But the guard hadn't been injured in here, and it was unlikely the attacker had come by to leave finger-prints on the magazine before leaving.

She glanced at the black wall clock. 1:22. Had she left home nearly an hour ago? What if David had awakened to find her missing?

Guiltily she reached for the phone again. After three rings, David answered groggily. "Caroline? Is that you?"

"David, I'm sorry. I only expected to be gone a few minutes, but I'll be longer."

"Why? Do you know what time it is? Where *are* you?"

"I'll have to tell you later." She heard a siren in the distance. "Bye."

He was still sputtering on the other end when she hung up, but she couldn't worry about explaining herself to him now. Already the EMS ambulance was pulling up. She ducked out of the guard booth and headed for her car, calling, "Follow me."

The driver had shut off the siren, but the red light still twirled in the darkness, throwing lurid color over the tombstones. The excitement had set off George again, and when they arrived at the hill, he was howl-ing like the Hound of the Baskervilles. The paramedics glanced at him warily. "It's my Labrador," Caroline said. "He won't hurt you."

One young man looked skeptical. "Would you mind getting him under control, lady, so we can work?"

"Certainly." Caroline climbed the hill with them and, not looking at the blood-drenched guard, took hold of George's leash. He went back down the hill easily.

Two uniformed policemen had arrived by then. One was taking her name and address when Tom pulled up. He jumped out of the car, his hair awry above a faded red Ohio State sweatshirt and jeans. "Caroline, are you all right?"

"Yes, but I'm awfully glad to see you!" By now nervous reaction was setting in full-force. Her voice trembled and Tom took her arm, leading her to her car. When he opened the door, George jumped in and Caroline sat sideways on the front seat, looking out at Tom and the officers.

"Are you going to faint?" one of them asked.

Caroline smiled. "Sometimes I shake, but I never faint. I'm okay."

"Can you tell us what you were doing out here, ma'am?" the other one asked, poised to write in a black notebook.

"I know what she's doing here," Tom said quickly. "Caroline, just tell us about finding the guard."

"I was at Pamela's grave, searching through the flowers." She saw a look pass between the two officers. "Then George started growling. He ran up to the tree and howled, time after time. I called for him to come. When he did, he jumped up on me and left blood on my jacket. I had my hand tangled in his leash, and when he ran back up the second time, he dragged me along."

"The guard was unconscious then?"

"Yes."

"Did you see or hear anything?"

"Nothing, Tom. But when I was in the guardhouse, I could tell that the coffee had been on the burner a long time. The pot was just about dry, as if most of the coffee had evaporated."

"So you think this could have happened quite a while ago."

"Well, certainly not within the last half hour. When I got here there was no sign of him in the guard house, and I never saw his car while I was driving around looking for Pamela's grave. He must have one, though. He couldn't patrol this whole place on foot."

Tom turned to one of the officers. "Would you go up and find out what they know about his condition? And see if you can find his car." Then he looked back at Caroline. "What time did you get here?"

"I'd say about twenty till one."

"And you drove all around the cemetery looking for the grave?"

"Only around the new section. I didn't think the Burkes or Fitzgeralds would have plots in the old section. That's taken up with families who have lived in town since before World War II."

Tom grinned. "You know, with you and Lucy around I feel like turning in my badge. You've made some very good deductions, especially considering the circumstances."

"I don't feel very smart. I feel like a fool, out here rambling around with a possible killer loose."

"You shouldn't have been out here. I told you *I'd* look for the bouquet."

"I didn't want to wait. You know the day after I found the bouquet on Hayley's grave it vanished." She paused. "And if the second black bouquet is on Pamela's grave, I couldn't find it."

"That's too bad."

Caroline looked at him sharply. "I know what you're thinking: there was no bouquet to begin with."

"I didn't say that."

"You didn't have to. But Tom, you can't deny one thing: that guard was shot near Pamela's grave. Maybe the person who sent the black bouquet came back to get it."

"And was discovered by the guard."

"Yes."

Caroline couldn't read Tom's expression before he looked at the officer coming back down the hill. "The guard's car's on the next street over," he told Tom.

"I didn't make it that far back," Caroline said. "That's why I didn't see it."

Tom nodded. "And the guard?"

"They got the bleeding stopped and started an IV, but the guy's still unconscious."

"What happened to him?"

"Shot in the chest. And it looks like by his own gun. It's missing."

2

Three days later Tom Jerome was convinced of one thing: the Hayley Corday case had suffered from some pretty sloppy police work. In spite of Millicent Longworth's abysmal lie detector test results, there was no concrete follow-up. In addition, little or no investigation had been done on the backgrounds of anyone who came in contact with the child, and glaring leads had been dropped for no good reason. For instance, a week after Hayley's disappearance a woman named Margaret Evans had seen a child fitting Hayley's description lying in the back of a Cadillac parked at a roadside rest outside of Chillicothe. The woman claimed she pecked on the Cadillac's window, but the child did not stir, leading Mrs. Evans to believe the little girl was drugged. Harry Vinton, the detective from juvenile in charge of the investigation, had dismissed the woman as a nut, claiming she was always reporting that she had seen missing children. However, Tom's research revealed no similar calls by Mrs. Evans. On impulse, he called the number listed for the woman, certain that in twenty years she would have moved. His heart leaped when a young woman answered, saying her mother was indeed Mrs. Margaret Evans, and although she was out of town now, she would probably be returning by Friday. After hanging up, Tom decided to do a little digging on Harry Vinton.

"Sure, I remember him," Al McRoberts, once on Juvenile and now on Homicide, told him. "Damn good cop until the drinking got to him. He retired, oh, let's see, seventeen-eighteen years ago, long before you came."

"A good cop, you say."

"Yeah." Al frowned. "Good because he was smart and he liked to show it. I mean, I know you can't get personally involved with cases or you'd lose your mind, but every one of them rolled right off Harry's back. No personal reaction whatsoever. Each case was like a puzzle to him, and he wanted to prove he could solve the puzzle. Aside from that, it meant nothing to him." He smiled crookedly. "How's that for a little dime-store analysis?"

"Interesting. Do you remember the Hayley Corday case?"

Al stared off, his prematurely aged face pale in the harsh morning sun. "Daughter of the artist, right? Killer cut off the head and burned the body?" Tom nodded. "I wasn't working on that one, but it does seem to me I thought Vinton wasn't showing his usual bulldoggedness about the whole thing."

"What do you mean?"

"Just that as I recall, he let that one go pretty quick after the kid's body was found."

"It was a Homicide matter then."

"I know, but that never stopped Harry before. Like I said, he loved attention. A prima donna. Normally he would have stayed with it, even on his own time, just to show he could solve the murder when no one else could."

"Didn't anyone think that was strange?"

Al rubbed his hand across his chin in thought. "Yeah, but we attributed it to him being all torn up over his wife at the time." Tom raised an eyebrow. "Oh, hell, what was her name? Something made up. She acted in a lot of local plays and seemed to think she was headed for stardom."

"I assume she didn't make it."

Al laughed. "Never stood a chance as far as I was concerned. I'm no judge of acting, but if the things my wife dragged me to see with her in them were any indication ... Well, anyway, she was young and sexy, a good twenty years younger than Harry, and she led him a merry life for a while. He left his first wife for her, spent what little savings he had, and then she dumped him and went to California. He started drinking bad. Then she got killed. Harry quit the force a couple of months later."

"To do what?"

"He played around at being a P.I. for a while, but he gave that up years ago."

"So what's he live on?"

"Search me. Maybe he had a windfall."

"Maybe," Tom said thoughtfully.

3

Harry Vinton rolled out of bed and looked at the clock. 11:30. Well, at least he was awake before noon for the first time this week. Hell, for the first time this month. What was the cause for all this get-up-and-go? Must be something exciting in the air, he thought, something he couldn't quite figure out until he had his morning coffee.

Groaning, he hauled his two hundred and fifty pounds out of the bed, wincing as sunlight cut through the open venetian blinds and right into his eyes. God, when was he going to remember to close those damn things before he turned in? Probably the first night he went to bed sober, which hadn't happened for a long time and wasn't likely to happen in this lifetime.

He plugged in the Mr. Coffee and listened to it hiss into action while he leaned over the kitchen sink, peering out at the young woman next door. She was loading suitcases into her car, her long blond hair pulled back in a ponytail, her skirt tight over rounded hips. He'd never seen her up close, but he guessed her to be around twenty-five, and from this distance she reminded him of Teresa, his second wife. They had the same cocky walk that said they knew they were sexy, the same way of flipping their hair around for attention. But in spite of her voluptuous body and self-awareness, the girl next door somehow seemed innocent. Teresa had been anything but innocent.

Which is part of what attracted you to her, Harry thought. His first wife had been loyal, kind, and dull as dishwater. The only time her plain little face showed any animation was when she was planning a garage sale, and she bore his once-a-week lovemaking with the abstracted air of a woman making grocery lists in her head. Then had come Teresa, a cocktail waitress who hung on his every word when he stopped by the bar after work and one night in the OK Motel acted thrilled when he told her he was going to divorce his wife and marry her. But domestic life wasn't for her. She craved attention, and although he'd done everything he could to hold her, she headed for Hollywood, certain there was a place for her on the silver screen. Harry laughed aloud at the memory, but there was no humor in the sound. He'd loved her, God only knew why. Poor Teresa. Teresa Torrance, that's what she'd called herself. But a year later, when she was stabbed to death by a mugger, the minuscule newspaper account had given her real name: Tessie Kuhn.

Almost nineteen years. Hard to believe she'd been gone for so long. If she hadn't been murdered, she would have come back. Harry knew that. She would have come back when she realized Hollywood didn't want her and he did. And he had money by then. Just eight months after she left, Hayley Corday had been kidnapped. That's when he'd seen his chance, his only chance, to ever have enough money to lure Teresa home. He had talked to her three weeks before her death, telling her he'd "come into money." She didn't believe him at first, especially when she asked him to send her some of his new-found wealth and he refused. Supporting her stupid Hollywood dreams wasn't the way to bring her back. But months in Los Angeles had weakened her confidence. No one was interested in putting her in a movie, a TV show, a commercial, or anything else, and she was back to waitressing again, this time in a cheap diner. Harry figured that if she'd lived six more months, she would have come home. But she didn't live.

He poured a cup of coffee, watching the blonde drive off. She sure traveled a lot, he thought without interest. The Corday kid would have been about the same age. She'd been a blonde too. Funny how he thought about her at the most unexpected times. No, funny how he thought about her *all* the time.

Well, hell, what else is there to think about? he mused, slogging back to the living room in his shorts and snapping on the television. For nineteen years he'd officially been a private investigator, but long ago he'd given up the pretense. After all, he didn't need the money. Well, for a long time he hadn't needed the money. But now his source was drying up, and pretty soon there wouldn't be anything left, thanks to bad investments. He could coast along for a couple more years. And then what?

The doorbell rang and he nearly jumped out of his chair. He never had company. Maybe it was a salesman. He peeked through the drapes to see a tall, slender man whose eyes immediately spotted the movement. Harry darted back, but the bell rang again. Why doesn't the bastard just go away? Harry fumed. He wasn't about to buy anything. But when the bell rang for the third time, he gave up. Still clad only in ancient, baggy shorts, he opened the door a crack.

"Harry Vinton?"

Harry looked into a pair of piercing gray eyes. "Who wants to know?"

"My name is Tom Jerome. I'd like to talk to you about the Hayley Corday case."

Two hours later Harry slammed down the phone for the fourth time. Not home. Or not answering. Must know it was him. No, that was impossible. He was just shaken.

He popped the top on a new beer and thought. What had happened? A confession? Because nothing could make Harry believe Jerome's story about the Corday kid's mother being harassed by someone claiming to be Hayley. Hell, no, that was a ruse. And a pretty poor one. He'd have expected better from the detective he'd heard so much about. Hot shit. That's what Jerome was supposed to be. Hot shit from Chicago. Hell, in his prime Harry could have run circles around him. The guy was an idiot.

Except he wasn't. Harry knew that. The man was downright scary with those eyes as cold and hard as granite. And he was on to something.

In spite of the fat that usually kept him too warm, Harry shivered. Then he dialed again. This time there was an answer.

"This is Vinton. I'm coming over there tonight to talk to you." He gulped beer while someone spoke. "I'm not coming about money. I'm coming about your big mouth."

He slammed down the phone. No one was a match for Harry Vinton, he thought, his big hand clenching into a fist. Not even Jerome. No sir. He was going to get to the bottom of this. And then he was going to fix it.

4

Chris Corday ordered another Scotch and water and glanced down the bar. She was toying with a damp napkin under her drink, keeping her eyes downcast as if she was completely unaware of him. He smiled to himself. Why did they always act like they didn't see you? Like they didn't know you existed? When all the time they were tensed, waiting for you to make the first overt move. Well, okay. He knew how to play the game.

He picked up his drink and walked slowly down the bar to her side. She glanced up, her silver-shadowed eyes trying to look startled. "May I sit here?" Chris asked with just the right touch of beguiling tentativeness. "Or are you expecting someone?"

"My friend was coming, but I guess he couldn't make it." Her voice was flat, midwestern, and faintly nasal. It had absolutely no charm. "You can sit down for a while."

Chris smiled his thanks, thinking what a lot of bull all this was and how he was too tired to get enthusiastic, even if she did bear a faint resemblance to Cheryl Tiegs. But what was the alternative? A night at the cabin alone, thinking about Hayley? He forced warmth into his voice. "Your drink looks a little watery. Can I buy you a fresh one?"

She appeared to think this over. "Well, okay. I guess I can stay for one more."

"Great. By the way, my name is Chris."

She smiled coquettishly. "I'm Renée."

It only took an hour to convince her to come home

with him. By this time she was on her fourth Manhattan and telling him about what a bastard her first husband had been, although he couldn't hold a candle to the second, who'd walked out on her last year. Chris listened, shaking his head in sympathy. The bar was getting crowded by then, and when someone jostled Renée's arm, making her spill her drink, Chris leaned near her. "Listen, this place is turning into a madhouse. Besides, the drinks are mostly ice. Why don't we go back to my place and have something decent?"

"Oh, I don't know if I should."

"Please?" Chris's blue eyes were full of sincerity. "I'm really enjoying talking to you."

Renée gazed back foggily. "Well, I guess it'll be okay. But just one drink. I have to go to work tomorrow."

As they stood up to go, she slung a huge bag over her shoulder, nearly hitting Chris in the face with it. "Is that a purse or a tote bag?" Chris asked, trying to hide his irritation.

She laughed a little drunkenly. "I hate itsy-bitsy purses. They don't hold anything. I can carry half my apartment in this baby."

On the way back to his place she leaned over, turned on the radio, and broke into "Every Breath You Take" with the Police. She closed her eyes as she sang, her face throbbing with emotion her flat voice couldn't match, and Chris wondered if the great body under her jeans and sweater was really worth all this. God, she sounded like a warped record. He took a deep breath, wishing he'd had at least one more drink. Then maybe she would be slightly more appealing.

"A log cabin!" she squealed and burst into hysterical laughter. "What a trip!"

"I didn't think anyone used that expression anymore." Chris remembered to smile at her. "It's humble, but it's home. Come in and let me fix you a drink."

When he opened the front door and flipped on the lights, Hecate raised up from her bed on the settee and glared at the girl, who shrieked as if she'd been stabbed. "What is *that?*"

"I believe it's called a cat."

"But its eye." Renée tensed. "I hate cats," she said in a frozen voice. "I absolutely detest them."

Hecate leaped off the settee, hissing fiercely. Renée screamed again, then swung her massive shoulder bag at the cat. Her aim was good, and Hecate hit the wall with a thud before scrambling up and darting out the door.

With a frigid look at Renée, Chris went after the cat, who had taken refuge under his jeep. "Sorry, Hecate. I guess she doesn't care for felines." Hecate's one good eye blinked at him accusingly. "Come back in and I promise to get rid of her."

But the cat only cowered lower. Timid under the best conditions, she was now terrified and would refuse to come near the cabin until morning, when she was hungry. Sighing, Chris went back inside, where Renée sat curled on the settee, her shoes lying on the floor in front of her. "This place is kinda cozy," she said sweetly. "It'll be even cozier when you fix me a drink."

Chris looked at her for a full ten seconds before he said quietly, "Renée, maybe this was a mistake. It's late."

"It's ten-thirty."

"But you said you have work tomorrow."

"Well, I can stay up past ten-thirty, for God's sake."

"Yeah. Sure. You're not a kid, right?" What the hell does it matter if you don't like her? Chris thought. Two hours from now you'll be driving her home and then you never have to see her again. "What'll you drink?"

"It isn't good to mix things. I'll stick with bourbon." Renée uncurled herself from the settee, looking at him coyly. "While you fix my drink, I'll be powdering my nose. If you show me the location of the powder room, that is."

"The *bathroom* is through here." He led her toward the bedroom, turned on the overhead light, and motioned to the far wall. "Right over—"

His eyes flashed to the bed, where a clown doll lay grinning at him.

"I might need a guide to lead me back to the living room," Renée was saying. "Otherwise I could get lost and—"

Chris strode to the bed, picked up the doll, and whirled on her. "Where did you get this?"

Renée's silver eyelids fluttered. "Where did I get what?"

"Twinkle. Where did you get Twinkle?"

She stiffened at the fury in his voice. "You mean that doll?"

"You know damn well I mean the doll."

"What do you mean, where did *I* get it? It's on *your* bed. I never saw it before."

"You carried it in that big bag of yours, didn't you? You put it on the bed when I went outside after the cat."

She took a step backward. "Look, I don't know what you're talking about." She was suddenly sober, and her eyes showed fear. "I swear I never saw that doll before."

"Liar."

Her tongue touched her lips as her eyes searched the corners of the room. "Your door was unlocked. Maybe someone came in and put the doll on your bed."

"*You.* You put it on the bed." He tossed down the doll and stalked across the room, grabbing at her shoulder, but she was too quick for him. She was already in the living room, screaming.

"You're crazy! You're a freak!" He stood watching as she struggled with the front door. Cold night air drifted in as she flung open the door and ran barefoot into the darkness. "You're nuts! I'm calling the police!"

She had made it out to his jeep when something whistled past her head and shattered the front window of the cabin. Instinctively Renée fell to the ground, huddling beside the jeep as another shot sliced the darkness, and another and another, all aimed at the cabin. Then there was silence.

Nearly fifteen minutes passed before Renée was able to uncoil her body. She was terrified and very cold. She was also curious about the abrupt silence within the cabin. Just moments after the shooting stopped, the cat emerged from beneath the jeep and dashed through the open door of the cabin, but even then there was no sound, no one coming to see if she was all right. The man and the cat seemed swallowed up in a void, which would have been just fine with Renée if she could have gotten away, but she remembered Chris had taken the keys out of the jeep when they arrived, and she couldn't walk barefoot the mile of darkness to the foot of the hill and the highway.

Her breath rattling in her throat, Renée half crawled, half ran toward the cabin. She hesitated before entering, then plunged across the threshold into the living room where Hecate sat licking Chris's closed eyes while his blood dripped onto the Oriental rug.

9

"**W**ELL, IF IT isn't the midnight prowler," Lucy said as Caroline entered the store.

Caroline laughed. "I guess I'm never going to live that one down."

"Well, Caro, creeping around cemeteries in the middle of the night isn't exactly in character, not to mention that you made the papers."

Caroline grimaced. "Yes, David was thrilled about that."

Lucy looked surprised. "Was he really mad?"

"Yes, not so much about my being in the newspaper as my going to the cemetery. I don't think he believes I'm in full possession of my faculties."

"You might have been killed."

"I couldn't have known that when I went there. I was only looking for the black bouquet. Has the guard regained consciousness yet?"

"Last night. Tom told me he claims he was going on his usual midnight round when he spotted two young hoods. He got out of his car and asked what they were doing. They started running and he went after them. He caught up with one near the tree, they struggled, and somehow the guy got the guard's gun away from him and shot him."

Caroline frowned. "What would two guys be doing out in the cemetery at midnight?"

"A drug deal, the guard says. Claims he saw briefcases changing hands—one obviously loaded with money, the other with coke." Lucy grinned. "Tom doesn't buy it. He thinks the guard's seen too much *Miami Vice.*"

"What makes him so sure?"

"That guard is about fifty-five and overweight. Now why would he chase and tackle some tough and probably armed young guy instead of simply firing a warning shot?"

"How do you know he didn't?"

"The gun was found near the entrance of the cemetery. It had been fired only once, and that bullet went into the guard."

"What does Tom think *could* have happened?" Caroline asked.

"He has no idea, except that the guard's face was scratched. There obviously had been some kind of struggle."

"The cemetery gates were unlocked," Caroline pointed out. "Is that important?"

"With the guard booth right at the entrance, they're usually left open. The owners of the place told Tom that. Nothing unusual there. Anyone could have gotten in. You did."

"Only because the guard had already been shot. But then I drove into the cemetery. I guess it wouldn't be any big problem to leave your car outside the cemetery away from the guard booth, then climb over the fence. It's only about six feet high."

"I think they're checking on that. But for now, that's all the police know." Lucy twisted one of the amber beads on her waist-length necklace. "Tom said you didn't find the bouquet."

Caroline caught Lucy's steady gaze. "No. I think I got there too late. It had been taken away by whoever shot the guard."

"The person must have been awfully desperate to get away with those flowers."

"Since the person who sent the flowers possibly murdered Pamela, I can understand that."

"Caroline, that's what you seem to be forgetting. Pamela was *murdered*. Even if you think there's a connection between Hayley's case and Pamela's, you have to leave this to the police."

"So they can wait around until the evidence vanishes?"

"You didn't find the bouquet either."

"I know. I'm sorry for snapping at you." Caroline crossed her arms almost defensively over her chest. "It's just that this situation is getting very hard to handle calmly. *I* know what I've seen, but no one else does."

"No one can deny that someone left a clown doll remarkably like Twinkle on Melinda's bed and a child dressed like Hayley came to your door, then called Melinda. I've never said this was in your head."

"No, you haven't." But you're not convinced about the connection between Pamela and Hayley, Caroline thought, feeling thoroughly frustrated with Lucy's stubborn downplaying of the situation. Then she reminded herself that Lucy was probably trying to help her keep some perspective and not leap to conclusions.

She forced a smile. "Well, I'm ready to forget

about black bouquets and wounded guards for now," she said lightly, laying her purse on a nearby dining table and withdrawing several skeins of embroidery floss. "I brought by some samples for Mrs. Reinfeldt's tablecloth. She said she wanted rose and willow, and I thought you might help me pick out the shades that would go best with her china."

A customer walked in just as Tina leaned over the balcony rail and called, "Mrs. Webb, your husband is on the phone."

"My husband?"

"He said he called the house and your cleaning lady told him you were here. He says it's urgent."

"Oh, my God," Caroline gasped. "One of the kids is hurt."

She bolted up the spiral wrought-iron staircase to the second-floor office, Lucy right behind her. Tina clicked off the hold button and handed the receiver to Caroline while Lucy motioned for Tina to go downstairs.

"David? What's wrong?" Caroline demanded.

"It's Chris."

Expecting to hear him say Greg or Melinda, she went blank. "Who?"

"Chris Corday. He's been shot."

"Shot?" Caroline felt as if she were listening to him from under water. "What do you mean, shot?"

"Caroline, last night someone shot Chris in his home."

She sat down on the edge of the desk. "Is he . . . dead?"

David sounded contrite. "No, honey, I didn't mean to scare you. He'll be all right. I just thought you'd want to know."

"Which hospital is he at?"

"Here at County. I found out when I came in to make my rounds this morning."

"I'll be right there."

"Caroline, there's no need for that. He'll be all right."

"David, he doesn't have any family. I'll be there in fifteen minutes."

David hung up without saying goodbye, and Caroline turned to Lucy. "Someone shot Chris last night."

Lucy's face sagged. "How bad is he?"

"I don't know, but I'm going to the hospital. Do you want to go, too?"

"Sure." Lucy was already reaching for her gray cape hanging on the coat tree. "Want me to drive?"

"No. My car's already warmed up from the drive over here." She reached for her purse, then remembered she'd left it downstairs. They pounded down the staircase. The customer had left, and while Lucy hurled a brief explanation at Tina, Caroline collected the purse lying on the dining table and headed for the car.

Traffic was unusually heavy although rush hour had ended two hours earlier. Caroline swore as she sat through a light a second time, unable to make a left turn.

"Take it easy, Caro," Lucy said softly. "David said Chris isn't in serious condition. This isn't a life-and-death matter."

"But he was *shot*, Lucy. It's awful."

Lucy threw her a severe look. "Caroline, just do me one favor. Don't let David see how upset you are."

"He'd expect me to be upset."

"Not *this* upset. You're wearing your heart on your sleeve, pardon my cliché."

In spite of her anger and fear, Caroline blushed with embarrassment. Lucy was right—she could see right through her. And so would David if she didn't pull herself together.

The light turned green and this time Caroline made it. They pulled into the hospital parking lot and miraculously found a place not far from the front door. By the time they spotted David lingering outside Chris's room on the fourth floor, Caroline felt she was in much better control. At least her heart wasn't thudding and she could draw a full breath without it hurting.

"Hi, honey," she said, going up to kiss David's cheek. "It was sweet of you to wait for us."

David smiled, although he looked strained. "I thought you might like to know a little more about his condition before you go in. I could have told you on the phone, but you didn't give me a chance."

"I'm sorry, David. I was just so shocked. How is he?"

"As I said, it's not serious. He was shot in the shoulder, but his doctor says the bullet went through the deltoid muscle without damaging bone, blood vessels, or nerves. A second shot grazed his temple."

Caroline felt almost faint with relief, although she tried to hide it.

"How long will he be in the hospital?" Lucy asked.

"Two or three days." David looked at Caroline, his gaze slightly distant. "I'll let you go in and visit now."

Caroline smiled at him. "Thanks. See you this evening."

David merely nodded and walked away. Lucy raised an eyebrow at Caroline before opening Chris's door.

"Knock, knock," she called. "Up to seeing two gorgeous broads?"

"Always," Chris returned, although his voice was gravelly with pain and fatigue. Caroline's heart contracted when she saw his ashen face and the purplish shadows under his eyes. He looked thin and old in his green hospital gown, bandages protruding around the neck. Another bandage covered his left temple. "Word travels fast."

"Caro and I have a hotline," Lucy bantered. "Every time they bring in a good-looking man, we come dashing over to see what we can do."

"You got a false alarm this time because I look like something the cat dragged in." Chris grinned, motioning to the single vinyl-covered chair beside the bed.

"You take the chair, Caroline," Lucy said quickly. "I'll perch up here on the patient's bed."

"I think sitting on the bed is against the rules." Caroline took the chair nevertheless.

"They can sue me." Lucy plumped down, letting her long, alligator-booted legs dangle over the side of the bed. "So, Don Juan, what jealous husband let you have it?"

Caroline was uncomfortable with the teasing, but Chris looked at her solemnly. "No jealous husband, Lucy."

"How do you know?"

Chris's eyes found Caroline's. "I admit I brought a

woman home with me last night." Caroline's stomach tightened. Why does that bother me? she thought furiously. Why do I feel like he's still my husband who's being unfaithful? "We hadn't been there more than ten minutes when I walked in the bedroom and discovered Twinkle."

All thought of the other woman vanished as blood drained from Caroline's face. "Twinkle?"

Chris nodded. "Big as life, old and dirty, lying on my bed grinning at me."

"Twinkle," Lucy repeated. "Hayley's clown doll."

"That's right."

Lucy gave him a hard look. "That is impossible."

Chris sounded surprised by her tone. "Why is it impossible? The doll appeared at Caroline's."

Lucy's gaze shot to Caroline. "I didn't know you'd discussed all this with Chris."

Caroline suddenly felt like a fifteen-year-old whose mother had found out she'd been skipping school. "Yes, I told Chris," she said with a defensive quaver, then with more vigor, "Of course I told him, Lucy. He's Hayley's father. This involves him, too."

Lucy studied her for a moment before turning back to Chris. "Okay, you saw a clown doll on your bed. Then what?"

Chris's eyes glinted. "Well, Ms. Prosecutor, I accused the woman I'd brought home of sneaking the doll in and putting it on the bed. She had this steamer trunk for a purse, and I did leave the cabin for a few minutes. It would have been possible. But she went crazy with denials, and when I got pretty aggressive, she headed out the front door. She'd been gone for about ten seconds when the glass shattered and I was hit in the shoulder. Then there was this terrible stinging in my temple. Even after I fell I heard other shots before I passed out."

"So you think she shot you?"

Chris looked exasperated. "No, Lucy, not unless she had a gun stashed in those skintight jeans. She left her purse inside."

"Maybe more time passed than you think."

"I wasn't drunk. I know exactly how much time passed. And what the hell's the matter with you, anyway?"

Caroline intervened. "What about Twinkle?"

Chris tried to shrug, then winced at the pain. "I don't know, Caro. The doll might still be at the cabin. I left it in the bedroom."

"Then it's all part of what's been happening to me," Caroline said softly. "It's all connected."

Lucy looked like she wanted to say something but was forcing back the words. They were all three silent for a moment before Chris said, "Lucy, I do have a favor to ask. They say I won't get out of here for a few days, and my cat needs care. Do you think you could take her to the vet for me? He'll board her until I get home."

Lucy's eyebrows drew together in despair. "Chris, that cat hates me. It won't even let me touch it."

"If you'll just try . . ."

"I'll take care of Hecate," Caroline said quickly. "I have more experience with animals than you do, Lucy."

Chris looked at her gratefully, almost tenderly. "Thanks, Caro. I really appreciate it."

"It's no problem at all."

Caroline made small talk as she and Lucy walked

back to the parking lot, but Lucy wouldn't answer. When they climbed in Caroline's car, Lucy reached over and put her hand on Caroline's when she tried to slip the key in the ignition. "Caro, you have to stop this," she said quietly.

"Stop what? I don't know what you mean."

"Oh, yes, you do. You're trying to revive the past."

"Revive the past? That's crazy."

"Is it? First you're convinced Hayley has come back from the grave—"

"I *never* said such a thing!"

"And now you're getting chummy with Chris again. Obviously you visited him at the cabin."

"Lucy, I wanted him to know what's going on, and he doesn't have a phone. If I wanted to talk to him, I had to see him."

"And did you tell David about this visit?"

Caroline took a deep breath and stared out the windshield at a young woman creeping across the parking lot with a crippled old man dragging at her arm. "No, I didn't," she said finally.

"See what I mean?"

"Yes, I guess I do."

Lucy leaned back in her seat and said gravely, "Caroline, I'm your best friend. There have been times in the past when I've let you down, but I'm trying not to do that now. I see where you're headed, and it's for trouble. You still have a lot of romantic memories of Chris, and you've rationalized the way he treated you the last year of your marriage by blaming it all on his shock over Hayley's death. And maybe that is what changed him, but I've been around him a lot more than you have the last few years, and I can tell you he's *not* the man you married. He's turned bitter and selfish. I think he might try to turn himself back into what he once was through you, but it won't work."

"What do you mean that he might try to change through me?"

"He was at his peak artistically with you. He wants that success back and I think he might do anything to get it, to get you."

"Anything like what?"

"Like lying about the doll."

"Lucy!"

"Well, think about it, Caroline. You go up there telling him about phone calls, about Twinkle, and wham! Twinkle's at the cabin, Chris is shot, and you're flying to his bedside like Cathy rushing across the moors to Heathcliff."

Caroline was astounded. "How can you even think such a thing of Chris?"

"Because I know him. Are you going to argue in favor of his virtues?"

"He does have some. And besides, Lucy, he was shot."

"Like I said, probably by some jealous husband. You *know* that isn't out of the question—he's been asking for it for years."

Caroline couldn't deny what Lucy was saying. "I guess it is something to think about, although I've never known Chris to lie before."

"You haven't really known Chris for a long time. Maybe you never did. In any case, Chris's problems aren't yours. You have David and Greg and Melinda to concentrate on." She paused. "You know, Caro, I'd give anything to trade places with you."

Caroline looked at her in surprise. "Lucy, you'd be

bored stiff with my life. Husband always gone, kids growing up."

"Still . . ." Lucy flashed her brilliant smile. "You're right. Madcap Lucille Elder would never fit in the domestic scene. Now, my dear, I have a design studio to run."

When they pulled into the store's small rear parking lot, Caroline glanced at the clock on her dashboard. "It's twelve-thirty. We could go get some lunch—"

"No can do. I've got an appointment in half an hour. But thanks for the invitation. See you soon."

The farewell was uncharacteristically abrupt for Lucy. What she said about Chris seemed to have a bigger impact on her than on me, Caroline thought, puzzled. Was Lucy really worried that Caroline would throw away her marriage for Chris? Because in spite of the recent contact that reminded her of her continued attraction to and even love for Chris, she knew what she had in David. She would never break up her home for Chris, and Lucy should know that. Still, as Caroline drove away, she glanced in the rearview mirror to see Lucy standing at the back door of the studio, her sad eyes following the car.

Caroline was so distracted by the events of the morning that as she drove by Melinda's school on her way home she almost didn't notice the empty playground. At this time it should have been full of children basking in ten more minutes of freedom before the one o'clock bell rang. Alarmed, she rushed home to find Fidelia sweeping out the garage. David had wanted Caroline to let the woman go, but Caroline insisted that if she really was up to something, it would be easier to keep an eye on her if she was still working for them. Besides, although she knew her faith in Fidelia might not be logical, she really could not believe Fidelia had possession of Twinkle or was sending black bouquets around the city.

"Bomb scare," she announced before Caroline had fully emerged from her car. "De school called and said dere had been a bomb scare. Not'ing to it, I'm sure, but dey can't take any chances. So I walked over and got Melinda."

"Oh, Fidelia, thank you so much," Caroline said. "And I bet you didn't wear a coat—just that skimpy little sweater."

Fidelia grinned. "I don't mind de cold. Besides, I took George on de leash. He was so excited he kept pulling me along. I didn't have a chance to get cold." Caroline laughed. "Melinda is in de kitchen talking to a friend on de phone. She tinks dis bomb scare is wonderful."

"I can imagine. It's a first for her."

Sure enough, when Caroline stepped into the kitchen Melinda was talking at machine-gun rate, her little cheeks flushed pink with excitement. She waved at Caroline, who smiled back as she took off her jacket and bent to pet George's head.

"My mommy's home now," Melinda was saying. "She wasn't here when they called from school, and Fidelia had to come get me. You should meet Fidelia. She's really neat. She tells the future." Pause. "Well, of course she can really tell the future. Honestly and truly, Hayley, she *can.*"

Caroline was across the kitchen in an instant, making Melinda yelp in surprise as she snatched the receiver from her hand. "Who is this?" Caroline demanded. "What do you want?"

After three beats of silence, the child said, "Hi, Mommy. I bet you're real sad Daddy got shot."

10

~

1

"**D**ETECTIVE JEROME, PLEASE."

Melinda was still staring at her with wide, frightened eyes as she cowered against Fidelia. While Caroline waited for Tom, she reached out and stroked the child's hair. "Sorry I scared you, sweetie, but someone is playing a terrible joke on us."

Melinda's voice shook as she fought tears. "I don't get it. It was just Hayley."

"That was *not* Hayley."

The little girl looked at her in complete confusion, and Fidelia turned her around. "What you say I read de cards for you while your mom's on de phone?"

"I guess that'd be okay," Melinda said without enthusiasm.

"Good. I feel hot today." Fidelia snapped her fingers to indicate psychic prowess, and Melinda smiled.

Fidelia was laying out the cards on the dining room table when Tom's low, intense voice came on the line. "Jerome here."

"Oh, Tom, I'm so glad you're in. This is Caroline."

His voice warmed. "Hi, Caroline. What's up?"

152

"We just got another phone call." She tried to be calm and coherent as she told him about the call to Melinda and the mysterious child's comment about Chris.

"You didn't recognize the child's voice?"

Should she tell him it sounded just like Hayley's? No, of course not, not if she wanted him to maintain any confidence in her. "It's not one of Melinda's friends."

"Do you know what she said to Melinda?"

"Just little-girl talk. Nothing about her background or anything personal about us. Not until I took the phone."

"But she mentioned Chris's shooting," Tom said thoughtfully, "and as far as I know, it didn't make the morning papers."

"Did you know that just before Chris was shot he found Twinkle on his bed?"

"The clown doll?"

Caroline heard the excitement in his voice. "Yes."

"No, I didn't know. Well, that throws a new light on things, doesn't it?"

"If the person who put the doll on the bed is the same one who shot Chris, I'd say it does."

"Caroline, I know David threw out the doll the night you found it. Do you know if he stuffed it down in a trash can or just left it on top?"

"I have no idea. The trash is collected about six in the morning. But I can ask him. Do you think someone picked up the doll from our trash?"

"I can't think of any other answer. Listen, Caroline, I'm going to check into Chris's shooting myself. I'll go by the hospital and question him, then search his house for the doll."

"It will probably have disappeared, just like the

bouquets." Caroline shuddered, thinking of her night at Rosemont Cemetery. "Lucy said the guard regained consciousness but that you don't believe his story."

"It's hard to take him seriously. I've been checking him out. Believe me, he's no hero. All he wanted to do was make two or three rounds a night, watch TV, and eat. Even if there had been a drug deal, which I find highly unlikely in this area, our man wouldn't have gotten himself mixed up in it."

"But why would he lie?"

"Because he's afraid of being hurt or killed, or else he was doing something he shouldn't."

"Lucy said he had scratches on him like he'd been in a struggle, but you don't have any other evidence."

Tom hesitated. "Actually, we do."

She knew from his hesitation he was reluctant to tell her what the evidence was, and she tensed. "What is it?"

"I didn't find out until this morning because I'm not working this case. But a few hairs were found on his clothes and under his nails, obviously from the person he struggled with."

"What kind of hairs?"

"Synthetic. Frizzy. Orange."

Caroline let out her breath. "Just like Twinkle's. Just like the wig Hayley wore on her last Halloween and the one that child wore to my door this Halloween."

"Let's not jump to conclusions, Caroline. There are probably a lot of orange wigs floating around."

"This one just happened to turn up at Pamela's grave where a man was shot."

"I considered not telling you, but I really think you

need to know everything since this whole thing started with you."

"Let's just hope it doesn't end with Melinda."

"It won't, Caroline. I won't let it."

As Caroline hung up she heard Melinda giggling in the other room before she came bounding into the kitchen. "Fidelia says I'm gonna be rich and famous!"

"A prima ballerina, no doubt," Caroline said, bending down to enfold Melinda in her arms. God, I'm frightened for you, she thought wildly. Why doesn't the little girl call me instead of you? Then she pulled herself up short. Because she knows having Melinda threatened would frighten me more than anything, since I've already lost one little girl.

"Either a prima ballerina or an actress," Melinda chattered on, pulling herself free of her mother's tight grasp. "I'm not sure—the cards don't say exactly, but those are the two things I'm best at."

"Did the cards say if Aurora is going to sprout?"

Melinda frowned, going over to look at her pot of dirt carefully placed in a circle of faltering sunshine. "I forgot to ask."

Fidelia was wrapping the tarot cards in a paisley silk scarf and slipping them in her purse. "I predict Aurora will indeed sprout."

"Did the cards say so?" Melinda asked hopefully.

"No, but I have belief. So must you, *ma petite amie.*" She winked at Caroline, then asked, "Did you want me to start on de basement today?"

Caroline shook her head. "No, we're having it painted in a couple of weeks and it would be best to wait until it's finished before you clean." She glanced at her watch. "It's nearly two o'clock. Why don't you just call it a day?"

"Fine. I'm baby-sitting for de Richardsons tonight and I could use a few hours' rest. Dose kids and de four cats dey torment to madness—"

"Cats!" Caroline exclaimed. Melinda and Fidelia jumped, clearly not sure what outburst to expect next, and Caroline laughed. "I didn't mean to startle you. I just remembered I was supposed to pick up a cat for a friend who's in the hospital."

"You mean we're gonna cat-sit?" Melinda asked.

"Maybe. This is a very temperamental cat. If I can't get her to behave, I'll have to board her."

"*I* can make her behave," Melinda informed her. "I love cats. So does George."

"It's just that cats don't love George back," Caroline said dryly. "Oh well, we'll have to do our best. I promised."

"I'll go get a box and put a nice pillow in it for the cat. What's her name?"

"Hecate."

"Wow, that's weird. Anyway, I'll go get a box for Hecate. There's a nice big one in the basement—"

She was already gone, racing through the house talking to herself. Fidelia looked at Caroline, her blue eyes shrewd. "I wish you'd talk to me. Maybe I could help."

"I don't want to talk about it in front of Melinda. But the next time we're alone . . ." She trailed off, clasping her hands together. "Fidelia, do you believe in ghosts?"

Fidelia's eyes did not waver. "Yes. Do you?"

"No."

"Your eyes tell a different story. Do you feel de presence of a ghost?"

"I feel something," Caroline said vaguely, losing herself in Fidelia's aqua eyes. "It feels evil."

"Surely you don't tink your little girl was evil."

"How did you know . . ."

"You're terrified when Melinda receives a call from a child named Hayley, den you ask if I believe in ghosts." She shrugged.

"I guess it is pretty obvious. You're right—the trouble does revolve around Hayley. I'm just not sure how."

Caroline watched Fidelia closely, waiting for any betraying signs of guilt at the mention of Hayley's name. Fidelia's leathery face remained impassive. Then she smiled. "You tink I have someting to do with dis trouble."

"No, I . . ."

"It's all right. I understand. I know about Hayley, and I work here. I was here de day de window upstairs was broken, and I know dere was more to dat business dan Melinda told me."

"What makes you think so?"

"You. You're nervous. You watch me. But you must believe, Caroline, dat I would not harm you or your family. However, if you want me to go . . ."

"No, actually, I don't."

"Den sometime soon you must tell me all dat is happening. You do not realize de power of de supernatural. Dere *are* such tings as witches, evil spirits which can be called up, death spells . . ."

"Oh, Fidelia, I can't really accept all that," Caroline said sharply, thinking what David would have to say if he heard this conversation.

"It is frightening, but it's real," Fidelia said calmly. "Just remember—I care about you and your family, particularly Melinda. I will help you if you wish it."

Caroline was tempted to say, "Yes, please help me," but realized that in doing so, she would be admitting she thought something supernatural *was* happening. Isn't that what Lucy had said? *"First you're convinced Hayley has come back from the grave . . ."* No, she could not let herself give in to such thoughts. They weren't rational, and her willingness to entertain them for even an instant frightened her.

"I've got it!" Melinda reappeared, her legs peeking from beneath the box Caroline's new microwave oven had come in. "Is this big enough?"

"Lin, Hecate is a cat, not a lion," Caroline laughed, grateful to turn her gaze away from Fidelia. "Couldn't you find something smaller?"

"Nope. You threw out everything this summer, remember?"

"Nothing good ever comes of being too efficient. And what's the nice pillow from the family room couch doing here?"

"It's all I could find, Mommy, honest. And the kitty *needs* a pillow."

"Oh, well, it has a washable cover. Go get your jacket while I put this stuff in the car."

"Can George come?"

He was looking at them appealingly from melting brown eyes, his tail slowly sweeping the air. "I'm afraid not. He'd probably scare the cat away."

Melinda bent to take his face in her hands. "Don't you worry, George. We're gonna bring that little kitty home, and then you can make friends."

"Or so we hope," Caroline muttered to Fidelia.

Ten minutes later, as they sped toward Longworth Hill, Melinda asked, "Who does Hecate belong to?"

"A man named Chris Corday. He's an artist."

"Oh, your first husband." In her amazement, Caroline accidentally pressed down on the accelerator.

"Whoa!" Melinda laughed as they surged forward. "That was fun!"

Caroline slowed down, overcompensating for her burst of speed as she gazed at Melinda. "How did you know about Chris?"

"Greg told me a long, long time ago. I found a picture of you in a long white dress with flowers in your hair. You were holding hands with a handsome man. I took the picture to Greg and he said you'd had another husband before Daddy, but I wasn't to ask you about it because it makes you sad to remember." Melinda cocked her head. "Does it make you sad?"

Caroline looked back at the road. "Divorce is always sad."

"Oh, I know that. Some of my friends' parents are divorced. But that's different."

"Why?"

"Because you and Daddy are still married. I don't even know Chris Corday." Melinda frowned. *"Corday.* You asked me if Hayley's last name was Corday. Did you think they might be related?"

Caroline said warily, "Yes, I thought maybe they were."

Melinda nodded thoughtfully. "You didn't think my friend Hayley was your little girl that died, did you?"

This time Caroline gasped, forcing herself to keep her eyes on the road. "Did Greg tell you about her?"

"Nope. Jenny did. Her mother knew all about it. She said you had a little girl that got kidnapped and killed. She said it was in all the newspapers—front page. But she didn't say the girl's name. Was it Hayley?"

"Yes," Caroline said reluctantly. "Melinda, how long have you known all this?"

"Years. Well, maybe not years. Maybe months. I don't remember."

"Could it have been last spring?"

"Yeah, I guess."

The child had begun twisting her hair the way she always did when she was nervous. Caroline reached over and took her hand. "Is that why you started crying at school?"

Melinda nodded. "I felt real bad 'cause I knew how much your little girl dying must have hurt your feelings. And I felt sad 'cause Greg and me had a sister we never knew." Her green eyes dropped. "And I guess I felt pretty scared, too."

"Scared that the same thing might happen to you?" Melinda nodded again. "It won't, baby."

"Well, of course not," Melinda said in her best grown-up voice. "I'm all over being scared. And, Mommy, my friend Hayley can't be your little girl 'cause she doesn't even look like a ghost."

"You're right, Lin. It was silly of me to even think such a thing."

"That's okay. Everybody's silly sometimes, even me."

Caroline couldn't help smiling as they turned off the highway and began the ascent of Longworth Hill. When they reached the cabin, Melinda was goggle-eyed. "Wow! A real log cabin like Abe Lincoln's. Did you ever live here?"

"I sure did, for eight years."

The cabin had been cordoned off, but there were no policemen present. Caroline was relieved. She didn't want Melinda alarmed, although the child seemed much stronger than she realized. Caroline still couldn't believe she had known about Hayley for months and kept the knowledge to herself. It just

showed how secretive children could be. Hayley had
been the same way.

"Look, Mommy! There's a black cat peeping at us
from behind that tree."

"That's Hecate. And honey, I forgot to tell you the
cat was in a terrible fight and lost an eye. She's not
very pretty."

"Oh, the poor sweetheart!" Melinda cried, darting
out of the car. "Maybe we can get her a glass one."

Melinda edged toward the cat, speaking in low,
sweet tones. She was about two feet away when Hecate hissed furiously, then shot up the hill toward the
Longworth mansion. "You bring the box, Mommy!"
Melinda shouted, already on the cat's trail.

Caroline wrestled the big box out of the car and
paused for a moment, staring at the cabin. Part of her
wanted to go in and look for Twinkle. Another part
was deathly afraid of what she might find. But a
closer look at the cabin door relieved her of responsibility. The door had been sealed off with a sign
reading CRIME SCENE. She knew she was not supposed
to enter the cabin and in fact might disturb evidence
that could reveal who had attacked Chris.

"Mommy, are you *coming?*" Melinda called down
the hill. She had Hecate cornered against the
Longworth garage and was gesturing impatiently at
Caroline. "She'll get away if you don't hurry."

Caroline trudged up the hill carrying the box. Even
from this distance she could see that the cat was terrified, but Melinda was crawling toward her, holding
out her fingers in a gesture of friendship. And miraculously, the cat wasn't running.

"Sweet little girl, you don't have to be afraid of
me," she was saying as Caroline cautiously approached. Hecate cast her a baleful glance, then

turned her attention back to Melinda, who was holding out one of the cheese treats George loved. "Why don't you try one of these? They're real, real good, and you look hungry. Come on, kitty cat. Everything's gonna be all right."

Caroline stopped in her tracks as Hecate stole forward. Her one jade-green eye studied Melinda and her ear twitched. Then she stretched her body forward, ignoring the cheese treat as she angled her head under Melinda's hand. "Oh, you just want to be petted, don't you?" Melinda crooned. "Poor little baby whose daddy's in the hospital. You haven't gotten petted all day!"

When Melinda sat down on the dry grass and pulled an unprotesting Hecate onto her lap, Caroline approached. "Looks like we won't need the box. She likes you."

"That's 'cause she knows I like her." Melinda stood up, carefully cradling the small cat. "See, there's nothing to worry about. I knew I could make friends with her."

At that moment a flapping black cape and straw sunbonnet flashed around the corner of the garage. "Here now! What's all this? What's going on?"

Hecate yowled and Melinda looked frightened as Millicent Longworth bore down on them. Caroline touched Melinda's shoulder. "You run on down to the car, honey. I'll be along in a minute." She turned to Millicent as Melinda fled. "Miss Longworth, I'm sure you don't remember me—"

"You were married to Corday."

"That's right. I'm Caroline. My last name is Webb now."

"Yes, yes, I know all that. What are you doing here?"

"There was a terrible incident last night. Chris was shot. He's in the hospital, and I came to collect his cat."

Millicent's slightly prognathous jaw lowered, and her voice softened to a normal tone. "The girl he was with came up here to use the phone after the shooting."

"She did?"

"Had to. He doesn't have a phone, and it's a long way to the foot of the hill. I almost didn't let her in. Sounded like a maniac out there banging on the front door. And of course he didn't want me to open the door at all."

"Your brother?"

Millicent's gaze grew guarded. "No. A caller. I don't like to mention names."

"I see. I didn't mean to pry." Encouraged by what for Millicent was downright chattiness, she couldn't resist asking, "Did you see anything, Miss Longworth? Anything that might help the police find out who shot Chris?"

"I saw nothing. I was in my house."

"What about your brother? Could he have seen anything?"

Millicent looked beyond her at the flat gray sky. "Garrison had a heart attack last night. The shock . . ."

"Good heavens, I'm so sorry. Is he all right?"

"I don't know. He's in the hospital."

Either the woman is a very good actress or she doesn't care about Garrison's heart attack, Caroline thought. And once again all the old questions began to assail her. Could Millicent have had anything to do with Hayley's murder? The police had thought so for a while until her alibi was established. And Caroline had to admit the woman was cold, even about her own brother. And there had always been something not quite right about her eyes.

"I don't like that cat coming up here," Millicent said suddenly, "even if cats were sacred to the Egyptians."

Caroline inwardly recoiled, uneasiness sweeping over her. "I understand. We're taking her away now." She turned her back and started quickly down the hill.

"Goodbye," Millicent said so softly Caroline could barely hear her. Then, "Your little girl is quite beautiful. Just like the other one."

2

"Daddy, can you do anything about Hecate's eye?" Melinda asked.

A slow, dreary rain had set in about an hour earlier and now, as they sat around the dining room table, it pattered against the window like a lost soul begging for admittance.

David, who had not uttered a complete sentence since he came home to find Chris's cat sitting on top of the refrigerator out of a delighted George's range, stretched his mouth into a smile. "The eye is gone, honey. It can't be fixed."

"I was thinking of a transplant," Melinda said earnestly. "Do we have enough money?"

Greg spoke without looking up from his plate. "They don't do transplants on animals, squirt."

"How do you know? Daddy's the doctor."

"I think Greg's right on this one. But don't worry

about the cat, Melinda. I'm sure it can see very well with only one eye."

"Maybe, but she just looks so weird she probably scares off other animals."

Greg grinned. "Not George. He's been planted in front of the fridge for two hours with that stupid, lovesick look on his face."

"George is special," Melinda said fondly. "He wouldn't let a little thing like her lost eye bother him. But boy cats might not be so nice." She dug a crater in her mashed potatoes and dropped in a few peas. "Daddy, me and Mommy saw the creepiest lady when we went to get Hecate. She looked like the wicked witch in *The Wizard of Oz.*"

"Millicent Longworth," Caroline told David.

"I guessed."

"She said her brother Garrison had a heart attack last night, but she didn't seem too concerned about his condition."

Greg speared his third piece of roast beef. "They the people who owned Longworth Mills?"

Caroline nodded. "They were very rich when I lived near them. But Millicent didn't know a thing about running the mills after her father died, and her brother, I understand, wasn't interested, so the operation was turned over to outsiders who fleeced them and ran the company into the ground. I don't know what they have left, but Millicent is certainly a pathetic creature."

"Scary's more like it," Melinda put in, pushing her plate away. "Is there dessert?"

"How about ice cream? I didn't have time to bake anything."

"Ice cream's fine with me," Greg said, sitting back and waiting to be served.

Caroline pushed back her chair, but David stopped her. "Sit still. Greg, fix your sister and yourself each a dish and eat it in front of the TV. I want to talk to your mother."

A look flashed between Greg and Melinda before he said easily, "Sure. Come on, squirt. Maybe you can talk George into moving so I can get near the freezer."

David listened intently, and when he seemed satisfied the children were in one of their frequent squabbles instead of eavesdropping, he looked at Caroline. "Why did you bring that cat here?"

She had been steeling herself for this all evening. "David, she's just here for a couple of days, and she won't be any trouble. Besides, I thought you liked cats."

"Don't evade me. Why did *you* have to be the one to take care of Chris's cat?"

Chris had been an unspoken issue between them ever since the marriage. Although David never said a word against Chris or openly expressed his jealousy, Caroline knew he saw Chris as a threat—the glamorous artist Caroline had loved and lost. It had taken him almost a year after her divorce to even ask her to dinner, and it was she who had proposed, not because she was lonely, but because she knew David loved her and she had fallen in love with his strength and kindness. But David never seemed to believe she could love him just as much as she had Chris, if in a different way, without the romantic abandon of youth and first love. So maybe Lucy had been right earlier. Maybe David had sensed her renewed interest in Chris, and it was making him miserable.

She smiled. "Chris asked Lucy to take care of the

cat for him, but she didn't want to. I volunteered because there was no one else. I brought her here instead of taking her to the vet's because I thought Melinda would enjoy having her around." That is almost the exact truth, she thought guiltily.

David clasped his hands behind his head and turned his face to the ceiling, sighing. "You know, I thought we'd put it all behind us. Hayley. Chris. But because of everything happening lately, it all seems like yesterday."

"I know, but that's not my fault."

His eyes met hers. "I know that, honey. I didn't mean to imply it was. It's just . . . unfortunate."

"David, I'd hardly use the word *unfortunate.* Someone is out there calling, breaking in, *shooting* people." She looked at David searchingly. "You do believe me now, don't you? That all of this is related?"

"I know someone left a doll on Melinda's bed and someone has been calling. I still think it's Fidelia."

"Fidelia was here today when the call came."

"It's possible to play a tape over the phone."

"David, Melinda was having a conversation with someone before I took the phone. You don't have a conversation with a tape recording."

"I guess not."

"And what about Chris?"

"Anyone could have shot him. We only have his word that there was a doll on his bed."

Caroline drummed her fingers on the table. "Have you been talking to Lucy?"

"You mean she said the same thing?"

"Yes. Quite a coincidence."

"Not a coincidence, Caroline, just common sense.

I'll bet you five dollars the police don't find a clown doll in Chris's cabin."

Caroline ignored the challenge. "Speaking of Twinkle, Tom wanted me to ask you if you stuffed the doll down in the trash, or put it on top of a trash can."

David lowered his hands and put his elbows on the table. "I never carry trash cans to the street. Too heavy. I just take out the trash bags." His forehead creased. "Let me think. It seems to me that I tried to cram the doll into a full bag, but it wouldn't fit. I just laid it on top."

"Then it might have fallen on the ground."

"I suppose. Which means you think someone could have picked it up—someone who's watching the house and who wanted the doll back in order to frighten Chris like they did you."

Caroline nodded.

"Well, I'm not convinced."

"Oh, David, why is it you just shut your eyes to what you don't want to be true?"

"I don't."

"Yes, you do. You always have. You seem to think if you don't admit something's wrong, it'll go away."

David shut his eyes and rubbed the lids for a moment. "Caroline, you went through hell over Hayley," he said slowly. "Now you seem to be obsessing on her again. It frightens me."

It frightens me, too, Caroline wanted to say, but wouldn't. She did not want David to think for even an instant that she doubted herself. "David, something strange is going on. You have to admit that."

"I do. Someone is trying to scare you with these phone calls. But as for them being related to Pamela

Burke's death and Chris's shooting"—he lifted his hands—"I just can't buy it."

"In spite of what the child said on the phone about Chris getting shot?"

"Hundreds of people could have known about that. It could have been on the radio for all we know."

"And this child just happened to hear it."

"An adult heard it and had a child call. What's happened to your power of reason?"

"I think it's still intact."

"Is it? What about today?" David looked into her eyes with an intensity she rarely saw. "Caroline, I have always believed Millicent Longworth killed Hayley. She's been a nut case for years. Now when someone—possibly Millicent—is trying to scare the hell out of you by making you think Hayley's come back, you take our little girl out to the place where Hayley was kidnapped and Chris was shot not twenty-four hours earlier. That doesn't seem too sensible to me."

Caroline knew David wasn't being completely honest either—there was an element of jealousy in his not wanting Melinda at Chris's home. However, he'd still made a good point—an excellent point. She was suddenly horrified at what she had done by letting Millicent see Melinda and taking the child to a crime scene. She ran a hand across her forehead. "David, I'm sorry. I guess with everything that's been going on I'm just not thinking straight." And there was also the fact that she had never really believed Millicent had taken Hayley. She had nothing whatsoever to base that faith on. It was just a feeling. And feelings can be wrong, she told herself.

"I was wrong to take Melinda up there," she said fervently. "I promise I won't be so careless again."

David came to kneel beside her chair. "You're the least careless mother I know. You've just been distracted." He hugged her. "Friends again?"

She looked down into the beloved dark eyes, now showing slight bags of fatigue. "Always."

"Daddy?" Melinda stood timidly in the doorway. "Are you through fighting?"

"We weren't fighting, kiddo, we were just talking."

"You always say that when you fight." Melinda approached, giving them her most angelic smile. "*One Hundred and One Dalmations* is on at the movie Saturday night. Could we go?"

David wrapped an arm around her thin legs. "Haven't you already seen that?"

"Yeah, but you watch John Wayne movies more'n once. Please?"

Caroline looked at David. "*Please?* We haven't done anything as a family for a long time."

David smiled. "Okay, but I doubt if Greg will be too thrilled."

"*Dalmations* is on at the place with lots of movies in one building. He said if Julie could come they'd see something else."

"John Wayne?"

"Tom Cruise." Melinda giggled. "He's *so* cute!"

"Cute or not, you're sticking with Walt Disney," David laughed. "So, Saturday night I've got a date with the two prettiest girls in town."

3

Millicent twirled in front of the mirror in her new blue taffeta party dress. "I look almost pretty!" she exclaimed to the maid, Sally.

"There's no almost about it," Sally said. "Pretty as a picture."

"I want to show Mother. Where is she?"

"I don't know, Miss Millie." Sally bent to tug at the hem of the dress. "She's probably in her bedroom."

Millicent ran down the hall to her mother's room, the taffeta rustling around her long legs. She tapped on the door, but her mother didn't answer. Millicent hesitantly opened it, wondering if her mother was taking another of her increasingly frequent naps. But the big canopied bed was empty. Frustrated, she strode down the hall to the sewing room. Not that her mother sewed much anymore. But maybe . . .

Then she spotted it—the attic door standing open at the end of the hall—and she was filled with unreasoning dread.

Slowly she walked up the steps to the attic, her beautiful skirt rustling, her heart pounding. When she reached the top, she stood perfectly still, watching how brilliant sunlight streaming through the leaded attic window played over her mother's body suspended by a rope from the rafter, one of her dainty white shoes dangling from a limp foot.

Millicent's heart slammed against her ribs and her eyes snapped open. At first she was blind, the images of her dream dancing in front of her like flickering flames. Then her heart began to slow as the shadowy rectangle of her bedroom came into focus. Yes, it was all right. Only the dream again. She should be used to it after all this time. She ought to be able to say, "It's only a dream about someone long dead" and wake herself up, but she never could. The nightmare

was just as vivid and spellbinding as it had been fifty
years ago.

Millicent drew a long, shuddering breath, her
mouth bitter the way it was when she had taken one
of her sleeping pills. But she hadn't taken one tonight. At least, she didn't think she had, although she
had been overcome with drowsiness after her evening
sherry and had gone to bed at 9:30. Was it possible
she *had* taken one, or even two, and didn't remember?

She tried to sit up and couldn't. Her right arm
seemed to be held fast up and behind her, and twisting around on the bed, she saw with horror that her
wrist was handcuffed to the brass headboard.

Someone moved in one shadowy corner. "Are you
scared?" a little girl asked. Millicent whimpered and
jerked, but the handcuffs held relentlessly. "You *are*
scared, aren't you? Real scared," the sweet young
voice went on. "Scared is an awful feeling, isn't
it?"

"Who are you?" Millicent gasped.

"Don't you remember?"

"Remember what?"

"It's bad to lie. You remember it. A long time ago
a little girl cried. She asked you to turn her loose and
take her to her mommy." Pause. "But you didn't."

Millicent peered frantically into the darkness.
"What do you want?"

"I want you to feel like she did so long ago.
Scared. Lonely. Don't you want to cry?"

Millicent's long white nightgown twisted around
her bony legs as she flopped on the bed, wondering
hopefully if she wasn't having another nightmare, but
knowing she wasn't. "I don't understand."

"Yes, you do. Just think real hard, Miss

Longworth. *Real* hard." A soft metallic sound came from the corner, as if a cap was being unscrewed. "She came up here to be friends, but she wasn't supposed to tell her mommy and daddy. It was a secret. It was all a secret."

Sick recognition filled Millicent although she knew what she was thinking was impossible. "You can't be that little girl. That Hayley."

"Why not?"

Millicent heard a splashing sound. "Hayley is dead."

"Oh." The childish voice seemed preoccupied, and slowly a pungent smell filled the room.

"What are you doing?" Millicent croaked.

"Sprinkling stuff around."

"Kerosene! It smells like kerosene!"

"Yes."

"My brother is here. My brother will—"

"Your brother is in the hospital."

Millicent began thrashing. "Let me up! Unfasten these things!"

"I can't. Then you'd run away."

Millicent quaked with racking dry sobs. "What are you going to do?"

"Burn you up."

"Burn me . . . That child was burned. Hayley."

"I know."

Millicent suddenly stopped thrashing. "I've tried to forget."

"I didn't forget."

"I tried to make amends. I'm sorry. I never thought it would come to that."

"What did you think, Miss Longworth? That you could hide her forever?"

"I didn't think about it. But I didn't want anyone dead. I asked God to make everything all right."

"God doesn't listen to bad people."

"But I didn't have any choice! I had to protect the family name. Father would have been so angry. So *angry!*" Millicent fell into muttering. "But I always thought she was pretty. Beautiful blue eyes. Eyes like Mother's. Mother is dead. Hayley is dead . . ."

"Oops, the can's empty."

Millicent's voice rose hysterically. "I know why you're here! Harry Vinton sent you!"

"Who?"

"The policeman. He gave me a lie detector test. I was lying. He knew it. He checked on everything. He figured it all out. Ugly, hateful man! But he said he'd help. He said for some money he'd cover everything up, make everything look all right. They left me alone after that. Everybody left me alone until last night."

"I didn't know about him. But he didn't send me."

Millicent lay still for a moment. Then she screamed, "Father sent you! He sent you to punish me. He didn't understand."

A match was struck and in its glow Millicent caught a glimpse of bright, frizzy hair. "Your daddy didn't send me. Maybe God sent me. Or maybe the devil."

Millicent's body whipped back and forth on the bed as the match was held against a piece of cloth. The cloth flamed. "Goodbye, Miss Longworth." The cloth, flung forward, exploded as it touched the kerosene.

Within seconds a wall of flame reached at the foot of Millicent's bed. She shrieked and in one violent convulsion dislocated her right shoulder. But there was no escape from the handcuffs, and while smoke billowed forward, she choked out a final curse at the God who had deserted her the day her mother hanged herself.

11

~

1

TOM WAS EXHAUSTED. He'd been called out at
5:00 A.M. on the arson-homicide at the Longworth mansion and watched them carry away the re-
mains of Millicent Longworth, who had been found
handcuffed to a brass headboard. This was the second
fire in two weeks. The work of a firebug? Tom didn't
think so. Now it was one o'clock and he was back at
his desk wondering if the tartar sauce on the fish
sandwich he'd downed in the car had been spoiled.
Something was not sitting right in his stomach. He
reached for his coffee cup, stared at it for a moment,
then put it down and rifled through the drawer for
Tums.

The phone rang. He bit the Tums disk in two when
he heard his ex-wife Marian's voice. "I want to talk
to you about the kids," she said without preamble.
"They have some crazy notion of coming to visit you
over the holidays."

"Sounds great to me. I haven't gotten to spend
much time with them since I moved down here."

"And whose fault is that?"

"Yours. You always manage to schedule some hysterical illness whenever they want to see me."

"My illnesses are not hysterical," Marian said coldly. "And besides, I don't want them around that woman you live with."

"Don't call her *that woman*. Her name is Lucille."

"I don't give a damn what her name is. I don't want my children around her."

Tom sighed, wondering where the gentle-voiced girl he'd married twenty years ago had gone. Everyone said they were too young to get married. Before long he knew everyone had been right. They were kids who within five years found themselves with two children of their own and nothing in common. Tom began spending more and more time on the job, and Marian started seeing other men, which she seemed to have forgotten in the four years since their divorce. Now she saw herself as the wronged woman, abandoned to care for two daughters while her ex-husband lived off a rich older woman. In spite of his anger, he couldn't help smiling. Marian's melodramatic imagination had been working overtime ever since he got involved with Lucy, and her antipathy had grown even stronger since last summer when he and Lucy went to visit the girls in Chicago. They had not only accepted Lucy but were enchanted with her ebullience and young ways, so different from their mother's hypochondriac moodiness.

Tom forced himself to keep his voice controlled. "Look, Marian, in spite of the fact that I've always had joint custody of the girls, I've been letting you call the shots ever since we got divorced. Guilt, I suppose, although why I ever felt guilty I don't know. But the children are in their late teens now, and I think it's time they started making some decisions for themselves."

"They aren't eighteen yet, and I will *not* have them subjected to your living situation."

"I'm afraid you don't have any choice. I remind you—*joint* custody. I have as much say in what they do as you, and if I have to exert my authority to help them do what they want—like visiting their own father—I'm damn well going to do it."

Marian slammed down the phone. Tom groaned and took out the roll of Tums again, wondering if you could overdose on the things.

He stared at the small bronze replica of the Sphinx on his desk, a present from Lucy because she said it embodied enigma, and enigmas were his stock-in-trade. Like the enigma of Hayley Corday's murder. Forcing Marian from his thoughts, he decided to call Margaret Evans, the woman who had reported seeing Hayley a week after her kidnapping. Her daughter said she'd be home by Friday morning, and it was already afternoon.

A woman answered on the third ring and identified herself as Margaret Evans. After introducing himself, Tom said, "I know it's been years since you first reported seeing a child you thought was Hayley Corday at the rest stop, but I would really appreciate it if you would tell me everything you can remember about the incident."

Mrs. Evans, a tart-tongued seventy years old, had waited a long time to vent her anger over Harry Vinton's dismissal of her report, and she wasn't coming forth with any details until she made Tom aware of just how affronted she had been all these years. "Fine time to get interested in what I saw," she grumbled. "It's too late now to do anything for that little girl."

"You're certain it was Hayley Corday you saw in that car?"

"I was inches away from her. *Inches.* I recognized her from the pictures on the news and in the papers. I told that smart-alec policeman in charge of the case it was Hayley, but he didn't believe me."

"Can you tell me exactly what you saw?"

"Why? Are you reopening the case?"

"Not officially, but I've been reading the reports from the Corday investigation, and I have a few questions." Tom decided flattery was definitely called for. "Please, Mrs. Evans. I'm not Harry Vinton, and I'm not going to brush aside what you tell me. You could really be a big help if you would just try to recall that night."

A deep sigh on the other end of the line as feathers smoothed. "All right. All I ever wanted to do is help. And it's not as if I don't remember what I saw. I'll never forget it."

"That's great, Mrs. Evans."

"It was the Fourth of July, and my husband and I were coming back from visiting my married daughter. That was her you spoke to on the phone the other day. Her husband died five years ago when he was up on the roof fixing the antenna. Rolled off onto the front lawn. Snapped his back like a matchstick."

"How awful," Tom murmured, thinking that aside from surveillance the only thing he didn't like about police work was garrulous witnesses.

"Yes, it was awful, and since she never had any kids, I insisted she move right in here with me. Anyway, Roy—that was my husband—Roy had to go to the bathroom. Kidney problems. I told him to wait until we got to a nice restaurant—those roadside park facilities aren't much better than outhouses—but he wouldn't listen. You know how men are. We pulled into the rest stop and there was only one other car in the parking lot. I told Roy I'd wait in the car. After a minute or two, though, I decided to get out and stretch my legs. I walked near that Cadillac—that was the other car, a brown Cadillac—and call it second sight, or the Lord's will, or whatever you want, but I knew I was supposed to look in that car, Mr. Jerome."

"Amazing." Tom gripped the phone. "What did you see?"

"A little girl wrapped in a blanket. At first I thought there wasn't anything unusual about a child asleep in the backseat of a car. Then I saw that her mouth was taped. I peered in closer and could see her eyes all sunken in, her skin pale. I thought she'd been drugged. Then it hit me. Hayley Corday. I was looking at Hayley Corday, the little girl who's been missing for a week."

"What did you do then, Mrs. Evans?"

"I ran around and looked at the license plate. Then I headed for the restrooms. I yelled for Roy. He said, 'Hold your horses' or something like that and I screamed, 'It's a matter of life and death!' He came running then. But just as he appeared, the car started and tore out of the parking lot like a bat out of hell. I wanted to follow it, but Roy wouldn't."

"Mrs. Evans, what was that license number?"

"Well, I can't remember *that* after nineteen years. But I told Harry Vinton. Isn't it in his report?"

"No, it isn't."

"Well, there you go. I told you how he acted. Practically told me I was imagining things. He probably wouldn't have written any of it down if I hadn't talked to another policeman there. Can't remember his name."

"You told your story to another policeman?"

"Oh, no, not the whole thing. I just mentioned that I'd seen Hayley Corday and that Harry Vinton had taken all the details." Therefore the report, Tom thought. If Mrs. Evans had talked to someone else, Vinton couldn't ignore the sighting—he had to file a report of some kind. But he didn't have to make it complete. And he didn't have to follow up on it. "I was calling again because I'd just remembered something else I thought he should know," Mrs. Evans was saying. "It was about the blanket the little girl was wrapped in."

"What about it?"

"Well, it wasn't your usual bed blanket. It was rough like it was handwoven, and it had an odd pattern on it. I don't know how to describe it without saying it looked African. Is that important? On TV mysteries things like that are always important."

"It could be very important, Mrs. Evans."

"Yes," she said with satisfaction. "I thought it would be."

"Mrs. Evans, you didn't see the person who drove away in the car?"

"Oh, no. And that puzzled me. He must have stopped there to use the restroom, but I didn't run into him when I went to get Roy."

"Were the men's and women's restrooms in separate buildings?"

Mrs. Evans was silent for a moment. "Yes, as a matter of fact they were quite a little distance apart. But you don't think a *woman* could have taken that child and . . . and done those *things* to her!"

"Anything is possible."

"Oh, sweet Jesus," Mrs. Evans breathed. "A *woman.*"

"Maybe. Mrs. Evans, can you remember *anything* else?"

"That's it."

"I want you to know how much I appreciate your giving me this information," Tom said in his warmest tone. "I know it wasn't a pleasant memory for you to dredge up."

"No, it certainly wasn't," she said crisply, then with a slight tremulousness, "Detective?"

"Yes?"

"Did I handle things wrong all those years ago? I knew Harry Vinton wasn't doing right by my information, and I wanted to come to police headquarters and find someone who would, but Roy, rest his soul, talked me out of it. He said, why make trouble for ourselves? And I went along with him. But I've always ... I've always thought that maybe I could have saved that little girl's life."

And you could have if Harry Vinton hadn't been in charge of the investigation, Tom thought furiously. The man had suppressed this woman's invaluable evidence, but that was not her fault. "Mrs. Evans, you did just fine," he told her kindly. "I wish everyone was as observant and cooperative as you."

"Oh, well ..." He could sense her relaxing. "That's good to know. I've worried for a good many years."

"Stop worrying. And thank you very much for the information."

Tom hung up, leaned back in his chair, and drew in a deep breath. Hayley Corday wrapped in an *African* print blanket? Of course, Mrs. Evans hadn't seen the blanket for almost twenty years, and her description amounted to a vague impression about the design, but no one could ignore the implications, not when old reports showed that Millicent Longworth had been touring Africa when her father died and she came home to take over the business. Still, he wanted to be sure. He picked up the phone and dialed again. "Caroline," he said in a moment, trying to sound casual. "How are you?"

"Okay. No more phone calls." Her voice was tight and worried, nevertheless. "Is this a friendly call or is there something I can do for you?"

"Both. Actually, I wonder what you can tell me about Millicent Longworth."

"Millicent? Why?"

"You'll hear about it on the evening news, so I might as well tell you. She was burned to death in her home last night."

Caroline gasped. "Not another fire!"

"And another murder. She'd been handcuffed to the bed."

"Oh, my God."

"Yeah, it was pretty bad. Her brother didn't know how lucky he was to have a heart attack and get away from there. Otherwise he might have been killed, too."

"Heaven only knows how the shock of his sister's death will affect him after what he's just been through."

"Did you know him?"

"No. I never even met him. He was living in Italy with his wife when Chris and I were married. Chris said his wife died and he came home just a few years ago because of heart trouble."

"But you did know Millicent."

"I wouldn't say I *knew* her. We'd met. I talked to

her for a few minutes maybe four or five times when I lived in the cabin."

"Didn't she travel around the world, too?"

"Yes. She and her brother were sort of a team until he got married. Then she went on traveling by herself. She came home the year Chris and I were married, the same year her father died. Now there was a tyrant."

"The father?"

"Yes. Of course, he didn't deign to even speak to Chris and me, and he was trying to get rid of the cabin, even though it wasn't on his land. He'd tried to buy Chris out several times and finally was resorting to calling in local political favors to get rid of us. He used to be in Congress, you know. He fought us right up until the week he died."

"So then Millicent came home."

"Yes. I wasn't surprised she and her brother were always on the go, never staying around their father, but I *was* surprised that Garrison didn't come back when the old man was gone. I guess there was no love lost between them, though, and Garrison was very happy in Italy. It's just strange that after all that extensive travel, Millicent became a recluse when she came home." Caroline paused. "You know she was a suspect in Hayley's murder."

"I know. And with good reason."

"But she was cleared. She was somewhere else the night of the kidnapping." Yes, according to Vinton, Millicent Longworth had been visiting a Mrs. Sally Rice that evening, Tom thought grimly. Mrs. Rice claimed Millicent had been with her from three in the afternoon until ten that night.

"Caroline, do you remember what kind of car Millicent had at the time of the kidnapping?"

Caroline laughed. "Now you're asking a tough one. That was a long time ago. But let me think. I do recall her father left a car that Millicent dutifully drove to the foot of the hill and back once a week to blow out the carbon, she once told us. Chris thought it was so funny she believed creeping down that steep hill at ten miles an hour would take care of the carbon. But if I remember correctly, the car was a Cadillac, one of those old models with the big fins."

"Color?"

"Gosh, Tom, I don't know. Dark."

"Black?"

"Maybe. No, wait. Chris said once if it were black it would look like a hearse. Let's see ... brown or dark green. Brown, I think. Why is that important?"

"Just wondering if she knew how to drive," Tom side-stepped. He'd told Caroline he wanted to let her in on everything, but this was one point he wanted to keep to himself for a while. If Caroline knew someone had spotted Hayley and she could have been saved ... well, he just couldn't let her know, with everything else she was worrying about.

"I think I know why you're interested in her driving. David says he stuffed Twinkle in a full trash bag and the doll could have fallen out. David always believed Millicent took Hayley, you know. It's possible she came here and found the doll in the yard."

"But how would she have gotten it in your house to begin with?"

"That's what I've wondered, too. But I suppose there are ways." She sighed. "It's hard to believe I just saw Millicent yesterday."

"You did?"

"Yes. Melinda and I went to the cabin to get Chris's cat. The cat ran up to the Longworth house and Melinda went after it. Millicent came out demanding to know what was going on. I explained about Chris getting shot and she said she knew—that the girl Chris had been with ran up to her house to use the phone after Chris was shot."

Ah, the charming and kind Renée, Tom thought wryly. He'd spoken with her yesterday about the shooting. "I don't know anything and I don't want to know anything," she'd told him hatefully. "You know, you meet a guy and go to his house for what you think'll be a nice evening and what happens? He goes berserk, then someone starts firing a machine gun at the house."

"It was a handgun."

"Handgun, machine gun, they both shoot bullets. And *then* after I've barely escaped with my life and go running for help, that crazy loon and fat toad up at that mansion aren't going to let me in. 'Don't open that door!' he kept shouting. Some scrawny old man opened it anyway. He was real sweet to me, but his lips were all blue. He looked sick. The woman kept flapping around yelling about privacy, and the fat toad turned his back and took off for the other room like he didn't want to be seen. If you ask me, it was him who fired those shots."

"Did you get a good look at him, Renée?"

She stared off petulantly for a moment, then, reconsidering the chance for more attention, relented. "Like I said, he was fat. And he had real black eyes like olives and grayish-brown hair that had gotten thin on top. That's all I could tell because he took off so fast. But I did see an Olds 98 parked in front of the house. I noticed because my mom has a car just like it. I suppose it was his—I can't picture that crazy woman or the sick old man driving."

"What color was the car?"

"White. And it wasn't new. My mom's isn't either."

"You didn't happen to notice the license plate, did you?"

Renée had looked at him with empty eyes, her jaw dropping. "You cops are a real trip. Sure, I'm getting shot at and I stop to take down a license plate number. Jeez!"

Jerking his mind back to his conversation with Caroline, Tom asked, "What else did Millicent say about the shooting?"

"Nothing that made a lot of sense. There was one interesting thing, though. She said *he* didn't want her to let the girl in. I thought she meant her brother, but she said it was a caller. When I asked who the caller was, she got cagy and said she didn't like to mention names. But she looked frightened. I think she'd let something slip."

"You're sure she didn't say anything else about the man?"

"Nothing. Why? Do you think he might have had something to do with the shooting?"

"You never can tell," Tom said vaguely as he thought of the white Olds 98 he'd seen sitting in fat Harry Vinton's driveway.

2

Caroline hung up the phone and ran a hand through her hair in frustration. Why hadn't she told Tom she was certain Millicent Longworth's death was connected with Hayley? First Pamela, then Chris, now Millicent—all people who had known her little girl. But she had no proof it wasn't coincidence.

One piece of tangible evidence might make her case more convincing.

When the phone rang ten minutes later, she thought it might be Tom again. Instead, Chris's whiskey-edged voice throbbed in her ear. "Caro."

"Chris! Are you calling from the hospital?"

"No, I was released this morning and took a taxi. I'm calling from a drugstore near home. I stopped by the vet's but he said you never dropped off Hecate. She didn't vanish after I got shot, did she?"

"No. I'm sorry I didn't let you know sooner, but I didn't think you would be released until tomorrow. She stayed here with us." She laughed. "After what she'd been through I thought being with a family might be less traumatic than staying at the vet's, but I'm not sure."

"I hope she hasn't been any trouble."

"Not at all. Our Labrador, George, has been the problem—he's in love with her and won't give her a minute's peace, so I'm sure she'll be glad to get home even if Melinda will hate to give her up."

"Your daughter liked the cat?"

"Melinda has a magic touch with animals. Hecate even likes her, although I don't think she's too crazy about the rest of us."

"I'll come by and get her."

"That isn't necessary. I'll bring her to you if you're sure you're up to taking care of her."

"I'm fine. My arm's in a sling, but aside from that I'm good as new and ready to take the cat off your hands. Besides, I miss her."

"Okay," Caroline said. "I'll see if I can coax her into the car and we'll be there in about half an hour."

As soon as she hung up, her heart began to pound. She was going to see Chris. The prospect unnerved her, especially when she thought of David's disapproval, but at the same time she felt exhilarated, more alive than since this whole Hayley business started. Chris could always do that to her, from the time they met when she was a seventeen-year-old student in an art-appreciation class where Chris was the guest speaker. Twenty-seven years she had spent loving him, in spite of the hurt, in spite of the years apart. In spite of David.

She pushed the thought of David from her mind as she went in search of the cat. There was no sense in writhing in guilt over feelings she could not change, even if she intended to do nothing about them. She would take Chris his cat, make sure he was comfortably set up in the cabin, and that would be the end of it.

Hecate was curled into the bookcase in the family room, George stationed six feet below in ardent admiration. "George, we're going to have to get you a proper girlfriend," Caroline sighed as she scooped the cat off the shelf. Hecate stiffened and spat, terrified she was going to be presented to the black monster that had trailed her relentlessly for days, but when Caroline held her high and tight against her chest, the cat relaxed slightly. George was determined to follow them out to the car but let himself be diverted by a few Milkbones Caroline tossed on the kitchen floor before she and the cat dashed out the door to the garage.

"Melinda's going to miss you," Caroline told the cat as they drove along the river road toward Longworth Hill. Hecate looked at her suspiciously with her one beautiful eye, then went into a deep study of the scenery on the passenger's side.

The smell of smoke still hung in the air around the

hill, and when Caroline reached the top she understood why. All that remained of the Longworth mansion was a few crumbling brick walls. Obviously there had been no automatic sprinkler system here like the one in Pamela's house. Even the beautifully tended lawn and Millicent's prized rosebushes had been scorched by the conflagration. Caroline shut off the car, simply staring at the ruins for a few minutes while her stomach turned. Poor, strange Millicent, who only yesterday had been tearing around the lawn in her black cape, jealously protecting the family home. Well, she didn't have to worry anymore. There was nothing left of the Longworth domain, nothing left of Millicent.

Chris came out on the porch just as Caroline was opening the car door. "It's a real mess up there, isn't it?"

His arm was in a sling, his face thinner and paler, but otherwise he looked fine. Hecate scrambled across her lap and shot toward him, a sleek black missile. "I had no idea the damage was so extensive." Caroline climbed from the car as Chris bent to scoop up the cat. "There's hardly anything left of the place."

"And it was built like a fortress, too."

Now that she was standing so near him, Caroline could see the deepening crow's-feet around Chris's eyes, the lines of strain making vertical slashes by his mouth. It seemed to her he had aged ten years in the past few days. "Have you heard the fire was deliberately set?"

Chris looked at her in surprise. "Are you sure?"

"Yes. Tom told me." She glanced up at the house again. "They also found Millicent handcuffed to the bed. She was murdered."

Chris's pale face went whiter. "I can't believe it."

"I know. Pamela Burke and now Millicent."

"But there can't be a connection, can there?"

Caroline shrugged. "Maybe not."

Chris set Hecate on the ground, where she began winding around his legs. "Well, it's going to be strange not having dear Millicent's binoculars trained on the cabin. Tending her roses and watching me have been her only sources of entertainment for twenty years. But I bet old Garrison's going to miss her. He seemed really attached to her."

"Do you know anything about his condition?"

"He was at County, too, and I had one of the nurses check on him for me." Of course, Caroline thought dryly. Women are always happy to do favors for Chris. "It was a mild heart attack. I just hope he doesn't have another one when he hears about his sister." He nodded at the cabin. "I made coffee. Care for any?"

I should go, Caroline thought. I should say no thanks and be on my way as soon as possible. "I'd love a cup," she heard herself saying.

As soon as they entered the cabin, Hecate jumped from Chris's arms and dashed to her spot on the settee, looking as if she had just reached the promised land. "I know she's glad to be back," Caroline said, following Chris into the kitchen. "George has made her life unbearable."

"Naw, she's just playing hard to get. She's probably flattered to death a member of the male sex still finds her appealing."

"Melinda thinks you should check into eye transplants and maybe some reconstructive surgery for her ear."

This time Chris threw back his head as he laughed.

"She sounds like a doll, Caro. I wish I could meet her sometime."

"Well, maybe you can someday," Caroline said vaguely, thinking of David's reaction to that suggestion. "Need some help with the coffee?"

"No. Thank goodness it was my left shoulder that got it. I can even paint. Whoever was out there that night didn't mean to kill me."

Caroline studied his face. "Why do you think that?"

Chris handed her a mug of coffee. "According to Tom, the bullets were from a .22 caliber Beretta. The ground behind my jeep was scuffed up, so apparently the sniper was hiding there, over fifty feet away from the cabin. If someone really meant to blow me away from that distance, he would have chosen a more powerful gun."

"Maybe he didn't know that much about guns. Or maybe he was just a bad shot. He did hit the cabin twice."

"*After* I'd already fallen. Why keep shooting when I was out of range? No, I really think the intent was to vent rage, but not kill me."

"That sounds like Lucy's jealous-husband theory."

"Jealous husbands don't carry around clown dolls."

Caroline sauntered over to the hutch bearing the blue country crockery Chris's grandmother had given them as a wedding present. It was sparkling clean and shone in the morning sun. "Chris, what about Twinkle?"

"The last time I saw the doll it was lying on my bed. But when Tom came to check the place over, he said it was gone, and according to him, the cops who came right after the shooting didn't see it, either."

She turned to look at him. "But you're sure it was Twinkle."

"Pretty sure. It certainly looked like Hayley's doll."

"And it vanished when your girlfriend ran up to Millicent's to use the phone?"

"It must have because the ambulance and the police got here fifteen minutes after she called and there was no doll then."

Caroline drained her cup. "Chris, do you think Hayley's murderer could have done this?"

Chris stood and walked over to the window. Hecate, sensing his distress, raised her head to watch him. "That's exactly what I think. I'm leaving town day after tomorrow for Taos. I think you and David should vamoose, too."

"We haven't discussed it, but it's a good idea." She stared at Chris's straight back, thinking. "You know, David always thought Millicent murdered Hayley, but she was murdered last night, too."

"That doesn't mean she didn't kill Hayley or shoot me."

"You don't believe she killed Hayley or you wouldn't have gone on living here."

"No, you're right. She had an alibi. So who killed Millicent?"

"I have no idea, but I have a feeling her death is related to everything that's been happening to me. Maybe even to Hayley's murder."

Chris turned to look at her. "I think so, too. But what in God's name could be the connection between the murder of a little girl and that of an old lady all these years later?"

Caroline tensed with the frustration of trying to explain feelings she couldn't prove. "I don't know. But

I'm so desperate to find an answer." Her voice broke. "There's Melinda, you see. She gets calls, she's approached by a child calling herself Hayley . . ."

Chris strode across the room and took Caroline in his arms. "Caro, don't fall apart. What happened to Hayley is *not* going to happen to Melinda."

"You can't know that. And I can't forget."

"You have to try."

"Can you?" she cried. "Don't you go over Hayley's murder every day?"

Chris sighed. "Yes, but I was the one who was supposed to be looking after her. If it had been you with her up on the hill, she would never have been taken. I know that. But unfortunately for Hayley, I was left in charge. And now she's dead."

"Don't say that!" Caroline raised her face to his. "Stop blaming yourself. I can't bear it."

"Really, Caroline? Don't you blame me?" Chris's voice was both incredulous and cynical. "Can you honestly say you have never blamed me?"

"Yes, I can say it! You loved her as much as I did. And you were a wonderful father, a wonderful husband."

Chris abruptly released her and turned away. "I wasn't as wonderful as you thought," he mumbled. "I wasn't a wonderful father *or* husband. That's why I've always said her death was a punishment."

The awful cold feeling Caroline had experienced so often during the past few days swept over her again. Chris was going to tell her something she didn't want to hear. Her immediate desire was to run out the door with her hands over her ears, but some deep, masochistic impulse made her stand still and ask, "Punishment for what?"

Chris wouldn't turn around to face her. "I wasn't

going to tell you. Not ever. And then when this whole thing started again, I had a superstitious feeling that my silence was causing it." He laughed half-heartedly. "Crazy, isn't it?"

"Just tell me," Caroline said flatly.

"Oh, Caro, I'm so sorry."

"Tell me."

Chris took a deep breath and walked back to the settee. Hecate crawled onto his lap, her tail swishing as if in fright. "It was when you went on the trip to Jamaica with your parents. They always hated me, and I guess I resented your going and taking Hayley."

"You *told* me to go. I hadn't been away from home since our marriage."

"I know. I didn't say my feelings were fair. They just *were*. So you were both gone with your parents, who could give you anything while I couldn't even support us. Little did I know that in just a couple of months everything would break for me. The gallery showing in New York. The great reviews. Anyway, one night Lucy drove up to see me." Oh, God, oh, no, a voice within Caroline moaned, but she looked back at him steadily. "Her painting wasn't going anywhere. She'd been told over and over she was competent, but that was it. She's always said none of that bothered her, but it wasn't true. The criticism crushed her."

"I figured that out a long time ago, Chris."

"Yeah, well, you would." Chris ran a hand through his hair. "She was at the bottom of the well, so we had a few drinks, then we smoked some. I guess we were both pretty stoned. And then . . . well, she told me she'd always loved me. Ever since we dated before I knew you. She was so fragile, so adoring. And you were—"

"In Jamaica with my parents, who could give me anything."

"Caro, don't make this harder."

"I wouldn't dream of it. Please continue."

Chris lifted his hands. "You can guess the rest. We both felt terrible afterwards. Then Lucy found out she was pregnant. She wanted to have the baby. She said she could pass it off as the child of a man she'd had a brief affair with. But I said no. She was your best friend, she told you everything. If she'd had a fling, you'd know about it. You'd see right through a story about a mysterious man. You'd figure out she'd gotten pregnant while you were away. You'd put it all together. Lucy was hysterical. She loved you. She said you were the only real friend she'd ever had."

"She had a funny way of showing it."

Chris ignored her. "So we decided she'd have an abortion. It didn't work out the way it was supposed to. Something went wrong. She could never have a baby after that. So you see, I not only had to live with the fact that I'd cheated on you, I had to take responsibility for the abortion and her sterility. It was just a couple of months after that when Hayley was kidnapped. I felt like it was some kind of retribution."

"So that's why you wanted me to leave you—because you thought it was fair punishment for what you'd done, what you thought you'd caused."

He nodded. Caroline stared at him. He looked miserable. She knew he *was* miserable. But at the moment she could feel nothing for him except contempt. She remembered how happily he'd greeted her and Hayley when they came back from Jamaica that spring. But already he'd been unfaithful and her best friend was carrying his child, a child he'd wanted aborted rather than have her find out the truth. And so, those last few weeks of Hayley's life, she'd been surrounded by lies, lies that almost twenty years later could still rock her world.

"Caroline, I know you can never forgive me, but if you would just try to understand."

Caroline looked at him coldly. "Chris, I've been trying to understand you for a long, long time. I made every excuse in the book for you. But even I can't live a fantasy forever."

She set down her coffee mug and numbly walked from the cabin she had once loved, knowing she would never enter it again.

12

1

HARRY VINTON WAS zealously attacking the kitchen drain with a plunger when the doorbell rang. At first he ignored it, but when it rang for the fourth time, he flung down the plunger with a curse and stalked into the living room.

The moment he swung open the door and faced Tom Jerome, he knew something was wrong. Very wrong.

"Got a few minutes, Vinton?" Jerome asked, his eyes granite gray in the fading afternoon light. "I'd like to ask you a few questions."

"You already did." Harry's voice emerged loud and strong, although he felt as if everything in his big gut was shaking. "Besides, I'm busy."

"Then I'll come back." Tom paused, his eyes skewering Harry like a pig bound for roasting. "And I'll keep coming back until I get what I want."

And he would. Something far back in Harry's mind tolled like a death knell, and he knew it was all over. After nineteen years, it was all over.

"All right." He stepped back to let Tom enter the living room filled with expensive but neglected furniture. Newspapers lay scattered over a good braided rug, and crushed beer cans littered the early American tables. Lucy would die if she saw nice furnishings abused this way, Tom thought absently. Clearly Harry had decorated the place with care, then stopped caring completely. A shame.

Harry sank down on a battered wing chair, and Tom noticed the tremor around his mouth. "So what is it you want this time, Jerome?" he asked gruffly.

Tom didn't ask if he could sit. He stood looking down on Harry. "Why did you suppress evidence in the Hayley Corday case?"

Harry tried to look affronted. "I don't know what the hell you're talking about."

"No? Well, what about Mrs. Margaret Evans? You know, the woman who spotted Hayley in the back of a Cadillac parked at the roadside rest outside Mayesville?"

"A crank."

"I don't think so, Vinton. I think the lady knew exactly what she saw and gave you a very accurate account of it, including the license number of the Cadillac. A brown Cadillac it was, just like Millicent Longworth's. But of course that information doesn't appear in your report."

"License number, hell!" Harry exploded. "She didn't give me any license number."

"She says she did. And I believe her."

"Millicent Longworth didn't even know that kid."

"Vinton, she lived next door Hayley's entire life. Don't give me this 'she didn't know her' crap."

"But Longworth was gone the night of the kidnapping."

"Oh, yes, the convenient alibi. She was visiting Sally Rice." Tom was bending over Harry, his piercing gray eyes above his high-bridged nose making him look like a bird of prey. "Funny, but I discovered that Sally Rice used to work for the Longworths. She was their maid for nearly twenty years. Very loyal to the family. What's even more interesting is that one month after the Corday murder, she moved to Florida into a nice Palm Beach condo. Of course she'd been living on a small pension, but I guess she was really thrifty with her money, right?"

Harry's throat made a loud gulping sound as he swallowed. "Just what the hell are you getting at?"

"I'm getting at the fact that you did a piss-poor job of looking for that little girl, even to the point of suppressing evidence. I'm getting at the fact that not long after her murder, you were able to quit the force and dabble at being a P.I. while living more comfortably than ever. I'm getting at the fact that you were at Millicent Longworth's the night before her murder."

Harry blanched, his breath rattling. "*Who* says I was at the Longworth place?"

"The girl who came to use the phone," Tom said, not feeling a twinge of conscience about stretching the truth. He was working on a hunch and at this point was interested mainly in catching Vinton's reactions. "She's seen you before—she recognized you."

"That is a goddamned lie."

"Then what are you so upset about?"

Harry hauled himself out of his chair, his face inches from Tom's. "How would you like some young hot shit making all these accusations about you?"

"I wouldn't like it, but I wouldn't go to pieces. Not unless they were true."

Sweat popped out on Harry's forehead. "What if I

was at the Longworth place? She didn't die that night."

"But the next night she did die in a fire that was deliberately set. She died handcuffed to the bed. What happened, Harry? Did her conscience finally get the best of her? Was she going to confess to killing Hayley and name you as an accessory?"

"Get out of my house," Harry spat.

"Gladly. But I don't think I need to tell you not to leave town. You may have gotten away with whatever you pulled in the Corday case, but you're not going to get away with Millicent Longworth's murder."

"I did not murder that woman." Harry's voice cracked. "I *didn't.*"

Tom smiled. "Then you don't have anything to worry about, do you?"

Harry stared as Tom calmly walked out the door and closed it behind him. He felt rooted to the floor as blood rushed from his head to his feet like lava surging down a mountain. How many times over the years had he envisioned this scene? A hundred? A thousand? So many times he thought that if the day ever came, he'd be cool in his practiced nonchalance. But he wasn't cool. He'd acted like a sixteen-year-old caught robbing the local convenience store—shaking, terrified, guilty as sin. Twenty years ago he could have handled Jerome. Now look at him—a befuddled alcoholic. He'd screwed up bad. He raised his meaty hand to rub the cold sweat off his forehead. Well, this was just great. If Jerome was only fishing, he'd learned everything he didn't already know. Except about Millicent's death. Shit! Arson-homicide. Who would have wanted to burn the old bat? Not him. He already had one death on his conscience—he wouldn't have added a second, even if she'd threatened to tell the police, which she didn't. But Jerome would never believe that. Hell, nobody who knew about his part in the Corday case would believe it.

His hands would not stop shaking. A drink, that's what he needed. A good stiff drink.

He tottered into the kitchen on unsteady legs and opened the cabinet. What would it be? His eyes fell on the half-full bottle of Ezra Brooks bourbon he kept for special occasions. That would do the trick. Twelve years old and mellow, pure velvet going down the throat. He poured a generous portion and with a sigh of pleasure tossed it down. It rushed through him, warm and comforting, and he poured another shot, gulping it as quickly as the first. The third he decided to savor. He'd sip his drink, turn on the tube, and think his way out of this mess.

Sitting in his big chair in the living room, he aimed the remote control at the television, not really paying attention as the channels clicked silently by. The evening news on the networks. Cartoons on a cable station, a movie on HBO. He paused at the movie. Arnold Schwarzenegger in something. He kind of liked Schwarzenegger movies. Lots of action, not a lot of stupid romance . . .

When he awakened, the room was in total darkness except for images dancing across the TV screen. Groggily he looked at the bottle of bourbon, which was empty. Then he tried to focus on the face of a gilt-and-crystal anniversary clock on the table beside him. It wavered, but he thought the little hand was around nine. He'd been passed out for hours. He tried to get up, then fell backward with the effort. God, he was soused. Paralyzed. Bound to be sick tomorrow. Still, pleasantly numb. He didn't have to think about

Hayley Corday or Millicent Longworth or Tom Hot Shit from Chicago.

Harry groaned at the memory of Tom and gazed at the TV, where a baseball soared in slow motion through the air to slam into the light board. Spheres of light plummeted against the night sky like glowing confetti while music soared in the background.

"That looks so pretty. I could paint that."

Harry jumped, the bottle rolling off his lap. The voice hadn't come from the television. It seemed to come from somewhere behind him. But of course he was hallucinating. He rubbed his eyes.

"Only I'd make it even prettier."

No, he wasn't hallucinating. At least he didn't think he was. "Who's there?" Harry struggled forward, his big legs pumping up and down with the effort. Suddenly a length of wire slipped around his neck and he was jerked violently backward. The stinging told him the wire was cutting his flesh.

"Sit still." A kid's voice, he thought in amazement. A little girl holding a wire around his neck. He touched the wire. If this was a hallucination, it was damned realistic. "Do you know who I am?"

"No," Harry croaked. The room was swimming. If he wasn't so damn dizzy and weak, he could get out of the chair, break free of the wire.

"Don't you remember Hayley Corday?"

"What is this? A joke?"

The wire tightened and jerked. "Not a joke."

Harry felt as if his thoughts were thrashing around, trying to come to some logical conclusion. After a moment he said in triumph, "This is a trick! One of Tom Jerome's dumb shit tricks."

"You shouldn't say bad words."

"Who the hell *are* you?"

"I didn't even know anything about you till I killed Miss Longworth, but she told me how you'd covered everything up, kept it a secret. Why'd you do it? For money?"

Harry made a feeble effort to push himself forward, but the wire cut more deeply into his skin. Already blood was dripping down the front of his tee shirt. He looked at it quizzically, almost as if it weren't his blood. "You killed Millicent?"

"Oh, yes. And Pamela. I didn't know I'd have to kill you, too." She made a clucking sound of disapproval. "But you were bad just like them, so you have to die, too."

Harry felt urine wetting his pants and soaking into the chair cushion. Drunk as he was, he knew this was no stunt. Hell, he was bleeding. And that voice! Childish, but deadly. He started to blubber. "Millicent Longworth was crazy. Always been crazy. I couldn't nail her for the Corday killing, but she did it. You can't believe anything she said."

"Oh, yes, I did believe her. It makes sense now. It all makes sense."

In a sudden, groggy panic Harry clawed at the arms of the chair. "You're crazy. You can't—"

His voice stopped as a knife neatly sliced across his throat, cutting his vocal cords. Blood splashed forward, all over his thighs, onto the braided rug.

"I have to stand behind you so I don't get blood all over me," the voice explained sweetly. "But don't worry. I know how to cut. It won't take you very long to die." The wire was released and Harry slumped forward. Then a strong hand pushed him from the chair. He landed on his knees and his right shoulder, all squishing into the blood-soaked rug. He managed to turn his head slightly. Moonlight streaming through a window outlined a wavering form beside him. Gurgling, he reached for it, but it hovered beyond his grasp. Dully, he let himself roll on his back.

He wasn't going to make it, and suddenly he didn't care. Is this the way Teresa felt before the mugger launched his last, fatal stab wound into her heart? he wondered dreamily. Is this the way that kid had felt as a cleaver rose to lop off her head? Well, he wouldn't feel sorry for them anymore because really it wasn't so bad. Kind of peaceful, actually. Peaceful and final. In some ways, it was better than life.

2

"Where are you going?" David asked as Caroline drew a black wool-jersey dress over her head and smoothed it across her hips.

She hesitated, then said boldly, "To Millicent Longworth's funeral."

"What for?"

"She was an acquaintance. I used to live near her, you know."

"I know that very well. I also know you never said ten words to her in all that time."

"Yes, I did."

"Let's not split hairs. Why don't you just be honest with me?"

"I think there's a connection between Millicent's death and everything that's been going on with us the last few weeks."

"And what good is attending the funeral going to do?"

"If there is a bouquet of black silk orchids at the funeral, I'll *know* there's a connection."

Caroline stood quietly, waiting for David to object. Instead he shrugged out of his blue cardigan and went to the closet. "I'm going with you. Is my gray suit back from the cleaner's?"

Caroline looked at him in astonishment. "I thought you'd have a fit."

David turned to grin at her. "Honey, I'm not quite the old fuddy-duddy you've always thought." Then he sobered. "I still think we should leave the investigating to the police, but except for Tom I don't think they're taking our problem too seriously."

"I didn't think you did, either."

"I know. You're hurt because you think I don't believe you about the flowers. I want to prove to you that I do."

Or else you want to prove that they really don't exist and I'm imagining this, Caroline thought. But whatever David's real motivation was, she was glad he had offered to go along.

Caroline went over to hug him. "David, thank you so much for not trying to stop me. But I really don't want the children to be alone."

"Why don't you call Lucy?" David tore the plastic bag off his newly cleaned suit. "She probably wouldn't mind baby-sitting for a couple of hours."

"No!" David glanced at her, startled, and she lowered her voice. "I mean, her mother hasn't been well and I think Lucy was going to see her this afternoon."

Caroline had not spoken to Lucy since Chris's revelation about their past affair. Lucy had called three or four times, obviously aware of what Chris had told her, but Caroline asked Greg or David to say she was busy and would call back. She knew that someday soon she would have to confront Lucy, but she couldn't do it when she was still so angry. "I could call Fidelia."

"No. I don't want her left alone here with the kids."

"Well, where does that leave us? I don't know of anyone else to call on such short notice, and considering all that's happening, I'm not going to leave Melinda in Greg's hands."

"Okay, I'll stay," David said, hanging his suit back in the closet. "But I don't like the idea of your going to this funeral alone."

"What can happen with me surrounded by a lot of people? I'll be fine. And you wait and see—this time I'll have a bouquet to bring home."

It was Sunday and Greg was glued to a football game on television while Melinda sat on the family-room floor cutting out paper dolls. "Where are you going, Mommy?" she asked when Caroline passed through the room in her high heels.

"To a funeral. I want you to stay here with Greg and Daddy."

"Whose funeral and why can't I go?"

"Can it, squirt, I can't hear," Greg said absently.

Melinda automatically stuck out her tongue at him and looked back at Caroline appealingly. "Please can't I go? I won't cry or anything. I don't even know who died."

Caroline dropped a kiss on her head. "I'd rather you stay here."

Melinda assumed her most long-suffering face. "Okay. You go on and have fun. I'll just sit here with my old paper dolls."

"Cheer up, kid," David said, walking into the room. "When Mommy gets back we'll go for ice cream."

"Oh, goody!" Melinda squealed, clapping her hands. This set off George, which in turn set off Greg. "It's impossible to watch anything in this house!" he blustered. "Noise everywhere!"

"Well, just go to Julie's then," Melinda shouted back. "Big grouch."

"Good luck," Caroline muttered to David as she slipped into her coat. "I think I'd rather be going to a funeral than hanging around here. At least it'll be quiet."

Millicent's funeral was being held in the old St. John's Episcopal Church on the west side of the city, the church frequented by most of the town's blue bloods for the past fifty years. Unlike Pamela's funeral, Millicent's drew no crowds. Caroline had no trouble finding a parking space. In fact, if she hadn't double-checked the obituary column that morning, she would have thought she was in the wrong place. Only a handful of cars were parked in front of the church. Caroline noticed a man going around taking license plate numbers and remembered Tom telling her the police did that at the funerals of murder victims, thinking the killer might attend. Probably several plainclothesmen had been doing the same at Pamela's funeral, but in the crush of people she hadn't noticed. As she climbed the steps toward the church doors, she saw only a handful of curiosity-seekers clustered around, studying everyone who passed as if they could detect Millicent's killer.

As she walked into the cool dimness of the chapel and sat down near the back, Caroline's heart suddenly beat harder. Although she had never been particularly religious, there was something about the soft organ music, the glowing gold cross above the altar, the slant of winter sun through jewel-colored stained-glass windows that filled her with a sense of something higher, more powerful than man. Is that power benevolent? she wondered. That seemed impossible in light of the brutal murder of her little girl. Yet here, in this quiet, compelling place, she could almost believe in a God who looked after the floundering humans who were His children, and who had a reason for taking away the innocent ones.

When Millicent's coffin, covered with a heavy maroon cloth, was wheeled in, the smattering of mourners turned to look at it with interest. Not grief—there was not a tear to be seen in the whole chapel—but interest. But that's only natural, Caroline thought. Millicent had spent her twenties and thirties traveling and after her return had become a recluse. Even Garrison, felled by his heart attack, had not been able to attend. David had found out for her that the old man was going directly from the hospital into a nursing home. No, those attending the funeral all seemed to be very old—probably friends of Millicent's father—or else merely the curious who hoped for an afternoon's entertainment. Caroline knew about the latter—professional funeral attenders who got some kind of thrill out of seeing other people grieve. Nearly two hundred had attended Hayley's funeral.

Which brought her back to her reason for being here. There didn't seem to be many flowers—only a few bunches arranged rather clumsily around the altar. She peered through the dimness, wishing she had sat closer to the front, but of course the minister was speaking now and she couldn't move. Impatiently she listened to him drone on, his sermon uninspired, the mourners fidgeting. At last the final hymn came. Caroline stood, pretending to sing, and glanced at her watch when Millicent's coffin was wheeled out. The whole thing had lasted twenty minutes, and it seemed like two hours.

Caroline had purposely left her purse open and dumped everything on the floor when she stood to leave. While the other mourners filed from the church, she was on her hands and knees, scrambling for her keys, lipstick, comb, billfold, and the dozen other things she always carried. When she came up with a Milkbone, she almost laughed. By this time the church had emptied and the minister had disappeared behind one of the mahogany doors to the right of the altar.

Like a thief she stole forward. Poor Millicent had commanded only about twenty floral offerings and none of those elaborate. Caroline walked down the line of pink, white, and yellow until she came to a small bouquet of black. Why hadn't she noticed it from the back? It stood out like a boil on a porcelain cheek.

With one last look around to make sure she was alone, she bent forward to pick up the bouquet. As she rose, the card dropped to the floor, but even from that distance Caroline could read the large, childish printing:

To Millicent
Black for Remembrance

13

1

"I'LL GET IT," Caroline called to Fidelia when the doorbell rang. Fidelia nodded, never breaking her back-and-forth strokes with the vacuum cleaner.

When Caroline opened the door, she was surprised to see Tom standing on the porch, his gray coat pulled tight against the November chill.

"Hello, Caroline," he said cheerfully, although she detected uneasiness in his eyes. He glanced at her wool skirt and low-heeled pumps. "Looks like you're going out."

"Yes. Unfortunately I attended a PTA meeting when they were choosing people to help with costumes for the Thanksgiving play. Everyone knows I do a lot of needlework, so when they asked for volunteers and all eyes were on me, I felt my hand shooting up in the air." She smiled. "No guts."

"Just think of it as your good deed for the year."

"I guess. I just don't feel like going to the school today to have a meeting with the director of the play."

"Well, before you go, I wonder if you'd take a few

211

minutes to talk with me about the flowers you found at Millicent's funeral."

"Of course, Tom. I'm a terrible hostess these days—I didn't even ask you in."

"No need to explain." Tom stepped in and glanced at Fidelia, who was finishing up the living room. "Is there somewhere we can talk privately?"

"The kitchen. I'll get you some coffee."

Tom sat down at the big maple table and Caroline got coffee mugs. "Cream? Sugar?"

"Black."

She tried to ignore the tremor in her hands as she poured the coffee, wondering what on earth Tom had found out about the flowers he had come by to pick up the afternoon of Millicent's funeral. That was only yesterday. Had he located the source already?

She placed the coffee in front of him and sat down, looking at him expectantly. "Okay. What is it?"

"First of all I want to ask you again if you recognized anyone at Millicent's funeral. Think really hard."

"I have, Tom. I didn't know *anyone.*"

"Wild hope, I guess. I thought maybe something had come to you."

"No. I keep thinking that if I'd been less intent on finding the flowers, I would have noticed someone suspicious-looking."

Tom smiled. "Suspicious-looking characters usually only show up in fiction. Serial killers tend to look perfectly normal. Take Ted Bundy or Albert DeSalvo, the Boston Strangler, for instance. If they hadn't looked so normal, they wouldn't have been able to get close enough to kill all those women."

"I hadn't thought of that." Caroline took a sip of

coffee. "So you do think we're dealing with a serial killer?"

"No doubt about it. Anyway, first of all, I haven't been able to turn up anything on the bouquet. As we said, the orchids could have been bought in any store selling silk flowers, not necessarily a florist's shop."

"Except that I doubt if too many stores sell *black* orchids, Tom."

"I know, and we're already following that up. As for the handwriting, there's not much to say. We have a handwriting expert we consult frequently. He seems to be pretty good. The trouble is, this is a child's printing. He says it's too crude to reveal anything useful."

"A child's printing," Caroline repeated. "Not an adult's printing made to look like a child's?"

Tom nodded reluctantly. "No."

"Oh, God."

"Don't forget that an adult could have had a child write it. But I didn't really come here to tell you about the handwriting. Do you remember Harry Vinton?"

Caroline frowned. "Of course. He was the detective in charge of the investigation of Hayley's kidnapping."

"Right. Well, this morning his sister found his body in his house. It's too early for an autopsy report, but it looks like he's been dead for at least thirty-six hours." His voice lowered. "Caroline, his throat had been slashed just like Pamela's and the house set on fire."

For a moment everything went black for Caroline. She held tightly to the table edges until her vision cleared. "If there was a fire, why wasn't he discovered sooner?"

"The fire didn't really catch. No kerosene this time. It amounted mostly to scorching around the body."

"And when his funeral is held, there will be a black bouquet reading, 'To Harry, Black for remembrance.'"

"I'd bet my last dollar on it."

Caroline stood up and paced over to the kitchen counter, her eyes falling on Melinda's pitiful pot of dirt called Aurora. "Pamela, Chris, Millicent, Vinton. All the victims have something in common— Hayley."

Tom made a steeple of his fingers, not looking at Caroline. "I see a stronger connection between Millicent and Vinton than the others. I've done a lot of digging on your daughter's case. Evidence was suppressed by Vinton—evidence incriminating Millicent Longworth. In addition, I'm almost positive Vinton was at the Longworth house the night before Millicent died, the evening after I'd confronted him with what I knew. I think Millicent paid him off a long time ago to save her skin. I also think he got scared that she was falling apart—maybe even responsible for the calls to you—and he went up there to have it out with her. Garrison had a heart attack that night—"

"'It was the shock,'" Caroline interrupted. "That's what Millicent said. Garrison's heart attack was caused by the shock. I thought she meant the shock of Chris's shooting. But maybe she meant the shock of finding out what she'd done to Hayley."

"That sounds logical."

"But, Tom, if Millicent killed Hayley, and for some reason killed Pamela, then who killed her and Vinton?"

"That's where my theory falls apart, although I know in my bones Vinton had something to do with Hayley's kidnapping."

"Then *who?* Who could have killed the three of them and shot Chris?"

"Of course, there's always the possibility that a jealous husband shot Chris."

"But the doll. He says there was a doll on the bed, and I believe him. Whoever shot him had Twinkle."

"Caroline, you have to consider that the doll you and Chris saw wasn't Twinkle." He held up his hand when she started to object. "I know you don't want to believe that, but you made other dolls almost exactly like Twinkle. We have to consider that your break-in and Chris's shooting are related—you were the parents of Hayley—but that those two incidents aren't related to the deaths of Millicent, Pamela, and Vinton. After all, what could be the connection between Pamela and Hayley, except that they went to kindergarten together?"

"I don't know, but there's something." She looked at him closely. "And you know there's something, don't you?"

"I don't *know* it. But I feel it." He stared out the window. "Still, I have to be objective, Caroline, and look at these incidents from all angles. That's what I get paid for."

Fidelia came to the kitchen entrance. "Sorry to interrupt, but I wonder if you want me to stay around until you get home dis afternoon."

Caroline shook her head. "I probably won't be back until around four, and you should be done by two, so there's no sense in your wasting all that time."

"I could come and pick up Melinda at tree."

"No thanks. I'll just make her wait and come home with me."

"She won't like dat," Fidelia laughed. "She'll miss her soap opera."

Caroline managed a smile. "It won't kill her just this once."

"Okay, I just wanted to make sure," Fidelia said, vanishing back into the dining room.

"I'm surprised she's still working for you," Tom said softly.

Caroline shrugged. "I have my reasons."

"Still doing your own investigative work, huh?"

"Please don't start sounding like David."

"All right. I can't tell you who to allow in your house. And I won't keep you since you've got an appointment." Tom stood, then shuffled uncomfortably, looking just past her eyes. "Caroline, I know Chris told you about him and Lucy."

"You know about them?"

Tom nodded. "Lucy told me the whole story when we started getting serious." His eyes finally met and held Caroline's. "You know what happened was an accident. She was stoned, depressed. Still, she had the abortion because she didn't want you to find out."

"And now she's sterile," Caroline said bitterly, "so I'm supposed to feel sorry for her and forget that she made love to my husband."

"She doesn't want your pity. She doesn't expect you to forget. She just wants you to forgive her."

"That's a pretty tall order, Tom. I trusted her implicitly."

"Is it too much to ask for someone who's been your best friend for over twenty years?" Tom smiled crookedly, making little commas on either side of his mouth. "I see both sides of this, honestly. It's just that I love Lucille and it tears me apart to see her suffering so."

"I'm suffering too." Caroline sighed. "Tom, you're a good man to plead Lucy's case, especially in light of the circumstances. But right now I don't know how I feel. I don't hate her, if that's what she's worried about. I of all people know what power Chris can wield over a woman. But whether things can ever be the same between us"—she shook her head—"I just don't know."

"At least you haven't said definitely they can't be the same." He took his keys out of his pocket, jingling them nervously. "I admire you a lot, Caroline. And I don't blame you for not wanting to deal with this situation right now. First we have to make sure your family is safe. Then you can sort out your personal relationships."

I wonder if Lucy realizes how lucky she is to have Tom? Caroline thought as she watched him walk back to his car. Just about as lucky as I am to have David.

2

The afternoon had been endless. With the news that Harry Vinton had suppressed evidence in the search for Hayley and almost twenty years later been murdered just like Pamela, she could hardly concentrate on what Miss Cummings, Melinda's teacher and director of the play, was saying about costumes and sets and what unlucky child was going to play the pumpkin, and a few times she caught the woman's eyes on her with a mixture of puzzlement and impatience. To make matters worse, when Melinda heard she'd have to stay at school until four, she lapsed into one of her rare sulking fits, grumbling and whining until at last Caroline had threatened to spank her. Now, furious and petulant, she hunkered in the bucket seat of the Thunderbird scowling for all she was worth.

"Melinda, I hate it when you act like this," Caroline said.

"You *embarrassed* me in front of Miss Cummings."

"You embarrassed yourself, acting like a bad-tempered three-year-old. What's the matter with you today?"

"I'm not three, I'm eight, and I'm old enough to go home by myself. You shouldn't have made me wait on you."

"I don't want you going to and from school by yourself."

"Other kids do."

"You're not other kids. Besides, you're only mad because you missed your stupid show."

"*Guiding Light* is not stupid! And you could have turned on the VCR."

"I forgot, all right?" Caroline took a deep breath. "Let's both just try to cool down."

"Fine with me." Melinda turned to stare out the passenger's window. "But I'm not three years old."

Caroline clenched her teeth and turned down their street. She'd tried counting to ten and was now working her way to one hundred, to no avail.

After they pulled into the garage, Melinda scrambled out of the car and stood by the door with ponderous patience while Caroline fished in her purse for the key. When they got in, Melinda went straight to the back porch to release George, chained as always by Fidelia when she left. He bounded into the house barking and nearly knocked down Caroline. "Stop it!" she snapped. "You calm down this minute!"

The dog looked at her in hurt surprise, and Melinda bent to stroke his head, muttering, "She's a big meanie today. Don't even listen to her."

"Why·don't you two go in the family room and watch TV?" Caroline suggested, trying to keep the shrillness out of her voice.

"*Guiding Light* is over and I can't stand *The Brady Bunch.* I'm going to my room."

"Good. Stay there until your mood improves."

Melinda flounced off with George in her wake. Suddenly the door flew back with familiar force and Greg hurtled into the room. "Hiya, Mom! Guess what happened today?"

"Greg, do you have to throw yourself into every room? Can't you just walk in like a normal person?"

"Well, yeah, I guess I could," he said, totally unoffended. "But don't you want to hear what happened?"

At that moment Melinda shrieked from upstairs. Caroline jumped and Greg's jaw sagged. Then he was running out of the kitchen, through the living room, and up the stairs with Caroline behind him. When they reached Melinda's room, they found her in the doorway, her small face white, tears pouring down her cheeks. "M-my room," she sobbed. "Something's been in my room."

Beyond her lay total havoc. The dotted-swiss curtains had been torn from the rods and shredded, the white flounced bedspread ripped and tattered, the little white rocker smashed against the wall. Her once-beautiful dolls gazed at them blankly from eyeless, noseless faces, and her stuffed animals' arms and legs lay ripped from their bodies, dripping stuffing.

George whined and trotted past them into the room, moving toward the dresser, which lay in shambles. Greg followed the dog, looking around him in wonder. Then, when he reached Melinda's mirror, his face paled.

"Mom, you'd better come look at this," he said softly.

Like one in a dream Caroline picked her way through the ruins to stand by Greg's side. And there she saw what had made him turn pale. Written on the mirror in what looked like blood was a message:

Help Me   Mommy

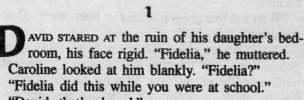

14

1

DAVID STARED AT the ruin of his daughter's bedroom, his face rigid. "Fidelia," he muttered.

Caroline looked at him blankly. "Fidelia?"

"Fidelia did this while you were at school."

"David, that's absurd."

Melinda, who had not let go of her brother's hand since they found the message on the mirror, shook her head vehemently. "Fidelia wouldn't do this, Daddy. She loves me."

"So she says."

"She *does*," Melinda insisted. "A kid knows who loves them."

"She's right," Greg put in. "Fidelia's okay. Besides, where would she have gotten the blood to write the message?"

But David's mind was made up. "We don't know that it's blood. Besides, George would have attacked any stranger who broke in."

"George was outside," Melinda told him. "I unchained him when we got home."

David nodded. "Don't you see the pattern? Every time something strange happens in Melinda's room,

221

Fidelia's been here and George is chained on the back porch."

"Fidelia wouldn't need to chain George," Caroline said. "She's not a stranger. He wouldn't attack her."

"But maybe you've got part of the pattern right, Dad," Greg added. "Maybe the person only comes in when George *is* chained outside."

"Or maybe it wasn't a person at all," Melinda quavered. "Maybe it was a ghost." All three of them looked at her in shock. "Well, a ghost wouldn't need a key."

"Who put this ghost business in your head?" David demanded. "Fidelia?"

"No, Daddy, she's never said anything about ghosts. I was just thinking that . . . well . . . since the writing on the mirror says 'help me Mommy' maybe it's the ghost of Mommy's little girl that got murdered."

David and Caroline exchanged a glance. She'd told him about Jenny's mother describing Hayley's murder to her daughter, and Jenny passing the information on to Melinda. David had been furious. "Maybe we should have told her ourselves," Caroline had said. "We could have softened it somehow, not gone into all the horrible details." But it was too late now. David bent down and hugged Melinda fiercely. "Honey, Hayley was your sister and she was a very sweet little girl. You can take my word for that—I knew her. So even if she had come back as a ghost, which we both know is silly, she would never do anything to hurt you. She would have loved you."

"Maybe she wouldn't like me because I took her place," Melinda said in a teary voice. "She prob'ly would have liked the dolls and stuffed animals, but they're mine."

"She wouldn't have hurt them any more than she would have hurt you. She loved dolls and animals." Caroline said the last with a glance at George, who sat cowering outside the bedroom door. After his first foray into the room with Greg, he had fled to the hall.

"If it wasn't a ghost George wouldn't be so scared, and the ghost doesn't like me. I'm the only one whose room got torn up," Melinda persisted, hugging what was left of a teddy bear to her chest.

"David, I think we should call Tom." Caroline forced her voice to steadiness. "I know breaking and entering isn't his department, but he's been in on this all along."

David nodded. "Greg, would you give Tom a call for us? I think your mother could use a few minutes to catch her breath."

An hour later, when the lab man had scoured the upstairs bedroom looking for evidence the intruder might have left behind, Tom sat down with David and Caroline in the living room. "You know there's no sign of any locks being tampered with," he said.

"I checked them first thing," David answered. "I think it's pretty obvious who's behind this."

"Maybe too obvious. Unless the cleaning lady is a total idiot, she would have made it look like a break-in." Tom leaned forward. "David, I think you folks should leave town for a while until we get to the bottom of all this."

"Leave town!" David burst out. "I have a practice to maintain. I'm supposed to be at my office right now. I can't just up and leave."

"I understand how important your practice is to you, David, but isn't your family more important? I can post someone outside your house, but I don't have the manpower to give all of you protection."

Tom looked at David intently. "Do you want to put your children at risk?"

"What kind of question is that?"

"Not an impertinent one. I just want to give you my professional opinion that your family is being stalked by someone who I think has already murdered three people. Now, if I were in your shoes, I wouldn't hesitate to turn my patients over to someone else for a while. Either that, or I'd let Caroline and the children go someplace without me."

David looked at him, appalled. "You really think our situation is related to those murders?"

Oh, David, Caroline thought in frustration. You still think I'm cracking up and nothing is going on besides Fidelia making mischief.

Tom was going on calmly. "Your wife isn't imagining things. All you have to do is take a look at Melinda's bedroom to know that."

"But the cleaning lady. She could just be sending black orchids to the funerals of anyone in the city who's been murdered."

"Why would she do that?" Caroline asked.

"Hell, I don't know. I told you I think she's crazy."

"Maybe she is, and we'll certainly question her," Tom said. "But, David, even if she *is* responsible for the havoc upstairs, she could also be responsible for the murders. She could be a very dangerous woman, and a lot could happen between now and the time we can put her away if we're able to make a case against her."

David looked down at his hands. "Okay, Tom. You're right—my family does come first, and if I have to take them away to protect them, I will." He looked at Caroline, his eyes tender. "We've never been to Miami. Would you like to go there for the week?"

"I'd love to," Caroline said.

"David, you need to be gone for more than a few days," Tom interrupted. "If that's all you can spare, make arrangements for Caroline and the kids to stay on until this mess is cleared up. I'm begging you."

David took a deep breath, then nodded. "They can stay as long as they need to. I can be ready to go by day after tomorrow."

Late that night when David had lapsed into the snoring that accompanied restless sleep and Melinda had kicked her for the fifth time, Caroline crawled out of bed, slipped on her silk kimono, and went downstairs. After hesitating for a moment, not certain where his guard duties lay, George left Melinda to sleep in the big bed beside her father and padded after Caroline.

The moon was bright so Caroline didn't bother with lights. She poured a finger of brandy and curled into the big easy chair beside the sliding glass doors in the family room. George settled down beside her, but he was restless too, raising his head every couple of minutes to listen.

The killer could be right outside, Caroline thought. After all, he must have the house staked out or he wouldn't know when it was empty and he wouldn't have been able to find Twinkle lying in the trash.

Poor Twinkle, once the beloved toy of a beautiful little girl, now a prop in a bizarre scenario of terrorization. It seemed too fantastic to be true, but it was happening nevertheless.

Caroline took a sip of brandy, her eyes straying to the bouquet of carnations David had sent yesterday to cheer her up. There were twelve, yellow and white mixed with baby's breath, standing in a cut-crystal vase that glittered in the moonlight from its place on the dark cherry coffee table Fidelia had polished that very morning.

The spicy scent of the flowers drifted over her. She loved carnations. Every year she put a bouquet on Hayley's grave. But there was something about the flowers. There was some association she couldn't quite make about carnations. What is it? she wondered wearily, finishing the brandy and leaning her head against the back of the chair. Something I should remember, particularly now with all that's happening.

And then it came to her. The rosette carved on so many old tombstones represented the carnation, and the carnation was the symbol of reincarnation. She sat up. For nineteen years she had been putting carnations on Hayley's grave and had never once made the connection. Or had she, subconsciously? Had she wished Hayley back, no matter what the consequences? And had she, like the grieving father in the haunting story "The Monkey's Paw," gotten her wish in a twisted and grotesque form? Had Hayley come back a murderer?

"No!" George leaped to his feet and barked. "Hayley has not come back," Caroline said fiercely. "It *can't* be true!"

But her words sounded hollow in the eerie half-light of a cold November night.

2

Melinda and Greg were unhappy. "Miss school for weeks!" Melinda wailed. "I was gonna be Pocahontas in the play."

"And I'll miss basketball practice. I'll be off the team."

"Lin, there will be other years you can be in the school play," Caroline told her. "And the same goes for you, Greg. The high school will still have a basketball team next year."

"But I'll be so far behind," Greg muttered. "A has-been. Forgotten."

"Look, kids, I'm sorry about this," Caroline said evenly, "but the police think we should leave town for a while."

"Why can't we just go to a motel and have a priest come and throw holy water around here?" Melinda asked. "Ghosts hate that."

David had already left for work, as usual leaving disputes with the children for her to handle. Even in an emergency he's not around, she thought angrily. She picked up the breakfast plates and headed determinedly for the sink. "There's more to all this than the destruction of your room, Melinda, but that's not the point. The point is that your dad and I have decided we're going to spend some time away from home and that's it. I don't want any more arguments."

"What about George?" Melinda demanded. "Are you gonna leave him here with the ghost?"

George, who had been lying peacefully in the sunshine beneath the window, raised his head and looked at them with what Caroline would have sworn was alarm.

"There is *no* ghost, but George is going, too. Daddy's going to rent a condo for a month where we'll be able to keep him."

"He won't like it," Melinda said darkly. "He'll run away."

"No, he won't. He'll love swimming in the ocean."

"In *Jaws* a dog got eaten by a shark."

"Melinda, that is enough! We're going and we'll have a wonderful time and that's final."

Scowling, the two of them left for school. Caroline had wanted them to stay home, but Melinda was to compete in the third-grade spelling bee that afternoon and Greg wanted to talk to the basketball coach about his upcoming "hiatus." Too frazzled to argue with them anymore, she relented, knowing that tomorrow they would all be safely on their way to Miami.

Greg had promised to drop Melinda off at the grade-school door before he went on to the high school, and when they were gone, Caroline sat down at the kitchen table feeling utter despair. Was there going to be anything left of her life when this nightmare was over? It had already damaged her friendship with Lucy, brought to full bloom inchoate problems between her and David, and now the children, particularly Melinda, were becoming increasingly contrary. Caroline had a feeling their touchiness sprang from fear they wouldn't admit, but no matter how they felt, she had to protect them from whatever menace hung over their lives.

She spent the morning packing. She attacked Melinda's clothes first, simply because it frightened her to look at the room and she wanted to get the packing over with as soon as possible. While she folded little cotton slacks and pullover tops, she thought about her musings last night. Reincarnation. In the cheerful wintery light streaming through Melinda's uncurtained window, the idea seemed not only fanciful but ridiculous. Resurrecting her daughter by putting carnations on her grave every year indeed! Maybe she *was* losing her mind. Well, if she was, it was no wonder considering what her life had been like ever since she heard that child's voice in Lucy's storeroom. But the train her thoughts were taking proved she desperately needed to get away. They all did.

Deciding Greg and David could pack for themselves, she hauled out her own large brown suitcase next and stood in front of her open closet door, trying to decide what to take. How hot was it in Miami at this time of year?

The doorbell interrupted her thoughts. She wasn't expecting anyone. Maybe it was Tom wanting to take another look at Melinda's room.

But it was Chris. He stood a little uncertainly on the porch giving her his rakish grin. "Hi, Caro. Hope I'm not interrupting anything."

"Actually, you are," she said shortly. "We're going out of town tomorrow and I'm packing."

"What I have to say won't take long."

"Are you going to tell me about someone else you slept with when we were married? Someone who slipped your mind?"

Chris's grin faded. "Bitchiness doesn't become you. Why don't you just get off your high horse and talk to me? Ten minutes. That's all I ask."

Caroline wanted to slam the door in his face but something prevented her. Maybe it was too many years of good manners. Either that or too many years of loving him. It was hard to do an about-face overnight.

She stepped aside. "All right, you can come in, but only for a few minutes. I really am busy."

George had followed her to the door and he bared his teeth, a low, menacing growl vibrating in his throat.

"George, stop it!" Caroline commanded. "This is a friend. It's all right."

The dog continued to look warily at the stranger, his hackles raised, as Chris stepped into the house. "He's a good dog, Caro," Chris said, holding out his partially closed fist for the dog to sniff. "Don't jump on him for trying to protect you."

George looked at her calm face, making sure the intruder really was a friend. Then he relaxed and allowed Chris to stroke his head, although his back legs remained tensed, ready to spring.

"You said you were packing?" Chris asked, continuing to pet the dog.

"Yes. Tom thinks it's best if we go away for a while until the police find out who's behind everything that's been happening." She paused. "Did Tom tell you about Harry Vinton and his suspicions about Millicent's death?"

"Yes. And he told me again I should leave town."

"I thought you were leaving for Taos a few days ago."

"I postponed the trip because I wanted a chance to talk to you. I want to get things straightened out before I go."

"I don't think that's possible," Caroline said shortly. "A few empty apologies aren't going to fix everything."

"Oh, Caro."

"Did Tom also tell you about Melinda's room?" Caroline asked to change the subject.

"No."

Caroline knew she was stalling, not wanting to get into the issue of Lucy with Chris, but she couldn't help herself. "Come upstairs. The police told me not to clean the room today in case they need to come back and check anything, so I can show you."

George trotted after them to Melinda's room, but he would not enter. Chris, however, stepped gingerly inside and let out a low whistle. "How did the creep get in?"

"We don't know. There was no sign of forced entry."

Chris's eyebrows drew together. "Then someone had a key?"

"So it seems, but I just had the locks changed. The only people with keys are David, Greg, and me."

"Lucy told me something about a cleaning woman you have. You don't think—" At the mention of Lucy's name, Caroline turned away. "Do you have to look like a stricken animal every time I say her name?"

Caroline whirled to look at him. "Sorry if my emotions make you uncomfortable."

"It was a long time ago."

"Well, I just found out about it."

"And that's a big part of what's bothering you, isn't it? That your best friend could keep a secret like that for so long."

"It doesn't do much for building trust."

"And it doesn't do much for your state of mind, either. I couldn't have chosen a worse time to tell you. Under normal circumstances you wouldn't be reacting this violently."

"Don't be so sure."

Chris sighed. "Caro, it was a mistake. We tried to correct it—"

"And instead you just made things worse."

Chris began walking restlessly around the room. "Yes, we made things worse. But how would you have felt if we'd told you? We would both have lost you."

"You mean *you* would have lost Hayley. I obviously was very easily replaced."

"Sure," Chris said angrily. "I ran right out and got married again. Never gave you a second thought." Abruptly he stopped pacing and stared at the mirror. "What on earth is this?"

"It says 'Help Me Mommy.' "

"I can see that. But it looks like it's written in—"

"Blood." Caroline came to stand beside him. "It was left by our visitor. Sounds like a message from Hayley, doesn't it?"

Chris looked at her sharply. "That's impossible."

"I know. At least part of me knows that. Another part says—"

"That Hayley's ghost came back and wrecked your daughter's room and left a message in blood?" Chris put his free hand on her shoulder. "Does that sound like Hayley to you?"

"No, but Chris, there were no signs of breaking and entering. And then there's George. Look at him. He won't come in here. Dogs are supposed to be sensitive to the supernatural, you know."

As if for confirmation Chris looked over at George, who crouched at the door, his tail tucked firmly between his legs.

At that moment the phone rang, and Caroline picked up Melinda's white Princess extension. Almost before she got out her hello, Tom's low voice was saying, "I don't want to alarm you, but I think you should know that some of the lab work we did in Melinda's room has come back."

"Yes?"

"There was only one set of fingerprints aside from

the ones we took from the family last night. Probably Fidelia's. No hair aside from the family's. But we did determine that the message on the mirror *is* written in human blood. Type O-positive."

"O-positive. That was Hayley's blood type."

"It's the most common blood type, Caroline. I just wanted to let you know this to emphasize that you're dealing with a real nut here and it's imperative for you and your family to leave town tomorrow and not tell *anyone* where you're going, particularly not Fidelia Barnabas."

"Fidelia! But you don't really think . . ."

"As I said, not unless she's stupid, but that doesn't change the fact that both days something has happened in your home, she's been in the house. Now, will you promise to keep your whereabouts secret?"

"I promise."

Tom hung up without even saying goodbye, and Caroline turned to Chris. "Tom says the message on the mirror is written in human blood. Type O-positive. That was Hayley's blood type."

Chris's face had gone parchment pale. "Caroline, there has to be an explanation for all this." He smiled weakly. "Besides, I don't think ghosts *have* blood, do they?"

Caroline giggled in spite of her fear and anger, although she was shaking all over. "I don't know. I guess I didn't pay enough attention to all those Friday night horror movies I watched when I was growing up." And then she burst into tears.

Chris wrapped his good arm around her, pressing her close to his chest as she cried. "Caro, everything's going to be better when you get away for a few weeks. They're going to catch who's behind all this and your life will go on just as smooth as before."

But my life can never be the same, she thought after Chris left. She could never forget that Harry Vinton had suppressed evidence that maybe could have saved Hayley. She could never forget about Chris and Lucy. There was no going back to the life she had before. The experience of the last few weeks had shaken the faith in people she had tried so hard to regain after Hayley's murder, and she didn't know if she would be able to restore it a second time.

In spite of their morning departure time, David had insisted on keeping office hours that evening as usual. Caroline was annoyed but not surprised. Raised in poverty, David had struggled to become a doctor and start a practice, and he held on to that practice with an almost paranoid tenacity, believing that if he turned loose for more than a week, the work of a lifetime would vanish in the blink of an eye and he would be back digging coal in a Kentucky mine just as his father had done until his early death. Caroline understood David, but that didn't make his near-constant absence any easier to bear. And she especially resented it tonight, when their home might be violated again.

She and the kids went to Pizza Hut for dinner, arguing good-naturedly over what toppings to choose. Caroline was relieved to see that Greg and Melinda had settled down about the projected trip, although they were still miffed that she wouldn't tell them where they were going except to a beach. Thank goodness she hadn't mentioned Miami this morning, she thought, since Tom said it was vital to keep their whereabouts a secret until the killer was found.

They got home around seven. Caroline sent Greg

up to pack while she assembled George's traveling paraphernalia, including vitamins, heartworm pills, and his favorite squeaky toy. Melinda sat at the kitchen counter coloring, and when the phone rang, she picked it up.

"For you, Mommy," she said. "It's not the ghost—it's a man."

Caroline took the phone, hoping whoever it was hadn't heard the part about the ghost. In a moment, though, she didn't care. It was the police calling to say David had been shot in the parking lot behind his office.

15

"**M**OMMY? WHAT'S WRONG? Mommy? Greg! Come quick! Something's wrong with Mommy!"

Caroline was aware of the receiver being taken from her hand and Greg's voice seeming to come from a great distance. Then he hung up the phone.

"What *is* it?" Melinda wailed.

"Dad's been shot, squirt, but he's not dead." By this time the room had stopped spinning and Caroline focused on Greg's frightened face. "Mom, we've got to get to the hospital. I'll drive."

"You don't have a license," Caroline said. "We'll ask the patrolman Tom put outside to guard the house to take us."

"Looks like he was guarding the wrong people," Greg said dismally. "Lin, put on your coat. You gonna be all right, Mom?"

"Yes, I'm fine." Caroline tried to smile. "Go get the policeman."

Melinda sat sniffling in the backseat as the young policeman drove with careless speed. None of them said a word.

Another officer was waiting outside the emergency room. He was middle-aged and looked like he hadn't smiled for years, but his voice was kind. "Mrs. Webb?" he asked as the three of them trailed up.

"Yes. What happened to my husband?"

"Why don't you have a seat first."

The waiting room was nearly empty, Caroline was glad to see. A television mounted high on the wall played to an audience of one woman. Caroline sat down on a black vinyl chair while Melinda and Greg hovered near her.

"According to your husband's nurse," the policeman began, "Dr. Webb said he was worried about something at home and asked that she call and cancel his last two appointments. He exited his office building by the back door that opens onto the staff parking lot. About twenty minutes later, after the nurse had made the calls and locked the front door, she went out the same way. That's when she found him about fifty feet from the car."

Melinda had started to whimper. "Let's go look for a Coke machine," Greg said. "I'll put the money in and you push the button." He took her hand and Melinda stumbled after him.

"How seriously is my husband hurt?"

"It's a thigh injury. He must have fallen and hit his head, because he was unconscious. I'm no doctor, but he didn't look too torn up to me. I'd say he's going to be fine."

Caroline realized she hadn't taken a deep breath since the phone call telling her David had been shot. So he hadn't been lying out in the parking lot with a hole in his chest like the cemetery guard, which is what she had been picturing.

"Do you have any idea who shot him?"

The policeman looked at her gravely. "Whoever did it was long gone by the time we go there."

"And there were no witnesses?"

"Only one other office in the building was open—a dentist's office at the front. Since the staff parking lot is at the back and surrounded on three sides by trees, there wasn't much chance of anyone seeing anything."

"But someone had been waiting for him." Just like they waited for Chris, Caroline thought. Someone who knew their habits, someone who had been watching.

Greg and Melinda returned, cans of Coke in hand. Melinda looked a little better, although she immediately wanted to know how Daddy was.

"I don't know yet, honey," Caroline said, taking the Coke Greg offered. She didn't want it, but it was sweet of him to think of her.

"Are they going to do an operation?" Melinda asked.

"We'll have to wait until the doctor talks to us before we know."

Melinda climbed up on a chair. "I'm a nervous wreck," she sighed.

Greg and the policeman laughed, and even Caroline couldn't stifle a smile. "I'm sorry everything is such a mess, honey."

"It's not your fault." Melinda looked at the policeman. "We have a ghost. She must have shot Daddy."

The policeman's smile faltered, and Caroline was relieved at that moment to see David's friend, Lew Ramsey, coming from the emergency room. His tired face creased into a smile. "Caroline, it's been so long. I'm just sorry we have to see each other under these circumstances."

"I know, Lew. How is he?"

"Lucky. He has a nasty wound in the right thigh,

but thank God the bone wasn't shattered. No vascular damage, either. If there had been, he could have bled to death out in that parking lot before someone found him. Most of the damage was to the quadriceps. We'll be keeping him for three or four days, then he'll be on crutches."

"Is he conscious?" the policeman asked.

"Yes. I suppose you'd like to question him."

"If it's all right."

Lew nodded. "I think he's up to it, although he's got quite a headache from that bump he took on the forehead. Go on in."

"When can we see him?" Caroline asked.

"Let's let the police finish with him first before his sedative really takes effect, then we'll get him settled in his room." He glanced at Melinda. "Not such a shock to see him lying in a regular hospital room, you know."

"Of course. We just want to say goodnight."

"Should just be a few minutes." Lew put his hand on her shoulder. "Get some color back in your face, girl. He'll be fine. He was shot at close range, but only with a .22."

"A Beretta, no doubt," Caroline said softly.

"What makes you think that?"

"Just a hunch."

Lew looked at her quizzically. "Well, I'm not that good at identifying bullets. The police will have to decide what kind of gun it was."

As he disappeared back in the emergency room, Caroline turned to see Lucy standing nearby. "Hello, Caro."

"How did you know?"

"Greg called me." Caroline looked at Greg, who was draining his Coke. So he'd known all along there was trouble between her and Lucy. She would have to realize he wasn't a child anymore but an increasingly perceptive adult.

Melinda rushed to Lucy. "Daddy got shot! His quadruped's hurt."

"Quadriceps," Caroline said. "It's a muscle in the thigh. But he's going to be all right."

"Thank God," Lucy breathed, picking up Melinda. Caroline noticed that her jeans were looser, and with only scant makeup, her face was almost homely. "Tom's gone to the parking lot."

"He probably won't find anything."

"He might surprise you." She hugged Melinda then set her down. "I want the three of you to come home with me tonight."

Caroline shook her head, piercingly aware of how strange it felt to be facing Lucy on these terms. Their voices were cautious, their eyes continually straying away uncomfortably.

"I really think we should be at home," Caroline said. "There's George . . ."

"He can come too."

"I don't think so, Lucy, but thanks anyway."

"You shouldn't go back there alone."

Caroline tucked her hair behind her ears. "Lucy, if this person wants us, he'll find us no matter where we are. Besides, Tom assigned someone to watch the house."

"It won't do any good, though," Melinda intoned. "You can't see a ghost if it doesn't want you to."

Lucy looked at her cautiously. "And you think a ghost shot your daddy?"

"Oh, yes. The ghost of Hayley."

Lucy's mouth opened and shut as she tried to come

up with an answer. Greg saved her the trouble. "Come on, Lin, let's check out the gift shop and see if we can get a present for Dad."

"A stuffed dog that looks just like George! He'd like that."

When they had gone, Lucy sat down beside Caroline. "I've wanted so much to talk to you these last few days."

"To say you're sorry? You don't have to. I know you are."

"It only happened once, Caro. It wasn't planned—"

Caroline stood up. "I don't want to hear the details."

The woman watching the television glanced at her briefly, then returned to her situation comedy whose laugh track blared annoyingly around the little room.

Lucy reached out and touched Caroline's arm. "I wasn't going into any details. I just wanted you to know that it wasn't an affair. It was one stupid night."

Caroline turned to face her. "When you found out I'd been talking to Chris about all the things happening lately, you acted angry. Were you jealous?"

Lucy's eyes widened. "*Jealous?* God, no. I just knew that if you and Chris started saying more than hello and goodbye to each other, there would be trouble. Either he would start trying to insinuate himself back into your life, or he'd tell you about us. I think he's done both."

Caroline sat down again. "There *is* something I've wanted to ask you the past few days. You've remained friends with Chris all these years. How?"

Lucy played with her dangling gold earring. "The

blame lay with both of us, Caro. He didn't rape me, and he didn't force me to have an abortion."

"But he was in favor of it."

"Yes, but the final decision was mine."

"Because of me." She studied Lucy. "How you must have resented me all these years."

Lucy finally pulled off the earring and sat looking at it in her hand. "I didn't resent you. It wasn't your fault. But let's not talk about that now."

Caroline popped open the Coke can and took a sip, glancing up at the television. "I'm glad you're here."

"You are?"

"Yeah. As Tom reminded me, over twenty years of friendship aren't easily forgotten."

"Tom talked to you about this?"

"Yes. He loves you very much, Lucy."

"I know."

"Is the reason you never married him that you're still in love with Chris?"

Lucy shook her head. "No, I don't still love him. I don't think I ever did. It was more like a delayed schoolgirl crush. I guess I never married Tom because I was afraid of totally committing myself to someone and then losing them, like you did Chris."

Caroline shrugged. "I can't guarantee that you won't—life is too unpredictable—but Tom isn't Chris. He's much more stable, less self-consumed. I think you should take the chance."

"I can't believe you're being such a good friend after how I deceived you."

Caroline sighed. "I admit it threw me, but I overreacted. I've already lost a daughter, and I could have lost a husband tonight. Maybe shocks like that make you realize you should value those close to you and not flagellate them because they're human. When I saw your face here in the waiting room, I felt more joy than anger, and I realized I can't turn against you because of one mistake you made twenty years ago. Besides, you already paid a terrible price." She gazed into Lucy's eyes. "You should have had that baby if you wanted it, Lucy, and let me handle the situation the best way I could."

"But I always thought of you as so delicate, so sensitive. Chris and I thought you'd fall apart."

"I did anyway, so it was all for nothing."

"Yeah," Lucy said softly. "All for nothing."

Greg and Melinda suddenly reappeared carrying a milk-glass vase full of red roses and baby's breath and a small gold box of Godiva chocolates. "I picked out a pink piggy bank, but Greg said this is what you give sick people," Melinda announced. "Also, he charged it to Daddy's account."

"I only had a buck fifty with me," Greg bristled.

"That's all right. I'll take care of the bill later," Caroline said.

Melinda looked hopeful. "Then maybe you could go back and get that bank. It was *so* cute. The pig was laughing—"

A nurse materialized at the door of the waiting room. "Mrs. Webb, you can see your husband now. I'll show you the way."

Officially children were not allowed to visit patients, but since David was on staff at the hospital, Melinda trooped down the hall with her mother and Greg, proudly carrying the flowers. Once they were in the room, however, she fell silent and shy. Caroline could understand why. David looked awful, deathly pale with forbidding circles around his eyes and a bruise on his forehead. He raised his head weakly when they entered, then let it fall back with a thump. Melinda was clearly alarmed and Greg didn't look too sure of himself either, so Caroline decided to be as lighthearted as possible.

"David Webb, you'll do anything to get out of leaving town!" He smiled wanly and she went over to kiss him. "Here I did all that packing for nothing."

"Not for nothing," he said huskily. "I want the three of you to go ahead."

"Not in the morning as planned. Maybe in a day or two."

"Stubborn as ever," David muttered, smiling. He peered at the children. "Are those gifts I see?"

"Candy and flowers," Greg said. "But you don't look much in the mood for candy."

"I will be tomorrow."

Caroline took the gifts from the children and placed them on a bedside table. Then Melinda began to cry.

"What's this all about?" David said, forcing heartiness in his voice.

"That ghost shot you," Melinda wailed. "You almost got killed."

David reached out his hand and she took it hesitantly. "Lin, a ghost didn't shoot me. I think it was just someone shooting at a stray cat. They missed and shot me."

"You're just fooling. People think kids don't know anything."

David smiled. "You're right. That was a silly answer. But a ghost didn't shoot me, honey. A real live person did, a person Tom's going to catch and put in jail."

"Did you see anything, Dad?" Greg asked.

"I heard something. A rustling in the trees. And I could swear I heard someone say, 'There he is.' Then my leg gave way and I hit the ground. But I can tell you one thing—whoever it was didn't mean to kill me. They could have finished me off easily when I was unconscious, but they didn't."

The intent was merely to frighten, Caroline thought. Someone wanted to frighten you like they wanted to frighten Chris. Then another thought struck her. It was Chris's left shoulder that had been wounded, not the right that would have interfered with his painting. And David had been shot in the leg. If it had been either shoulder, his ability to perform deliveries, especially caesarians, might have been impaired.

The nurse stuck her head in the door. "I'm afraid I'll have to shoo you out until tomorrow. Dr. Webb has had a sedative and he really needs to sleep."

"Of course," Caroline said. "Kids, say goodbye to Daddy."

Melinda, her tears dried, gave him a smacking kiss on the cheek. Greg gravely shook hands, then quickly brushed his lips against his father's cheek before heading out the door.

"He hasn't kissed me since he was seven," David said. Then, "Melinda, would you mind waiting outside with Greg for a minute while I say something to Mommy?"

"Okay. I love you lots and lots."

"I love you too, sweetheart."

When she had gone, David suddenly gripped Caroline's hand and held on with surprising force. "There's something I didn't want to tell you in front of the kids."

Caroline braced herself, trying not to wince as he squeezed her hand. "What is it, darling?"

"That voice I heard saying 'There he is'—it seemed to be speaking to itself, and it was a child's voice. A little girl's."

16

1

"**Y**OU'RE A HARD lady to find," Tom said as Fidelia Barnabas stood in the open doorway, her rough-woven beige caftan swaying around her slim body in the cold air.

"I've been out of town," she said. "Has something happened at de Webb house?"

"How did you know?"

"I can't think of anything else dat would bring a police lieutenant here."

"As a matter of fact, a couple of things have happened in the last two days. May I come in and talk to you about them?"

Fidelia moved aside. "Please."

Tom stepped into a small room with hardwood floors dotted with cheerful, patterned rugs. Several primitive paintings hung on the white walls, and the furniture was simple and austere, the kind you buy and refinish yourself. On a round table beneath a window lay ten pink, highly polished cowrie shells. "Would you like some herb tea?" Fidelia asked politely. "Or maybe something stronger."

"Nothing, thanks." Tom sat down on a cane-backed chair while Fidelia sank gracefully to the floor, her shining black hair spreading over her right shoulder and hanging to her waist, her narrow bare feet peeking from beneath the caftan.

She fixed him with uncannily light blue eyes. "What's happened?"

"You cleaned for the Webbs day before yesterday, right?"

"Yes."

"About what time did you leave the house?"

"Two o'clock. I offered to stay later, but Mrs. Webb told me to leave at two. You heard her."

"Sometime before four-fifteen, Melinda's room was ransacked, her dolls torn up, some furniture broken. Also there was a message left on the mirror. 'Help me mommy,' it said. It was written in human blood."

Fidelia looked at him steadily. "*Human* blood. And you tink I did it?"

"You were there."

"I see." Fidelia looked away for a moment, her dangling silver earrings catching light from the small fire burning in her white-stone fireplace. "Does Caroline tink I did it?"

"No, but you can understand why I have to question you. Where have you been the last two days?"

"Visiting relatives in Cincinnati. My papa's people." She pronounced *papa* with the accent on the second syllable.

"When did you leave here?"

"About five o'clock day before yesterday. I got back dis morning."

"Can you give me the name of someone who will vouch for you?"

"Certainly. My cousin." Fidelia went to the telephone, picked up a small address book, and began

copying information on an index card. She handed it
to Tom. "Name, address, phone number."

"Thanks."

"You know, no one but Caroline and I believes
someting other dan a person is behind all de terrible
tings happening."

Tom put the index card in his pocket and looked at
her closely. "Something other than a person. Do you
mean a ghost?" Fidelia lifted one shoulder and said
nothing. "I don't think Caroline believes a ghost is
responsible."

"Maybe she doesn't admit it, but dat *is* what she
believes."

"Has she received any encouragement in that belief?"

Fidelia smiled. "You mean, am I trying to convert
her to voodooism? No. But she did ask me if I believe in ghosts and I said yes."

"You think spirits of the dead come back?"

"Yes."

Tom looked at her coolly. "Don't you think believing in ghosts or spirits returning is a little unusual?"

"Where I come from, no it is not. But I suppose
you do."

"I've never seen a ghost, Miss Barnabas."

"Have you ever seen an idea?"

Tom's mouth quirked. "Touché. But I really didn't
come here to discuss the supernatural. Can you prove
you didn't damage Melinda's room?"

"No. I have no alibi. I was home alone. Packing
for my trip. But you're welcome to look me over for
cuts."

"Cuts?"

"I would have had to cut myself to get blood for
de message on de mirror. What type was it?"

"O-positive."

"I am A-positive. But I'll be happy to let you check if you don't believe me. Of course, I could have kept a container of someone else's blood in my purse all day, hoping Caroline would leave—she can tell you I didn't know she was going to Melinda's school until I got dere dat morning. And certainly I wouldn't expect anyone to suspect me even dough I was alone in de house."

"Okay, okay," Tom said. "A little farfetched, I admit. Still, if your alibi doesn't check out, I will want that blood typed. And I also need your fingerprints to compare with prints found in Melinda's room. We turned up five sets. Four belonged to the family."

"And de last is mine. But of course I'll submit to any tests you want. I have noting to fear." Fidelia, still standing, looked at him calmly. "You said a couple of tings had happened to de Webbs. Someting must have happened yesterday or you wouldn't want to check wit my cousin. What is it?"

"David Webb was shot last night."

This time color came and went in Fidelia's light-brown skin. *"Bon Dieu!* Is he dead?"

"No. He was shot in the thigh and the damage was mostly to the muscle. He should be fine."

"What luck!" Fidelia breathed.

"He was shot in the parking lot behind his office. The bullet was from a .22-caliber Beretta, and ballistics shows it was the same gun used on Caroline's ex-husband, Chris Corday. Before he was shot, David thinks he heard someone say, 'There he is' in a little girl's voice."

Fidelia closed her eyes. "I was wrong. I tought Melinda was de focus of de evil, but it's touching de whole family." Her hands clenched in her lap. "Dat family is in great danger. We have to help dem."

"I advised them to get out of town and they were going until David got hurt. Caroline won't leave until she's certain he's all right, and of course David can't go anywhere for a few days. He lost a lot of blood."

"Dey can't escape evil of dis level by leaving town."

"Do you mean supernatural evil?"

Fidelia lowered her head, rubbing a hand lightly across her forehead as if trying to clear her thoughts. "I'm not sure. I'm not a psychic, Mr. Jerome. My mama was. She was what in de voodoo religion is called a *mambo*, a female priest, healer, and protector against sorcery or witchcraft. She understood dese tings much better dan I do and she tried to teach me. My papa, who had been raised a Baptist, didn't approve. Maybe dat's why I didn't learn as I should have. But I still have feelings about de presence of evil, about how de evil is working."

Tom wasn't sure he believed her, but something in him wanted to. Wasn't she describing what he experienced so many times in homicide cases and labeled "hunches"? "What do your feelings tell you now?" he asked, a little embarrassed by the question.

"Dey tell me dat whoever, or whatever, is plaguing de Webbs isn't satisfied."

"What does he—it—want?"

Fidelia took a deep breath. "Revenge. And Melinda."

2

Tina hugged her sweater closer around her as she stood at the open storeroom doors, nervously watching the movers unload a huge antique tester bed. One of the men stumbled on the truck ramp and Tina gasped, ashamed of herself for being more worried about the bed than the man.

"Just take it slow and easy," she said.

"We know our job," the one who'd turned his ankle snapped.

"I'm sorry. It's just that this piece is so valuable."

"Yeah, yeah. You could probably feed a kid for a year on what this old bed costs. Hell, two kids. *My* two kids." They were off the ramp and entering the storeroom. "So where d'ya want this *valuable* piece?" He looked at his partner, who snickered at the high humor.

"Over to the right by the wall."

"Clear over *there?*"

"Yes, clear over there. Please."

"Hell."

They staggered through the storeroom, twice bumping into other pieces of furniture. "Be *careful,*" Tina wailed.

"So you wanna carry this yourself or what?"

"No. I just want you to watch where you're going."

"Yeah, yeah. We know what we're doing."

But as they neared the wall, the bed listed dangerously to one side. Trying to right it, they completely lost control. The men grunted, the loud one cursed furiously, and both bed and men lurched toward the north end of the wall, crashing into two tall stacks of crates. Tina shrieked as with a tremendous cracking of wood the bed crashed onto the concrete floor. The men collapsed, the staked crates raining down on them and bursting open.

Tina rushed forward. "Are you all right?"

The quiet one was already on his feet, but the loud

one was flailing in the debris like a man trapped in quicksand. "I'm suing!" he shouted.

Tina grabbed his arm and pulled him up. "I told you to be careful."

"Big damn deal. I've got a concussion. Hell, I've got brain damage."

"You had that before you got here."

The man glared and Tina knew she'd blundered. Now was not the time for sarcasm. And he did have a grand bump raising on his high forehead. "I'm sorry, really. Is anything broken?"

The doors to the showroom burst open and Lucy ran into the room. "What in the name of God . . .?"

"They dropped the bed."

"The *bed!* They dropped the *bed!*"

The loud one was smoothing down his curly hair, which looked as if it had not come in contact with shampoo for at least a week. "What about me? Huh, lady? What about me and Hal here? Any concern for us? Hell no, all you care about is some old relic."

Lucy stalked toward them. "How could you have done this?"

"Easy." He looked at his partner. "C'mon, Hal. We're goin' to the hospital." He gave Lucy a murderous look. "And *you'll* be hearing from my lawyer."

"And you'll be hearing from mine!" Lucy shouted back as the two trailed out of the storeroom.

Tina looked with despair at the bed lying on its side amid the pile of broken crates, which held so many of Lucy's personal belongings and old paintings, things she didn't have room for at the condo. There was no way to determine how much damage had been done to the bed until the mess was cleared away.

"Do you know how much that bed cost?" Lucy cried.

"Yes. I also know it's insured. Don't go to pieces."

"Money can't replace that bed. The workmanship. The sheer age of the thing."

She looked like she was going to cry. "Lucy, it may not be as bad as it seems." She bent to pick up an old photograph album. "Let's just get all this stuff out of the way."

"I'll clean it up."

"It'll take you forever alone."

"Tina, go back out front," Lucy said sharply. "I'll take care—"

Tina knelt and, shoving aside a canvas, picked up a battered clown doll. She stared at it for a long, still moment. Then she turned slowly to face Lucy.

3

It was midnight. The evening had been quiet at Sunnyhill Nursing Home, but the quiet was always short-lived. Garrison Longworth laid aside his worn copy of *Portrait of a Lady*, removed his reading glasses, and sighed as he heard that woman down the hall, the one they called Blanche, start her nightly tirade. It always began with sweet importunings for her daughter Rose to read to her. A nurse had told Garrison Rose died in a car wreck over fifty years ago, but as with so many senile people, the distant past was more real to Blanche than the present, and in her memory Rose still lived. Soon the importunings would become more strident. Then Blanche would begin cursing, move on to screaming, and finally have to be restrained and sedated. Always the same, Garrison thought. So distressing. And so *loud*.

Would he have to listen to this woman's torment until the end of his days?

Resignedly he tossed back the covers and tottered on stick legs to his bathroom. The bathroom was a joy to him, modern and pristine, not like the facilities at home, which had been hopelessly outdated. *Home.* His eyes misted over. Home was nothing more than a pile of rubble now. And Millicent had gone up in flames with it.

He flushed the commode, bared his teeth to the mirror to make sure they didn't need a second flossing, then flipped off the light and crept back to his room. There wasn't much moon tonight and he was glad the night-light burned steadily by the bed. He was afraid of the dark, but the nurses wouldn't let him keep on the overhead light all night. Every time they caught him asleep, they turned it off and he woke up in terror.

Blanche down the hall was now shouting. "Goddamn it, Rose, I said I wanted a story! *Mildred Pierce.* I want to hear *Mildred Pierce* and you're going to read it to me, not go off with that boy to screw in the bushes!" Good lord, Garrison thought. Not only did the woman have a foul mouth, but common tastes as well. *Mildred Pierce!* What an appalling choice of reading matter.

"Hi, Garrison."

Garrison felt as if he were plummeting down a tunnel toward the very depths of hell. Wind roared in his ears. Something seemed to growl nearby. He stood frozen.

"Aren't you going to say hi to me?"

He could not turn around. He could not face the atrocity he knew stood behind him. He uttered a feeble cry, but his door was shut and Blanche down the hall had already begun to scream. No one could hear him.

"You knew I was coming to see you, didn't you?"

How sweet her voice was. How sweet and relentless. And yes, he had known she was coming, ever since Harry Vinton told him Caroline Corday had been receiving calls from a child named Hayley. That's when he'd had the heart attack. And then Millicent had been murdered. Yes, he knew she was coming.

A rope slipped around his stringy neck and pulled tight, letting in just enough air to allow him to breathe. "You were supposed to be a good man, Garrison. You said you were a good man. But good men don't do what you did."

Garrison struggled for breath against the rope. Suddenly he could hear his father intoning Bible verses just like he did before every meal, and then he realized it was he who was talking, not Father: " 'And I looked, and behold a pale horse: and his name that sat on him was Death, and Hell followed with him. And power was given unto them over the fourth part of the earth, to kill with sword, and with hunger, and with death, and with the beasts of the earth.' "

"Hayley's a beast of the earth now. That's what you made her. She didn't have to be. She had a mommy and a daddy who loved her. She was going to first grade. But you took her. And you hid her. And you did things to her. Bad things. Things an old man shouldn't do to a little girl. Aren't you ashamed of yourself?"

Ashamed? Was he ashamed? It didn't seem he should be. But other people, people who didn't understand, they might think so. And Father might think so. Father. " 'And the devil that deceived them was cast into the lake of fire and brimstone, where the beast and the false prophet *are*, and shall be tormented day and night for ever and ever.' "

"You're going to be tormented. Even after I get through with you you're going to be tormented. All this time nobody knew. They all thought you were in Italy with your wife. Nobody knew you came home because you were crazy and she left you. Millicent kept you hidden and nobody knew, nobody except Harry Vinton. He found out, didn't he? But he didn't tell anyone except Millicent so she'd give him money. Isn't that right? And Millicent never told on you." The rope jerked, nearly pulling Garrison off his feet. "And *I* never told on you."

Down the hall Blanche was shrieking, "Goddamn it to hell, I want a story! Not a shot! I don't want any goddamn shot!"

Garrison closed his eyes. Only God could save him now. Only God could stop this misguided one who didn't understand him. " 'And the third angel poured out his vial upon the rivers and fountains of water; and they became blood.' "

"Stop it!" the voice hissed. "Stop saying that stuff! I can't stand it anymore. Talk. Say you're sorry. Say it!"

"You don't understand," Garrison quavered. "You never tried to understand." He started to cry.

"You're a murderer. You murdered Hayley."

"No, I didn't."

"Murderer!"

" 'I *am* he that liveth and was dead—' "

"Just like Hayley, Garrison. *She* that liveth and was dead."

" '—and, behold, I am alive forevermore—' "

A pain shot down Garrison's left arm. A fiery, paralyzing pain. He gasped before his eyes fluttered and he sagged, held up only by the rope around his neck.

Down the hall Blanche was subsiding, crooning, "Sweet little Rosie. My sweet little girl. My good little girl."

"Garrison. *Garrison!*" The rope was released and Garrison fell forward onto his face. A scream of childish rage filled the room.

An exhausted nurse coming back from Blanche's room heard the unfamiliar voice and pushed on Mr. Longworth's door, but it wouldn't open. None of the room doors had locks. It had been jammed shut. "Mr. Longworth," she called. "Mr. Longworth!" Nothing. She ran down the hall calling "Joe!" until the large orderly appeared. "Longworth's jammed his door shut with something. If you can't push it open, we'll have to break out his window."

But when they reached the room, the door opened easily. The nurse stepped in and turned on the overhead light. For a moment she was rigid. Then, like someone in slow motion, she sank to the floor in a faint. The orderly ignored her, mesmerized by the sight of Garrison Longworth's fragile body crumpled on the floor with a rope around its neck. Beside him rested a bouquet of black orchids whose petals fluttered in the cold wind coming through the open window.

17

1

"**B**UT, MOMMY, WE *want* to go to school."

Caroline looked at Melinda and Greg in disbelief. "I never thought I'd see the day when I had to talk you into staying home."

"But this house is haunted," Melinda explained. "We're scared here."

Greg was tossing an apple from hand to hand. "I'm not scared. I just think I ought to go to school today."

Caroline studied them. Well, the house had been broken into twice and now they knew someone was stalking the family. No wonder they were afraid to spend time in a place where someone left messages written in blood on the mirror.

"I'll tell you what," Caroline said. "You two go on to school—you might actually be safer there surrounded by people than you would be here. This evening we'll go to a hotel."

"The big one downtown with the indoor swimming pool?" Melinda asked excitedly.

"Sure."

"But what about George?"

"I'm afraid he'll have to be boarded at the vet's for

a few days. But they're very good to him. He won't mind."

Thd kids looked slightly cheered as they left for school, and Caroline had to admit she felt great relief at the thought of getting out of the house, even if they were only going a few miles away.

She made three calls, one to reserve a couple of rooms at the Carlyle Hotel, one to the vet reserving space for George, and one to Fidelia. Then she went upstairs to pack, this time for a short stay at the Carlyle. At ten o'clock she dressed to visit David.

She was supposed to tell the policeman watching the house wherever she was going, and he insisted on driving her to the hospital. "I'm here to protect you, not the house," he said. "We don't want you getting shot like your husband did."

David was propped up in bed watching a morning talk show when she arrived. "How're you feeling, honey?" she asked, thinking he didn't look as ghastly pale as he had last night.

"On the mend." He clicked off the television. "Do they always have bizarre topics on these talk shows?"

Caroline smiled. "Yes. They're quite an education."

"Tom called this morning and told me about the bullet they found in my leg. Looks like Chris and I got nailed by the same nut."

"It seems so. I guess you still don't remember seeing anything?"

David shook his head. "No. Whoever it was kept herself hidden in the trees. If the wind hadn't been just right, I probably wouldn't have heard the voice."

"You're sure it was a child's?"

"It sounded like a child's, but it couldn't have been. Not a young one, that is."

"I see." She glanced over at the roses the kids had brought last night. "Melinda is going to call you when she gets home from school," she said.

"Don't you mean right after *Guiding Light?*"

"I didn't know you knew which soap opera she liked!"

"Caroline, I don't live in a total fog. She talks about it all the time." He reached out and touched her hand. "But considering how much time I spend away from you and the kids, I'm not surprised you think I don't know anything about our homelife."

"You've been very busy the last few years," Caroline said carefully.

"I've been a fool the last few years. I guess an incident like this makes you sit up and reevaluate. All I could think about last night was, 'What if that bullet had killed me? What if I'd never seen Caroline and the children again?' And believe me, it scared the hell out of me to think it could have been all over and I've all but ignored the three of you lately."

Caroline's hand tightened around his. "I know why you've worked so hard. I know you felt like you had to prove something to yourself."

"And to you. You could have been married to a famous artist, but you ended up with me. I wanted to show that I was worthy of you."

Caroline's eyes filled with tears. "Oh, David, you never had to prove anything to me. Yes, Chris was a glamorous figure at one time and he could have been famous. But you're the person I've always counted on. You're the one who pulled me together after Hayley, not Chris. And if you think the kids and I care if you make a few thousand dollars less each year or don't deliver more babies than any other doctor in the western hemisphere, you've very much mistaken. We love you. All we've ever wanted is some of your time and attention."

"From now on you've got it." David's eyes twinkled at her. "You'll probably be begging me to go to the hospital and get out of your way."

"Don't count on it." Caroline leaned forward and kissed him. "I love you, David."

"I love you too, honey."

"And Melinda will call soon."

"I'll look forward to it. And speaking of calls, have there been any more lately?"

"No."

"Do we still have a policeman watching the house?"

"Yes. The one on duty today is named Mercer. The kids are very excited about his presence. Melinda wants him to keep the siren on at all times."

"That should make us popular with the neighbors. Lucy called about half an hour ago and said she'd like to drop by this afternoon, but Tina's out with the flu. She's determined to spend the night at the house with you, though. I think it's a good idea. I don't like your being alone."

"We're going to the Carlyle Hotel. We'll be fine. You just concentrate on getting well."

She asked Mercer to drive her directly home after she left the hospital, thinking how odd it felt to be riding around in a patrol car with a policeman for a chauffeur. When they stopped at lights, people in neighboring cars looked at her suspiciously, as if she'd just been picked up for something.

When they got back to the house, Caroline invited Mercer in for a sandwich and coffee, but he said he preferred eating in the car "where I can watch everything." Caroline had the feeling he just felt hesitant to impose on her by sitting around the house, but she didn't argue with him. She took out a roast beef sandwich and thermos of coffee to the car, wondering if he was even going to come in to use the bathroom or sit out there in misery all afternoon.

At one o'clock, Fidelia arrived. Caroline had already eaten her own sandwich and was putting on a fresh pot of coffee when she heard the familiar crisp tap at the door.

"Fidelia, thank you so much for coming over. I didn't hear your car in the driveway."

Fidelia rolled her eyes. "I know—you can hear dat old clunker a mile away. But I couldn't get it started dis morning so I took a cab." Fidelia looked at her closely, then enfolded her in her strong, thin arms. "I'm sorry about your husband. Lieutenant Jerome told me what happened."

"Did he mention the child's voice my husband heard before he was shot?" Fidelia nodded. "It was Hayley, you know."

"Or someone working on her behalf."

Caroline frowned. "I don't understand."

"Sometimes spirits have humans do deir dirty work."

"Like murdering people?"

"It has happened."

"Then you're saying there really could be a little girl who is being *guided* by Hayley?"

"I'm saying it can happen."

"But *why?*"

"Hayley was murdered. Her murderer was never caught. De souls of de unavenged often come back for retribution."

"But David didn't have anything to do with her

murder. Or Melinda, but she gets the calls from the child."

"You married again. You started a new life, had other children you love. Maybe Hayley doesn't like dis."

"Melinda said basically the same thing. But why, after all these years, would she come back?"

"You told me dat she is always on your mind. You've never been able to forget. From what I've heard, your first husband was never able to forget, either. Maybe all de energy you devoted to tinking about her somehow gave her spirit de strength to come back."

"Fidelia, this all sounds so fantastic."

"Only because you are not used to tinking dis way. I grew up wit it. Dat's why you wanted to see me today, isn't it?"

"Yes." Caroline walked over to the kitchen table and ran her fingers over the smooth wood. "I was up all night and I spent the whole morning thinking about it. The police haven't been any help. Now I'm turning to you. What can I do to stop this?"

Fidelia folded her arms across her narrow chest. "Voodoo teaches belief in de *loa*," she said slowly. "De *loa* are gods who act like what you call guardian angels. Dey can protect you from evil. But in order for a *loa* to attach itself to you and your family, you must take part in a ritual service and let de *loa* possess you during a trance state."

Caroline stiffened, thinking of the voodoo rituals she had seen in the movies. Glaze-eyed people chanting, dancing, someone biting off the head of a chicken. "Oh, Fidelia, I don't know about taking part in a ritual," Caroline said hesitantly.

Fidelia stepped closer. "I understand your fear be-

cause it's something new for you, but it's necessary."
Her aqua eyes held Caroline in an almost hypnotic
gaze. "Before de *loa* can help you, you must take
part in de ritual. You must meet with de cult and let
a *houngan*—a male—or a *mambo*—a female—guide
you."

Caroline's palms began to sweat. Already she felt
as if she were stepping off into an abyss of magic and
potions. "Do you know a cult group?"

"Oh, yes." She smiled. "Are you surprised?"

"Frankly, yes. David always said you practiced
voodoo, but I didn't believe it."

"I don't talk about it because it makes many people nervous. But it's noting to be afraid of. Will you
participate in de ritual?"

Caroline was suddenly uncomfortable. Although
she had invited Fidelia here to talk about the possibility of a supernatural agent being behind the killings,
actually being confronted with Fidelia's intensity and
the knowledge that the woman not only practiced
voodoo but also wanted her to participate in a cult ritual unnerved her. "I don't think I'm ready for what
you're talking about. I'm afraid."

"Are you more frightened of a voodoo ritual dan
you are of de danger your family is in?"

"Well, no, but this kind of ritual you're talking
about. It seems so—"

"Pagan?"

"I guess."

"Does your Christianity teach you to believe in
ghosts?"

"No, of course not."

"But you believe in dem neverdeless."

"I'm not sure."

"As long as you have doubt, isn't it best to try everyting to stop dis craziness? What can it hurt?"

"Nothing, I suppose."

"Den I will arrange it." For a few minutes Caroline had felt as if she were in an alien, exotic world. The reality of the cheerful kitchen and the smell of fresh coffee had disappeared with the talk of *loas* and cults and possession. But suddenly Fidelia smiled and said in a matter-of-fact voice, "As long as I'm here, I might as well get a little cleaning done. Dat all right wit you?"

Caroline blinked at her. "Sure," she said faintly. "Whatever you want."

"Good. De bedroom windows are dirty. I'll start with dem."

Ten minutes later the phone rang. It was Tom. "Caroline, I sent someone to Harry Vinton's funeral this morning.

She took a shaky breath. "Were they there?"

"You bet. A big bouquet of black silk orchids with a card reading, 'To Harry, Black for remembrance.' "

"So there's no doubt that all the murders are connected."

"I would say that's not an absolute certainty except for one thing."

"What's that?"

Tom was silent for a moment before he said, "I didn't go to the funeral myself because I was called to Sunnyhill Nursing Home."

"A nursing home? Whatever for?"

"Garrison Longworth. He died last night."

"A heart attack?"

"Yes. But he had a rope around his neck and beside him was the familiar bouquet and message."

"Oh, dear God," Caroline breathed. "But how

could someone have gotten to him there, with all those people around?"

"Apparently someone came in early in the evening, hid until around midnight, and then killed him. Or tried to. They didn't get a chance because the heart attack got him first."

"Was there any hair?"

"Not that I know of yet. But we haven't gotten all the lab reports back yet."

"If there is hair, it'll be orange synthetic. And there won't be any fingerprints. There won't be anything."

"Caroline, the killer came within minutes, maybe seconds, of being caught last night. This wasn't the neat job the others were. In fact, a nurse heard a scream she swears didn't come from Longworth. She said it sounded angry. Probably rage that Garrison died before he could be murdered."

"What kind of scream?"

"She said it sounded like a child's." Tom waited a moment, then said, "Caroline, are you all right?"

"Fine and dandy."

"Look, I know what a shock this was. I'm just telling you because I want you to realize how essential it is for you to leave town. And don't tell me you can't go until David gets out of the hospital. I want you and the children to leave tonight."

"We were going to a hotel downtown."

"That's not good enough."

"No, I guess it isn't." Caroline sighed. "Okay, Tom. I promise that we'll leave just as soon as the kids get in from school."

Caroline hung up. Immediately the phone rang. Tom again? She picked up the receiver with a shaking hand.

A deep-voiced woman said, "Mrs. Webb?"

"Yes."

"This is Donna Bell, the nurse at Melinda's school. Your daughter is quite ill."

"She's sick?" Caroline repeated dumbly. "But she was fine this morning."

"She's throwing up violently. She said she ate something a little girl gave her this morning. I wonder if she doesn't have food poisoning—"

Caroline slammed down the phone. A little girl gave Melinda something? Didn't arsenic poisoning mimic food poisoning?

Without even grabbing her coat, Caroline dashed outside to Mercer. "We have to get to the school. Melinda's sick. Maybe she's been poisoned."

The mile to Melinda's school seemed like ten. When they pulled up in front, Caroline ran inside, not even waiting for Mercer to follow. A self-important hall monitor directed her to the nurse's office. Caroline stepped into the small office to see a plump, older woman sitting at a scarred desk filling out forms.

"Mrs. Bell?"

The nurse looked up, smiling. "No, Mrs. Porter." Her voice was high and fluty. "Can I help you?"

"I'm Caroline Webb, Melinda's mother. Donna Bell called me a few minutes ago and said Melinda is very sick."

The nurse's creamy forehead puckered. "Donna Bell? Is she a substitute here?"

"No. She said she was the nurse."

"I'm the only school nurse, and your daughter hasn't been brought to me."

Panic raced through Caroline. "Then where's Melinda?" she demanded in a high, frightened voice. "Where's my little girl?"

Mrs. Porter stood up. "Calm down, dear. I'm sure there's been some kind of mistake. Whose class is she in?"

Caroline went blank, fear taking over. Her hands trembled. "She's in the third grade," she managed.

The nurse looked at her disapprovingly and said in a tone Caroline imagined was reserved for mental patients, "Then she would be in Mrs. Mailer's class, Mr. Stewart's class, or Miss Cummings's class."

"Cummings! She's in Miss Cummings's class."

"Very good." The nurse beamed. "Let's see if we can find her."

Caroline followed the stout woman down the hall. Oh, Melinda, please be in the classroom, she begged silently. Please don't be missing, fallen into the hands of—

"Why don't you just peek through the window here and see if you can spot your little girl," Mrs. Porters said. "That way we won't disturb the class."

Caroline moved to the window, her eyes running frantically up and down the rows of little seats. And there sat Melinda, tongue showing between her lips the way it always did when she was working on arithmetic problems. "She's there," Caroline breathed in relief.

"See?" Mrs. Porter said perkily. "Everything is fine, just as I knew it would be."

"I want to take her home anyway."

Mrs. Porter frowned. "Don't you think that would be alarming the child over nothing?"

Melinda would want to know why she was being jerked out of class, Caroline thought. It would cause a scene and probably alert whoever was watching them that Caroline was frightened, perhaps even planning to leave town. No, it would be better to leave her alone for an hour until school was out. Then after today, they would be out of the city and hopefully out of danger as well.

"I guess I will let her stay," she said reluctantly.

Mrs. Porter beamed some more. "Excellent. And my dear, you really shouldn't let yourself get upset over every little thing. Very bad for the digestion, you know."

Caroline gave the patronizing woman a long, cold look. "My digestion is the least of my problems right now, Mrs. Porter. Thank you for your help."

2

Fidelia doused the corner window of the master bedroom with Windex and reached for the paper towels. It was amazing how dirty these windows had gotten since she cleaned them a month ago. They always said electric heat was cleaner than gas, but if the heat in this house was any indication . . .

She heard a soft footfall down the hall and paused. Slow and stealthy, she thought abruptly. Not Caroline. George? He'd been lying in the entrance hall when she came upstairs. She glanced out the window again to see him standing in the backyard.

She laid down her towels. "Who's dere?"

Silence.

"Mrs. Webb? Greg?"

Nothing.

Fidelia's mouth went dry. There was evil in the house—it was as palpable as a strong, cold wind.

"Hayley?"

The grandfather clock in the hall ticked mournfully, as if it were measuring the last few seconds of her life. Funny how it had never seemed so loud before.

"Hayley, you have noting to fear from me," she called, trying to sound as fearless as her mother would have in this situation. She looked out the window again to see George, his head tilted curiously toward the bedroom window. "I only want to help you, *pauvre chèrie*, not destroy you. Don't you want help? Don't you want peace?"

"You can't help."

A child's voice, but calm, sure. Frightening.

"But I can. I have friends who can."

Childish laughter with a razor edge.

Fidelia knew she had an uncanny ability to sense evil; what she did not have was an ability to fight it, and it was practically staring her in the face right now. The situation was beyond her control, and she was more frightened than she had ever been in her life. She knew she had to get out of the house immediately. But first she had to get down the hall to the stairs.

She crept through the bedroom, pausing after every step to listen. Someone, or something, was very close. She just wasn't sure where. Her leathery skin had turned frigid, and she felt as wary as a helpless zebra being stalked by a lion, every sense humming as she tried to escape the predator. When she reached the door of the bedroom, she hesitated. Would it be better to lock herself in the room? No. Spirits didn't recognize locked doors. It was sunlight she needed. Fresh air and sunlight, where the evils couldn't follow.

With a deep breath, she plunged from the room, her sandals slapping against the gleaming hardwood floor of the hall, the floor she had waxed only last week. When she landed on the rectangular Oriental rug she had always admired, it flew out from under her, throwing her violently down. She had only one brief, startling glimpse of her assailant before pain flashed behind her eyes. Then she was dragged to the spiral staircase and pushed down to the marble entrance hall below.

1

"**Y**ET WHO WOULD *have thought the old man to have had so much blood in him?*"

Lady Macbeth's words kept running through Caroline's head. Who would have thought skinny, leathery Fidelia to have had so much blood in her? And who would have thought she could lose so much and still be alive?

In what seemed like seconds after Caroline and Mercer had walked in the house to find Fidelia limp and broken at the foot of the stairs, men were busting through the front door with a stretcher, IV bottles, blood pressure equipment. Then Tom arrived.

"There was a pile-up on the interstate. I couldn't get here as soon as I expected. What happened?"

Mercer explained about the call from the school and their returning home to discover Fidelia. Caroline heard him talking, but she couldn't say anything. She sat on the couch staring at her right hand, which had gotten covered with blood when she felt behind Fidelia's ear to find a fluttery pulse. Numbly she walked into the kitchen and poured dishwashing liquid over her hands before turning on the faucet. She rubbed until the stains were gone. She was just finishing when Tom came in.

"Are you all right?"

"I don't think I can take much more of this, Tom."

"I know. I called Lucy but there's no answer at the store. I'll try again in a little while and she can come to stay with you."

"Okay." Caroline went over and sat down at the table. "What have you found out?"

Tom sat down beside her. "Fidelia was struck in the upstairs hall. There's blood all over the floor."

"But she's alive."

"Very much so. The paramedics said all the blood is from a scalp wound. They bleed like the devil. It wasn't as bad as it looked."

"Thank God."

"I'm sure you noticed that her throat wasn't cut and there was no burning. No gunshot wound, either. I'd say it wasn't the intruder's intention to hurt her. Maybe Fidelia just surprised him."

"But why push her down the stairs?"

"Maybe he didn't. Maybe she just fell. Or maybe she saw something and he decided he had to get rid of her. But if so, he didn't hang around to make sure she was dead."

"It wasn't one of her usual days to work," Caroline said. "I asked her to come today because I wanted to talk with her. After we'd finished, she said she might as well do some cleaning upstairs while she was here. If she hadn't . . ."

"Where is her car?" Tom asked quickly as Caroline's voice broke.

"At home, I guess. She said there was something wrong with it. She took a cab."

"So it wasn't her regular day to work and her car

wasn't outside. Also, since she was upstairs, she wouldn't have heard someone come in down here."

"George would have. He was inside when I left for the school, but when we got back, he was outside."

"Could Fidelia have put him out?"

"Not without chaining him. She was very careful about that."

"Which means that someone George knew put him out. Otherwise, he would have attacked an intruder."

"I think so, yes."

Tom drummed his fingers on the table. "Well, clearly that bogus call from the school was a trick to get you and Mercer away from the house."

"The school!" Caroline burst out, looking at the clock over the kitchen counter. "It's three-twenty. Melinda got out twenty minutes ago and no one was there to pick her up!"

"I'll send Mercer. If she's left the school, what route will she take?"

"Elmwood to Parkhurst, then left onto our street. But I really think *I* should go."

"You sit here with me and calm down," Tom ordered. "Mercer can handle Melinda."

After Mercer left, Tom asked for more details about the call from the so-called school nurse. "She said her name was Donna Bell," Caroline explained. "She had a deep, kind of raspy voice, as if she were a heavy smoker. She sounded middle-aged."

"Have you ever heard this voice before?"

"Not that I remember."

"And you immediately left for school. What time would you say that was?"

"About one forty-five."

"You locked the door before you left?"

"No. I don't think so. I was too frightened. I thought Melinda had been poisoned."

"By a little girl." Tom shook his head. "I'm going back upstairs and see how things are going with the lab guys. You stay in here. I don't want you looking at all that blood right now."

Caroline nodded, pain flashing through her at the thought of Fidelia's wire-thin body plummeting down the stairs. Fidelia with her strange aqua eyes, her strong brown hands, her dangling silver earrings. Fidelia who had wanted to help by using voodoo, who had wanted her to participate in a ritual.

In a few minutes Tom came back, sat down, and looked at her intently.

"Caroline, I don't suppose you've been in your bedroom since you got back."

"I haven't been upstairs at all. Why?"

"There's a message written on the mirror."

"In blood," Caroline said tonelessly. "And it says, 'help me Mommy.' "

"That's right."

"That's what she came here to write."

"What *who* came here to write?"

"Hayley. She came here to write that message and Fidelia caught her so Hayley hit her."

Tom's gaze didn't waver. "Caroline, if Hayley had been here, she would have been a ghost, and ghosts don't have to hit people to get away. Fidelia was attacked by a *person.*"

"You don't even believe in ghosts, do you?"

"That is beside the point."

"I don't think so. No, I don't think so at all. I think that's what's giving you all so much trouble. You won't admit that Hayley has come back. It explains everything."

"It doesn't explain much to me. Why would she kill Pamela Burke?" He leaned forward and looked at her earnestly. "Caroline, you've had a big shock. A lot of big shocks. You're not thinking rationally."

"Now you sound like Lucy and David. But Fidelia knew. She was going to help me. Hayley couldn't allow that."

Tom sighed. "I'm not going to argue with you. But—"

Mercer walked in, his face taut. "I can't find her."

Tom jumped up. "You can't find Melinda?"

"I went over every route she could have taken, but there's no trace of her."

"Maybe she went home with a friend." Tom whirled on Caroline, who felt turned to stone. "Does she have a friend whose house she might have gone to?"

"Jenny. She used to go to Jenny's sometimes."

"The number?"

Caroline had it written down on a pad that she managed to find for him. He called and spoke to Jenny's mother, then by the change in his tone of voice, Caroline knew he was talking to Jenny. When he hung up, he looked at her solemnly.

"Jenny says Melinda left the playground with a little blond-haired girl she'd never seen before."

2

In those first few paralyzed seconds after Tom announced Melinda had left school with a little blond-haired girl, a hundred scenes flashed through Caroline's mind. Melinda born with a head full of curling, chestnut hair; Melinda toddling after Greg as he headed off to baseball practice and crying brokenheartedly when Caroline caught her and made her stay home; Melinda trundling down the hall on Halloween in her bunny costume, huge ears flopping; Melinda talking devotedly to her dormant bean sprout Aurora, willing it to grow. And now she was gone with the horror Hayley had become.

"What little blond friends does Melinda have?" Caroline looked at Tom blankly. "Caroline, listen to me. What little blond friend could Melinda have gone home with?"

"No one."

"Little blond girls are a dime a dozen. There must be someone."

"Hayley."

Tom strode over and grasped Caroline's shoulders. "Snap out of this. There's no reason to panic. Most lost children are found within fifteen minutes."

"It seems to me I was told that the last time, when Hayley disappeared."

"This isn't the last time. I need a picture of her."

Caroline went to her purse and riffled through the plastic photo section in her wallet. "Here's last year's school picture, and here's a shot of her at the Fourth of July picnic we had in the backyard."

"Good. Now, Caroline, I need to know what she was wearing."

Caroline was amazed at how perfectly she could picture Melinda that morning standing in the kitchen begging to go to school because she was afraid to stay in the house. "A skirt. Red-and-navy-blue plaid on white," Caroline said as Mercer took notes. "A navy-blue turtleneck sweater. Navy-blue tights. A camel-hair coat."

"Was she carrying anything?"

"A lunch box. A Barbie lunch box. And a book bag. It was red."

"You mean like a backpack?"

"No, like a little briefcase. She loved it because she thought it was like her daddy's medical bag."

Tom turned to Mercer. "Call Juvenile and have them get out some cruisers."

When he went to the phone, Tom forced her to look at him. "Caroline, Hayley Corday is dead. Melinda *can't* be with her. You've got to get that idea out of your head so you can help us. Now tell me what little blond girls Melinda knows."

Caroline dragged her hands through her hair. "Tom, it's no use. She didn't go home with any of her friends. She would have called."

"She's eight. Eight-year-olds aren't known for their sense of responsibility. Now *think!*"

"All right. Let's see. There's Beth Madison. She's a blonde but Melinda has never liked her. Then there's Cookie Stevens . . . no, Cookie moved away last year." From deep in the house she heard the doorbell ringing. Mercer, who had just hung up, left the room. "Stephanie Crane. She's new this year. She's in the school play, but I don't think Melinda knew her very well—not well enough to go home with her. Let's see, maybe Carol Braxton. She's in Melinda's class . . ."

Mercer appeared in the kitchen doorway. He held a young teenaged boy by the arm.

"What is it?" Tom asked.

"This boy just brought a delivery. Show them, kid."

The boy, pale with terror, stuck out a bouquet of black silk orchids tied with a black ribbon. Tom was beside him in an instant, jerking away the card that had been stapled to the ribbon. " 'To Melinda,' " he read. " 'Black for remembrance.' "

For the first time in her life Caroline fainted.

19

1

SHE AWAKENED ON the living room couch. Something damp was lying across her forehead, and Chris sat on the floor beside her, his blue eyes burning at her.

"Is Melinda . . ."

"She's not back yet."

"What are you doing here?" Caroline mumbled, sweeping the cloth off her forehead.

"I called to say goodbye before I left for Taos and see how everything was going. Tom answered and told me what happened."

"What time is it?"

"After six. When you passed out, they called a doctor. You came to for a few minutes, hysterical, and he gave you something to calm you down."

"I don't remember any of that. Is Tom still here?"

"No, he's out questioning people who might have seen Melinda. So's Greg. When he got home, he took the dog. He said if anyone could find Melinda, George could."

"I guess that's true."

"There's another detective here—a woman from Juvenile named Ames. She seems nice."

Caroline smiled thinly. "They don't usually put a detective on the case for twenty-four hours after the child disappears. I remember that. Not unless they suspect foul play."

"Don't think about that now, Caro. She's going to be all right."

"Yeah, sure."

"Tom finally got hold of Lucy. She's gone to the hospital to tell David."

Caroline struggled to sit up. "I don't want David to know! He's helpless and there's nothing he can do."

"Melinda's picture will be on the six o'clock news. You didn't want him to find out that way, did you?"

"No, I guess not."

The phone rang once. Then Caroline heard a woman talking in the other room. The detective, answering one of the many calls that would come in after Melinda's story appeared on the evening news. "Is the phone tapped?" Chris nodded. "But the kidnapper hasn't called."

"Not yet."

"Probably not ever." Caroline rubbed a hand across her forehead. She felt as if all sounds were coming to her from far away. It wasn't an unpleasant sensation—only strange. "Hayley's killed her, you know."

"I don't know anything except that I don't believe in the supernatural."

"Oh, Chris, you're trying to sound all hardheaded and reasonable, but it won't work. The black bouquet should tell you something."

"All that bouquet tells me is that things are happening differently. Always before the flowers turned up at the funeral."

"Not in Garrison Longworth's case."

"But there was a body. There's no body this time. I think the flowers are a warning."

"A warning that my daughter is going to be killed."

"No. I know it sounds crazy, but I wonder if the killer can't go through with it, if he's begging to be caught."

"Chris, that's such a cliché."

"Clichés get to be clichés because they're true so often."

Caroline closed her eyes. "Then why was Melinda taken to begin with?"

"Maybe it's all part of a plan, but the murderer can't take the final step. He can't murder a little girl."

"I wish I could believe that. Chris, who was the boy who brought the bouquet?"

"Just some fourteen-year-old who didn't know what the hell was going on. He said he was walking home from school when a little blond girl gave it to him along with five dollars and this address written on a piece of paper. He thought the black flowers were strange, but then she was such a little girl, maybe she thought they were pretty. He didn't see her get in or out of a car—she was just walking down the street."

"I'm surprised she didn't send Twinkle along with the flowers."

"Caroline."

"Well, if you don't believe Hayley is the killer, then it must be the person who kidnapped her. That's the only one who could have Twinkle."

"If it *was* Twinkle we found. We're not absolutely sure of that."

"*I* am."

Caroline had heard a car pull up outside but wasn't

really paying attention until the kitchen door opened and she heard David call, "Caroline!"

She swung her legs off the couch and rose, still dizzy after the sedative the doctor had given her. She swayed and Chris steadied her. "David, I'm in the living room."

David hobbled in, Lucy staggering at his side as he leaned against her. "He refused to stay in the hospital, Caro," she said breathlessly. "The nurses are screaming bloody murder, but here he is."

David's eyes flickered over Chris. Obviously Lucy had already told him Chris was here. "Where else would I be when my little girl has disappeared?" he asked, his voice breaking.

Caroline rushed to him, crying. "David, I'm so glad you're here, even if you shouldn't be." She helped him to the couch, where he dropped heavily. "Are you in much pain?"

"No." She could tell he was lying by the sweat covering his forehead. "Any news?"

"Nothing."

"Where's Tom?"

"Questioning people who might have seen Melinda leave the school."

"The school," David said with disgust. "They did a great job of looking after her."

"I shouldn't have let her go today. I should have brought her home after I got that call about her being sick. I should have been there to pick her up—"

"Caroline, stop it," Chris said. "It's not your fault. None of this is your fault."

David shot him an icy stare. "What are you doing here?"

"Trying to help Caroline."

"Caroline doesn't need your help. I'd like for you to leave."

"We'd rather he didn't." Caroline looked up to see a tall woman of about thirty standing in the doorway. Her brown hair was drawn back in a French braid, and her hazel eyes studied Chris intently. Obviously she was Detective Ames from Juvenile. "Lieutenant Jerome and I would like for you to remain here, Mr. Corday."

Chris looked at her in surprise. "I don't mind staying, but why do the police want me to?"

"For your own protection. You've been attacked once by the person who probably took Melinda. We don't want to risk another attack, and it would be easier for us to keep an eye on you here rather than assigning someone to your home."

"I see," Chris said. He turned to David. "Look, I know you don't like me, and in your place I wouldn't want me here, either. But if the police want me to stay . . ."

David looked away. "Then stay. I guess it doesn't matter at a time like this."

The phone rang again and Detective Ames went to answer. They all froze until they heard her say, "Dr. and Mrs. Webb don't want to do an interview for tonight's news. Please don't call again—we're trying to keep the line open."

Keep the line open, Caroline thought. Keep the line open for Hayley to call.

2

After almost two hours of questioning, Tom had come up with nothing from the people who lived around the school, so he headed back to his office to gather up all his notes on the Webb situation and drop off the note that had come with the flowers for the handwriting expert to look at. As soon as he walked in, Al McRoberts told him there was a woman insisting on seeing him. "I don't have time," Tom snapped. "Someone else will have to handle it."

"She's determined to see *you*," Al said. "She won't talk to anyone else. It might be important, you never know."

"Damn," Tom muttered. Peering through the glass wall of his minuscule office, he saw a washed-out-looking woman of about forty twisting her hands and looking as if she were about to burst into a screaming fit. "I guess I can spare a few minutes. No word on Melinda Webb?"

"Not a thing."

"Okay. I'll get rid of this one fast."

Tom was gritting his teeth but he hid his impatience as he walked into the office. The woman gazed up at him with eyes that must have once been the color of blue gentians but now bore the habitually bleary red hue of an alcoholic. "Hello, Mrs. . . ."

"Stanton. Annalee Stanton."

"Mrs. Stanton. I heard you have something important to tell me."

She leaned forward, placing big-knuckled hands on knees covered by a faded blue wool skirt. "It's about my little girl, Detective. My little girl, Joy."

"All right. How old is Joy?"

"Six. And she's missin'."

"Then you should be talking to someone in Juvenile."

Annalee Stanton shook her head, making the faded blond bangs dance on her high forehead. "No. I got to tell you."

"Why me in particular?"

"Because you're Lucille Elder's boyfriend. I seen a picture of the two of you at a party in the newspaper."

Tom looked at her suspiciously. "And what does Lucille have to do with this?"

"I got to start at the beginnin'. If I don't start there, you won't understand. And I'll get mixed up. I do that so much these days." Her hands had begun to shake and she looked around the room, then leaned forward conspiratorily. "You don't have nothin' to drink here, do you? I run out about noon and didn't get the money I expected, so I couldn't buy no more." Tom looked at her coldly. "Hey, a drink would calm me, make me tell my story better. Is it such a big deal?"

By now Tom felt like gnashing rather than merely gritting his teeth. He had the feeling the woman's suppressed hysteria had more to do with imminent DT's than with her missing daughter, but he remembered the bottle of Scotch a rookie had given him for his birthday. It was cheap Scotch, and Tom hated Scotch anyway, so four months later it was still in his desk drawer. He rummaged until he found it, poured a shot into a Dixie cup, and watched as the woman grabbed for it eagerly, downing it in one gulp.

"That was good. Another one'd be even better."

"Mrs. Stanton, I'm very busy . . ."

"Just one more, *please*. My nerves are shot to hell. One more blast and I can tell my story."

The second shot went down as fast as the first. Then the woman pressed her lips together in satisfaction, sat back, and regarded him from eyes surrounded by a hundred little dry lines and broken veins. "Okay, like I said, Joy's missin'. Has been since this mornin'."

"And you're only now reporting it?"

"Well, sometimes she's gone for hours at a time. On jobs, that is."

"A six-year-old has a job?"

Mrs. Stanton's jaw set. "Are you gonna let me tell this or are you gonna ask a bunch of dumb questions?"

Tom spread his hands. "Tell your story. I'll keep my mouth shut."

"Okay. First of all, you got to understand that Joy's dad died two years ago and left a ton of bills but no life insurance. Just like him, the bastard. He never was no good." Her eyes blurred even more with martyrdom and she was breathing faster.

"Yes, Mrs. Stanton?"

"Well, that's why I got to take money where I can find it. I just want you to understand that up front."

"I do. Please go on."

Mrs. Stanton cleared her throat, although her voice remained raspy. "Around Halloween this woman come to me and said she wanted to play a trick on someone and she wanted to use Joy. She was a classy-lookin' woman, but I was pretty leery at first. But like I said, I need money and she offered twenty dollars just to take Joy around on Halloween. Well, Joy'd been whinin' for days about not havin' a nice costume—I told her to put a paper bag on her head with holes for eyes, but that wouldn't do for *her*; I guess I've spoilt her no end—and this woman said she'd buy Joy a costume *on top of* givin' me the twenty bucks. So I says, 'Sure, why not? God knows we can use the money.' She got Joy in pretty early and Joy was all giggly and happy, tellin' me what a good time she had. So the next time the woman asked me if she could use Joy for one of her tricks, I said, 'Yes indeed. For a good price, that is.' "

"Mrs. Stanton, what did Joy do for this woman on Halloween night?"

"She said she just struck up a conversation with a little girl. Told the kid her name was Hayley—you know, like Hayley Mills—and she lived in a log cabin and her dad was a painter. Bunch a crap like that. Then she went to someone's house and said treats or tickles, whatever the hell that means."

Tom's heart was pounding. "Mrs. Stanton, who was this woman?"

"I got to tell my story first. If you don't hear it all, you won't understand."

"Mrs. *Stanton,* cut the bull!"

The woman drew back indignantly. "If you're gonna be hateful, I won't say another word."

She's enjoying this, Tom thought angrily. Her hour in the sun. He felt like wringing her neck, but he forced himself to smile. "I'm sorry. Go ahead."

Mrs. Stanton looked around nervously. "How about another slug of that Scotch? You scared me, talkin' harsh like that and me so upset anyway."

This time Tom gave it to her willingly. Anything to keep her talking. "I'm sorry I frightened you. So what happened next, Mrs. Stanton?"

"Well, today she wanted two things—she wanted Joy for the day and she wanted me to make a phone call. I was startin' to feel pretty uncomfortable about her and her tricks, but she offered fifty dollars at the end of the day when Joy and me was finished. I was s'posed to call a woman named Webb and say I was Donna Bell, the school nurse, and her little girl Melinda was real sick. We rehearsed and I was pretty good, if I do say so myself. I sounded damned classy." She smiled blearily. "But the woman said she'd have Joy back by three. When it got to be five, I started worryin'. Then I saw on the news that a kid named Melinda Webb was missin'. That was the name of the kid I'd called about. She was gone. Joy was gone. I got the super—he's a special friend of mine—to let me into the woman's apartment."

"You know the superintendent of the woman's apartment building?"

"Hell, yes. It's the same as mine. She lives right down the hall, although she hasn't been around much the last couple of days. She talked to me a couple of times and told me where she worked. That's how she seen Joy, too, there in the buildin'. Anyway, I went in and there was all these black silk orchids layin' around—"

"Whose apartment were you in?" Tom barked, unable to contain himself any longer. "Dammit, who *is* this woman?"

Mrs. Stanton flinched. "Your girlfriend's assistant, Tina Morgan."

20

1

BY EIGHT O'CLOCK a knot of reporters stood doggedly in front of the house, video cameras poised. The terse statement Tom had given out three hours ago hadn't helped—they were still waiting for some juicy tidbit for their eleven o'clock reports. The phone, which had been ringing incessantly for an hour, had fallen mercifully—if eerily—silent, and David was sitting with his arm around Caroline's shoulders to stop her shaking, when a furious Greg appeared with Mercer, the officer who had been with them all day. "Why do I have to stay here?" he demanded. "Why can't I be out there looking for Lin?"

"You've already done enough," Tom said. "You tracked Melinda to Maple Drive and found a woman who saw her getting in a Volkswagen."

"But the woman didn't see who was driving. She just saw some blond-haired kid with Lin. If you'd let me keep questioning people—"

"We have men on the streets doing that. Besides, we think we already know who was driving."

"You do? Who?"

"Tina Morgan."

Greg looked from Tom to Caroline. "Tina! That's crazy!"

"I know it seems that way," Caroline said. "But Tom has a lot of evidence that points to Tina."

"I don't believe it." Greg sat down without removing his leather jacket. George gazed around, waiting for his next command. "Why would Tina do something like that?"

"We don't know," Tom said. "But everything fits. Apparently Tina hired a six-year-old blond girl named Joy Stanton to play what she called tricks on your family. It was Joy dressed in a clown suit who approached Melinda on Halloween night."

"And the person who got into the house and tore up Lin's room, left messages in *blood* for cripe's sake, that was Tina, too?"

Tom nodded. "Tina helped Lucy redecorate this house. She had access to the keys."

"But the locks were changed."

"Somehow she got a copy of one of the new keys. And the fact that it was Tina explains why the dog didn't attack her earlier today although he was in the house. She made a big point of making friends with him when she worked here."

"I should have known yesterday," Lucy said. "Some crates in my storeroom were knocked over and a clown doll came tumbling out—a clown doll like Twinkle that Caroline gave me ages ago. I'd forgotten I still had it—it's been packed away for over ten years, ever since I moved into the condo—but Tina must have found it some time ago. She went absolutely white when it fell on the floor. Then she recovered and accused *me* of using it to scare your mother. She's a quick thinker and a very good actress. I was standing there defending myself like crazy."

"Where does Tina live?" Greg stormed.

"We've already searched her apartment, Greg, and we have someone watching it now."

Greg shook his head. "She shot my dad and now she's stolen my little sister." He pounded his fist on the chair arm. "Damn!"

George started reflexively barking, picking up on Greg's mood. "Settle down, Greg," Caroline said. "Why don't you take George out to the kitchen and give him a drink? His tongue's practically out on the floor. And he needs his dinner."

"How can you be so calm?" Greg demanded.

Caroline started to cry quietly and David said, "Gregory, shut up and go feed the dog."

"I'm sorry, Mom." Greg looked at the rest of them defiantly. "Okay, I'll give George his dinner, but I'm not going to sit around doing nothing. As soon as he's finished, I'm gonna get some of the guys together and we're gonna keep looking."

"I told you already I have men working on it," Tom said.

Greg glowered at him. "It was George who tracked Melinda to Maple Drive, not your men."

"But he lost the scent there, after she got in the car." Tom looked at Greg patiently. "You and George did a great job. But you're only fifteen and Tina's still out there. Like you said, she shot your father and she's taken Melinda. Now you're not going to do anybody one damn bit of good by making yourself the next easy target."

"He's right, Greg," David said. "Please don't make this harder than it already is."

Greg glowered, particularly at Chris, who was still

lingering uncomfortably in the living room. "Well, hell," he muttered and stomped off to the kitchen with George following.

The phone rang for the first time in twenty minutes. Please, God, let that be Melinda, Caroline prayed. Please let her be at a friend's and those flowers be a prank just like the call from the school.

"Ames will get it," Tom said, but Greg didn't know he wasn't supposed to answer the phone and beat her to it.

"Mom!" he shouted from the kitchen. "Mom, pick up the phone, quick!"

"Melinda," Caroline gasped, already reaching for the phone on the end table. "Melinda, sweetie, is that you?" she cried into the receiver.

"Hi, Mommy," the child said. "Melinda is still alive, but not for long."

Chills rippled down Caroline's back as she fought for control. "Is this Joy," she blurted, "or Tina?"

She heard a sharp intake of breath.

"Tina, we know you have Melinda. We *know*. It's all over."

"Not until you find me," she said in her normal voice. "Not until you come and talk to me. *Alone.*"

"Talk to you about what? I don't know where you are."

"Yes, you do."

"Tina, please let my little girl go. *Please—*"

"*Alone.* No police."

The line went dead.

2

Twelve-thirty. Caroline tossed on the bed. She had lain there an hour, vainly trying to rest while Detec-

tive Ames and Tom waited downstairs for more calls.
David, with the help of medication his pain required,
had fallen into an uneasy sleep beside her. Greg had
retreated in surly silence to his bedroom, and Tom
had sent Lucy home to get some rest in case Melinda
wasn't found and she was needed early in the morning. Chris had been asked by Tom to stay rather than
return to his lonely cabin where another cruiser
would be required for surveillance in case Tina decided to attack him again.

Every time Caroline started to drift into sleep, she
saw Fidelia's body in the hall, surrounded by a pool
of blood, and she jerked awake. Was Melinda already
lying in a pool of blood, too? Or had her kidnapper
decided to make her wait for death, just like Hayley's
had done? Hayley's death could have been prevented,
Caroline thought. I sat back and let the police handle
everything, and look what happened. "But I will not
let it happen again," Caroline murmured, climbing
out of bed. "This time I won't leave it to others. If I
think clearly, I can come up with *something*. I have
to."

She pulled on jeans and a sweatshirt and went
downstairs, George trailing along behind her. Detective Ames was in the family room. "Where's Tom?"
Caroline asked.

"He finally located Tina's boyfriend, Lowell Warren. He was in Washington at a conference. He told
Tom that he'd left his wife and he'd bought a house
for him and Tina. Maybe she's gone there."

"Why didn't anyone tell me?"

"From what Tom's said, you've been under siege
for weeks. You're ready to collapse from exhaustion.
He said to let you get as much rest as possible.

There's nothing you can do. He's checking the house."

"Do you really think she's taken Melinda there?"

Detective Ames's eyes slid away. "There's always that chance."

But you don't think so, Caroline thought. Of course Tina would know she would be found there. If she was thinking rationally, that is. But maybe she wasn't. "I'm going to make coffee," she said dispiritedly.

The young woman smiled, her eyes slightly shadowed from weariness. "Good. I could use some."

How many pots of coffee had they consumed in the past eight or nine hours? Caroline wondered as she plugged in the percolator. While it perked, she sat at the kitchen table, racking her brain for anything about Tina that might give her a clue as to where she had taken Melinda. She had not shown up for work yesterday morning, nor had her car been located at any area hotels or motels. But she must have been waiting for Melinda on Maple Drive. Caroline just couldn't understand why Melinda would have gone with her. She'd been warned over and over not to go anywhere except with the immediate family. Yet, obviously she'd left the schoolyard with Joy Stanton, and together they'd disappeared with Tina.

When the coffee was finished, Caroline took some to Detective Ames. The woman was on the phone again, and when she hung up she looked disappointed. "That was Tom," she said as Caroline handed her the coffee. "Tina isn't at the house."

"No, I didn't think she would be."

"Tom said there isn't a sign of her even being there. Mr. Warren told him Tina hadn't moved in yet.

It might cause problems with the divorce. He's been living there by himself for a couple of weeks."

"I see. How did he take the news about Tina?"

"He had a fit. Didn't believe it, of course. He only gave us the address of the house because he wanted to prove that Tina wasn't there hiding a child." She frowned. "Still, Tom said he got the feeling that Mr. Warren was really shook, like part of him knew something was wrong with Tina. Maybe he just hadn't wanted to admit it. Of course, that's pure speculation."

"That's all any of us can do now—speculate. No one even knows why Tina would do all of this."

"Tina or whoever she is."

Caroline looked at her blankly. "Her name isn't Tina Morgan?"

"We don't know for sure that it isn't, but Tina Annette Morgan of Indianapolis has been missing for over nineteen years. She disappeared when she was six."

"Nineteen years? Six years old?" Caroline repeated slowly.

"I know. Too close to your daughter to be a coincidence. We contacted the mother of the Morgan child. She said Tina had dark hair and eyes. That's awfully thin evidence, but still . . ."

"Good God!" Chris stood in the doorway, blond hair falling over his forehead. "You mean Tina is some kid that disappeared about the same time as Hayley? Maybe taken by the same pervert?"

"*Maybe,* Mr. Corday. We don't have any proof."

The phone rang again and the woman picked it up. "No, Mrs. Webb does not wish to appear on your talk show tomorrow," she was saying as Caroline went back to the kitchen in shock. Chris trailed after her.

As she sat down at the table, he poured two cups of coffee and joined her.

"Chris, what in the world is going on?" Caroline moaned, putting her head in her hands.

"I don't know, Caro. I don't get this at all. Maybe this woman isn't the same Tina Morgan. I mean, where would she have been all this time? And if the kidnapper killed Hayley, why wouldn't he have killed Tina?"

"Who knows what line of logic those people follow? If any. And maybe the two kidnappings are totally unrelated. We don't even know exactly when Tina Morgan disappeared."

"They aren't unrelated, Caro. You know that. The woman put flowers on Hayley's grave and sent the same kind of flowers to the funerals of people who knew Hayley."

"But *Tina!* She seemed so normal. So capable. But she's killed three people and injured four. Now she's kidnapped two little girls, one of whom she means to murder."

"I told you before, Caro, there's something different about her method this time. The flowers came first. Then the phone call. Maybe she's cracking and can't kill again."

"That's a comforting thought. I wish I could believe it." Caroline raised her head. "I keep remembering the day of Pamela Fitzgerald's funeral, when Tina was so kind to me. Or seemed to be. Obviously she'd planted the black bouquet and was watching for my reaction. When I nearly fainted, she took me outside and we went for coffee and a drive. She told me about her little girl who had died of leukemia last summer."

"Where's her husband?"

"There wasn't one. She had to go through it all alone."

"Do you think she's taken Melinda as a replacement?"

"So she can kill her?"

Chris grimaced. "I guess not. I'm just trying to figure out why she's done all this."

"Because of Hayley. It all has something to do with Hayley. I just wish we knew more about Tina's background."

"Can't Lucy come up with anything? She must have checked her references."

"No, she didn't."

"Shit. Good old 'Go by your instincts' Lucy. That philosophy could have gotten her in a lot of trouble this time."

"Tina gave her a very plausible reason for there being no references, and you know how charming she is. Was. You *wanted* to believe her." Caroline went silent in thought. "She said she'd worked in New York City."

"Talk about looking for a needle in a haystack." Chris leaned back in his chair. "Where did Tina take you on that drive?"

"To the wildlife preserve."

"The old munitions manufacturing site? I'd nearly forgotten it."

"Me too. I wasn't too happy when we ended up there. It's such a depressing place." Caroline's jaw dropped. "Oh, my God! Talk about mental blocks! That's where she's taken Melinda. I was just too upset over finding another bouquet to wonder why she'd taken me all the way out there, then asked if I hadn't been there before. That's an odd question to ask someone who's lived here all her life. Chris, she was calling attention to the place. She must have known even then she was going to kidnap Melinda. She led me right to the hiding place. That's why she said on the phone I knew where to find her!"

"We have to tell Ames."

He started to rise, but Caroline grabbed his arm. "No! She said to come alone."

"You can't go out there alone!"

"Lower your voice!" Chris sank down on his chair. "Chris, she wants to talk to *me*. If the police go roaring out there, they might frighten her into killing Melinda, if she hasn't already."

"They won't go *roaring* out there, Caro. They know how to handle situations like this."

Caroline leaned toward him. "Chris, this is my little girl we're talking about. What if it were Hayley? Would you risk getting her killed because you thought you should follow procedure? Last time we did everything just the way the police wanted us to, and Hayley is dead. *Please,* Chris, please just let me go and don't tell Detective Ames."

Chris stared at her for a moment. "Okay," he said reluctantly. "But Tina only said no police. She didn't say anything about me."

"No, Chris, I don't want—"

"You either go with me, or I tell Ames."

"Dammit, Chris!" Caroline glared at him. "All right." The phone had rung again, and Caroline heard Detective Ames speaking in the other room. "But hurry. We have to get out of here without her knowing."

They got up quietly from the table. Chris slipped out the kitchen door while Caroline took her jacket off the coat tree and looked at George, who had skittered up to her dragging his leash. "No, you can't go," she whispered, jerking the jacket over her sweatshirt. The dog stood on his hind legs, placing big paws on her shoulders. He was so strong, so protective. "Okay," she said. "I guess you've shown you're better at finding Melinda than anyone."

"Mrs. Webb, where are you going?" Detective Ames said, coming into the kitchen just as Caroline was dashing out the door. "Mrs. Webb!"

Caroline ignored her. Chris was already revving the jeep and she clambered in with George.

"Caroline, this is not a family picnic!" Chris snapped. "You *and* the dog?"

"He's got a little better nose than you or I have. Now get going before Ames shoots the tires or something to stop us."

They roared out of the driveway, leaving Detective Ames staring after them. The roads were almost deserted so deep into the night and the trip seemed to take forever. Caroline kept telling Chris to drive faster, but when they finally pulled off the highway into the wildlife preserve, she had a sudden quiver of misgiving. Tina had a gun. She was capable of anything. Maybe they shouldn't have come. Maybe they *should* have left it to the police. Then she thought of Melinda alone, possibly being tortured, and her misgiving vanished.

The starless night was so dark that at first she had trouble picking out the silhouette of the brick boiler house rising three stories against the depthless sky. When she was a teenager the deserted area had been *the* place for area teenagers to park, and more than one ghost story had been spun around the crumbling buildings where dynamite had once been manufactured. Of particular ghoulish interest had been the huge, echoing boiler house. Someone was always prowling around in there at night looking for vampires, werewolves, or other indescribable monsters. For a while the old building was strictly patrolled to keep out intruders. But as time passed surveillance slackened, although Caroline knew the place was not the popular attraction it once had been.

"Let's try the boiler house first," she said to Chris.

"Isn't it kind of obvious? You know there's a whole network of tunnels under the preserve, not to mention all those little buildings where dynamite is stored."

"Chris, she said I knew where she was. I don't think she'd expect me to find her in a maze of tunnels. Besides, those storage houses are locked."

"Locks can be broken."

"Chris, the boiler house. *Please.*"

Chris pulled off beside the main road and stopped the jeep. They couldn't risk Tina hearing the engine or the crunch of tires on the gravel road running beside the boiler house. Before they climbed out, Chris reached under the seat and withdrew a gun. "It's my old .38," he explained, and Caroline remembered he was an expert marksman. His deadly skill had always seemed a contradiction of his artistic personality—maybe that's why she had forgotten about it over the years.

"Do you always carry that around with you?"

"Only since I got shot. Let's go. And you stay *behind* me."

Quickly she and Chris and George emerged from the jeep and silently crept toward the hulking old building. George began to growl low in his throat as they drew near. "Please don't bark," Caroline whispered. As if understanding, George subsided, although he strained at the leash through the overgrown lot separating the boiler house from the road. He headed straight for a window while Caroline and Chris struggled through a tangle of dead honeysuckle vines that cracked beneath their weight and dragged at their ankles, almost throwing them down.

When they neared the window, they saw a faint glow. "It's a fire," Christ murmured.

"Oh, God. Sometimes she sets her victims on fire."

"Don't think about that. It's probably a fire for warmth."

As they crept up to the window, Chris withdrew the gun from his jacket pocket and pushed Caroline down. "For all we know, Tina's standing right there looking out at us," he whispered. "Stay low."

Caroline closed her eyes while Chris crawled forward and peered in the window set low in the wall. Breath hissed in his throat. "Tina's in there."

"And Melinda?"

"I don't see her, but most of the building is dark. I can't see much of anything except Tina sitting in front of a small fire, staring. But Melinda is there, Caro. She has to be."

"What'll we do?"

"Just what they do in the movies. Take her by surprise."

Almost before Caroline realized what he was doing, Chris had picked up a big rock lying near the brick wall. With all his strength he crashed the rock through the window. Barking wildly, George hurled himself into the room, and as Chris followed, gun aimed, Tina stood up and screamed. It was a shrill nightmarish sound Caroline would never forget.

"Where is she?" Chris shouted, his voice echoing in the cavernous building as Caroline crawled through the broken window. "Where's Melinda?"

"Mommy!"

Caroline's head jerked to the right. Somewhere in the shadows was her daughter. George tensed to run in her direction, but Tina shouted, "She's wired with dynamite!"

Caroline froze. "You're lying."

"Oh, no, I'm not. There's lots of dynamite stored out here. All you need is forty pounds of pressure to detonate it, and I have a detonator. I stole it from a Burke Construction Company site. Wouldn't Pamela have gotten a kick out of that?"

Melinda's voice, high and tearful, floated out of the darkness. "It's true. There's wires on me and Joy." George lunged, but Caroline held his leash firmly.

Chris's eyes narrowed. "Unwire them, Tina."

Tina looked back stonily, her beautiful face haggard and somehow different in the flickering light of the fire. "No."

"If you don't unwire them, I'll kill you." Tina stared at him, and Chris pointed the gun at her chest.

"No, don't shoot!" Melinda shrieked. "That's Hayley, your little girl."

The gun quivered in Chris's hand.

"What's the matter, Daddy? Don't you recognize me?" Black waves washed across Caroline's vision as she heard a little girl's voice come out of Tina's mouth. Hayley's voice.

"Hayley is dead," Chris said firmly. "Her body was found nineteen years ago."

"You mean *a* body was found nineteen years ago." Tina stepped forward, nearer the fire. "The body of a six-year-old girl, burned, missing her head, and beside her my locket with your pictures inside."

Caroline closed her eyes. The type of necklace

found on the body was a detail the police had never made public. She took a deep breath and tried to speak, but nothing came out. She thought she was going to faint again.

"You're Tina Morgan," Chris said hollowly. "You're Tina Morgan who disappeared from Indianapolis almost twenty years ago."

"I knew Tina. Just for a little while. Just until . . ." She trailed off, staring at them emptily.

"Just until what?" Chris asked.

"I'm keeping Tina alive. She's alive inside me. I guess in a way I am Tina. Sometimes I forget that I'm not." She shook her head slightly, as if clearing it. "But I don't always forget."

Caroline had started to shiver. "You say you're really Hayley."

"I'm both now."

"I see." She swallowed. "Were both of you taken by the same person?"

"Oh, yes."

"Who?" Chris demanded.

"Garrison Longworth."

"Now I know you're lying," Chris said. "He was in Italy."

Animation returned to Tina's face. She smirked. "Oh, was he? I suppose you took Harry Vinton's word for that and let it go." Tina now spoke in an adult voice. "He came home that summer because he'd flipped out. Probably did something to a little girl over there and his wife left him. He was ashamed and he wanted his presence at the mansion kept a secret. Mommy was gone all day, you were busy painting—neither of you ever saw him. But I did. He played with Twinkle and me, but he said it was a secret. It was all a secret." Her cocky expression faded.

"And then he tricked me. He dressed up like Twinkle and he took me and hid me up here in the tunnels. Millicent knew he had me, but she didn't do anything. Not even when I begged. I guess Harry Vinton figured it out, but they paid him to keep quiet. And Pamela saw me. When Garrison was leaving town with me, she saw me in his car. But she didn't do anything. She just walked away."

Caroline and Chris stood rigid, gazing with shock at the young woman in front of them. At last Chris said in a flat voice, "You-cannot-be-Hayley."

She smiled. "Why not, Daddy? Because I don't look like your little girl? Well, I'm all grown up now. My hair is dyed and I wore colored contacts. But I don't have them in now, and if the light weren't so bad in here, you'd see that my eyes are blue, just like yours."

"They *are*," Melinda called. "I saw them."

"You shut up!" Tina snarled.

Her sudden anger frightened Caroline even more. She had to keep Tina's mind off Melinda. "Whose body was found and identified as yours?"

"Tina Morgan's, I guess. Garrison picked her up in Indianapolis. I remembered the name of the town because it sounded like Indians lived there. That's what I thought, even though I didn't see any. Anyway, he picked her up one night. Said he would take her for ice cream. Then he said she was just an ugly little girl. Not pretty like me. Not worth keeping." Her voice quavered. "But I thought she was pretty. I liked her."

Tina seemed to choke, then she regained control and went on. "He said he was bringing us both back here to my house. I was so happy. But he only brought us back to the area so he could murder her.

He made me watch him kill her out in the woods. He cut off her head and burned her up, all because nobody would help me. If any of them had told about me, he couldn't have hurt her. She died because of me. Because of them. Pamela. Millicent. Harry Vinton. *Garrison.*"

Tina's face worked. Tears glistened in the firelight. Her stomach plunging, Caroline realized she really was looking at Hayley. With a mixture of elation and horror, she thought, She's my little girl. And she's a murderer.

"Garrison said I should see violence because the world is full of violence," Hayley continued. "He also said I should see what would happen to me if I tried to get away. But it was so awful. She screamed and screamed. There was so much blood. Her head . . . the fire . . ." She shivered, then she smiled. "Do you know even Millicent thought it was me he killed? He didn't want her to know the truth. But she wouldn't have told on him anyway. She was crazy, you know."

"But there was an autopsy," Chris said faintly.

Hayley shrugged. "She was a child. No head, no teeth. Burned—no fingerprints. Right age. My necklace."

"But the blood type was the same," Chris persisted.

"I've thought about that. That's the only way they could have told the other girl wasn't me. Either she happened to have the same blood type or Harry Vinton paid a pathologist to say she did. Some people will do anything for money."

How matter-of-fact she sounds, Caroline thought numbly. How frighteningly matter-of-fact. "What happened after Garrison killed the little girl?" she asked, stalling for time, wondering how in the world they were going to save Melinda, Joy, *and* Hayley.

"Garrison took me to California. He told me my parents didn't want me anymore. If they'd wanted me, he said, they would have come looking for me. But you didn't."

"Yes, Hayley, we did," Caroline cried. "We even hired private detectives to look for you after your body had been identified. But there wasn't a trace."

"So *you* say. Anyway, gradually I began to forget about this place, although I never completely forgot you and Daddy. Sometimes I thought I must have dreamed you. All that seemed real was Garrison." Again the choking sound. "He hurt me. He hurt me so much."

Caroline felt a wave of nausea as she thought of her beautiful child in the hands of a sexual pervert. "I'm so sorry," she whispered.

"I was so confused," Hayley went on, almost to herself. "He bought me things. He took me places. He taught me. He said that's how a real lady learned—from a tutor. That's how I know so much about interior decoration—he bought books and books on antiques and porcelain and crystal for us to go over. But he *hurt*. And the older I got, the more I hated him for hurting. He always said it was the price I had to pay for his taking me in when my own parents didn't want me, but I knew it wasn't right. He never let me out of his sight. He never let me watch television or listen to the radio. But he did let me keep Twinkle." She glared at Caroline. "And you put Twinkle in the trash! I drove past your house every night and one night I found Twinkle with the garbage!"

So it really had been Twinkle Caroline had found

in Melinda's room, not Lucy's doll. Caroline had known she was right. "I'm sorry about Twinkle," she said. "It was a mistake."

"It doesn't matter. I got him back."

Chris had lowered his gun, and Caroline saw that his hand trembled. So he believes her, too, she thought. He knows he's looking at his daughter. "How did you get away from Garrison?"

"We'd moved. We did that a lot, I guess so people wouldn't get to know us and get suspicious. We were in Maine, this really deserted place. It was miles and miles to town, and Garrison never let me go there. Besides, I knew what would happen to me if I tried. But one night he . . . he *really* hurt me. Worse than ever." Caroline shuddered. "I don't know what came over me," Hayley said dreamily. "I just ran in the living room and picked up a poker from the fireplace and started beating him. I thought I'd killed him. I meant to. Then I got Twinkle and the car keys and all the money he kept in the bedroom and took off. I was only fourteen. I ran the car into a tree halfway to town and had to walk the rest of the way. Then I got a bus. I went to New York. And I became a working girl, as they say nowadays."

"At *fourteen?*" Caroline gasped.

Hayley cocked an eyebrow. "Lots of men like young girls."

"I can't believe all this," Chris said.

Hayley looked at him fiercely. "Who else would have Twinkle? Who else would have known 'treats or tickles'? I really scared you with that, didn't I, Mommy?"

Caroline's mouth had gone completely dry. Her voice scratched. "Yes, Hayley, you did."

"And in the storeroom, too. Lucy was so wrapped

up in what she was doing, she didn't notice I'd slipped away for a minute when I saw your car pull in the parking lot."

"That was very sneaky of you."

"I know. And how about me getting that job with Lucy in the first place? You see, I started remembering everything a few years ago, but I wasn't going to do anything about it. I thought you didn't want me, and I had a boyfriend and a little girl I loved, so I didn't need to find you. But then Valerie died. And then *he* left me. After all, I was just a former prostitute. He didn't think he owed me anything. And I knew if you'd tried to find me so long ago, or if Millicent or Pamela had told what they knew, none of it would be happening. So I decided to come back here to make everything like it should be. But I had to be clever. I got the key to your new house, Mommy. Then you had the lock changed, but when your husband called you about Daddy getting shot and you ran upstairs in the store, I got your new key out of your purse and traced it to have a copy made. And I watched everyone. *Everyone.* I was only surprised about Garrison. I couldn't believe he'd come back here. But I was glad because it meant I got to kill him."

She had stepped closer to the fire and her blue eyes sparkled with febrile light as her hand clenched. "But he did it again, you know? He got away from me one more time. I never did get to kill him like I wanted to."

Caroline tensed. Were those tires on gravel she'd heard outside? Had the police followed them? Hayley didn't seem to notice anything, though, and Caroline asked quickly, "What about the cemetery guard?"

Hayley gasped and looked up, as if she were seeing him. "I was getting the flowers off Pamela's grave. And suddenly he was there. He threw me down on the ground. He started trying to take my clothes off. Ripping them. He slapped me. My wig—my Twinkle wig—he tore it off and laughed. And I kept fighting and I got his gun and I shot." Her teeth clenched. "I wish he'd died, too. But there are things worse than death. I know."

Caroline wanted to cry and scream and run all at the same time. "Hayley, I'm so sorry about everything that's happened to you," she said softly. "Especially about Valerie."

Hayley's face crumpled. "I had a little girl. She was the only person who ever loved me. And she died."

Caroline took an infinitesimal step forward. Hayley raised a gun that had been hidden in the folds of her full skirt and pointed it at her. "You don't want to shoot me, Hayley."

"No, but I will."

Caroline pushed down her fear, forcing herself to speak calmly. "Hayley, Valerie wasn't the only person who loved you. Your father and I loved you."

"So much that you stopped looking for me?"

"I told you, we didn't stop looking for you."

Hayley eyed them coldly. "I do not believe you."

"It's true." Now she heard it distinctly—the sound of someone moving beyond the broken window, feet snapping dry vines. She was closer to the window than Hayley, who still didn't seem to hear anything, but she spoke louder to cover the sound. "I always felt you weren't dead. I should never have stopped looking for you."

"No, you shouldn't have," Hayley said viciously.

"And you shouldn't have had more kids to take my place, especially another little girl."

"Hayley, darling, this isn't Melinda's fault," Caroline said, moving forward a little. "You can't punish Melinda for our mistake."

"Mistake? You call what happened to me a *mistake?*"

"It was my fault." Chris's voice sounded a hundred years old. "This was all my fault. If I hadn't left you alone on the hill that night . . ."

"But you did, didn't you? That's why I shot you. For punishment. But I didn't mean to kill you. If I'd meant to kill you, I would have." Hayley's twisted smile reappeared. "Ask me why I didn't kill you."

"Why didn't you kill me?" Chris responded dully.

"Because you're my daddy." She sounded like a little girl again. "You didn't mean to hurt me. The others did."

"Not Fidelia. Not my husband," Caroline said.

"And I didn't kill them, did I? Lucy said you were going away. I had to shoot your husband to keep you here. And that cleaning lady just got in the way. And she saw me."

Caroline inched closer. She could see the sweat glistening on Hayley's face now. "But even though she saw you, you didn't kill her. So far you haven't killed anyone who didn't hurt you a long time ago. Joy didn't hurt you, and neither did Melinda, so you can't kill them."

"Oh, yes, I can."

"Would Valerie want you to kill your own sister?"

Hayley suddenly looked confused. "I loved Valerie. She loved me." It sounded like a litany. "But when she died, nobody helped me. Not even then. He went away. I was alone again. Just like before. I was alone."

"But you're not alone now," Caroline went on desperately. "Daddy and Mommy are here."

"You don't even live together anymore!" Hayley's hands clenched around the gun as she looked at Caroline. "And *you* had other kids. The boy isn't so bad, but *her!*" She waved the gun in Melinda's direction.

Caroline's heart skipped a beat. "Hayley, listen to me. Things can't be the way they used to be, even if you kill Melinda."

"*I* know that," Hayley sneered. "Do you think I'm stupid? Well, I'm not. I never meant for you to find out about me. I just wanted to be around you as Tina. And I wanted to marry Lowell and have another baby."

Caroline took a deep breath. "You wanted to have another baby just like I did after you disappeared."

Hayley went rigid. "It's not the same!"

"It's exactly the same."

She was enraged. "No, it isn't! My little girl died. *I* didn't die. You just decided I did because it was easier. Then you had another little girl to take my place." Her voice rose to a shriek. "I *hate* her!"

"No, you don't," Caroline shouted. "You love her or you would have killed her already!"

"I *will* kill her!"

"No. You can't kill her. You want me to stop you. You've wanted me to stop you all along. That's why you said 'help me, Mommy' in Lucy's storeroom and wrote it on the mirrors. You didn't even try to keep your identity a secret from Joy's mother. You thought she'd tell long before she did."

"That's not true."

"Oh, yes, it is. But now you're stopping yourself. You can't kill a little girl who loves you."

"She doesn't love me."

"Yes, I do," Melinda called. "I loved you when you were Tina. You were so nice to me and George. I thought you liked me. You said if you had a little girl, you'd want her to be just like me."

"No, I didn't." Hayley seemed to waver. "I don't remember."

"You did say those things," Caroline said. "Hayley, you can't kill your own little sister."

"I will ... I ..." As Hayley raised her hands to her head in confusion, the gun pointed at Caroline.

A shot exploded from the shadows at the far end of the boiler house. Shards of brick flew as the bullet hit a wall. Caroline screamed. The little girls shrieked. Hayley flinched, looking wildly around her. "You brought the police!"

"No, I didn't!" Damn them, Caroline thought frantically. They'd found another way in and were going to frighten Hayley into fatal action. "Hayley, I *didn't* bring them!" Caroline's eyes searched the darkness. "Please stop firing!"

"Drop the gun!" A man's voice. Footsteps echoing on the cold concrete floor. "I said drop the gun!"

Hayley spun around, and in the bright light of the fire Caroline could see a dynamite detonator.

"Chris!" Caroline cried, but her voice was drowned out by the shattering sound of Chris's gun firing beside her. Hayley stiffened, whirled to look at him in hurt astonishment, then fell forward.

"I only hit her in the thigh!" Chris shouted. The little girls were screaming in the darkness while George barked hysterically. Vaguely Caroline was aware of the men climbing through the broken window as she and Chris ran to Hayley. He laid down his gun and gently turned her over.

Her nose was bloodied from the fall and she looked at him with eyes exactly like his own. "I couldn't do it. I was only going to run away." Then, with the lightning movement of a cat, Hayley grabbed his gun, put it to her temple, and fired.

Epilogue

~

AND SO SHE had lost Hayley again.

Caroline had only kaleidoscopic recollection of the time after Hayley's death: Tom arriving with the second police car, the first having found them after Detective Ames issued an APB on the jeep; the fire department roaring up to dismantle the bomb wired to Joy and Melinda; an ambulance coming to carry away Hayley's body; Chris driving her and Melinda home to leave them reluctantly with shocked and speechless Greg and David.

The funeral was a nightmare. Crowds gathered to see the burial of a woman who had murdered three people and kidnapped two little girls. They hurled epithets as well as stones, cups, and empty cigarette packages. *I don't think I'll ever be able to like people again,* Caroline thought stonily as she walked to the graveside. Police struggled to subdue the crowd without interrupting the ceremony, but their efforts were useless. Not even the first snow of the season falling in a heavy veil over the rolling, brown-grassed knolls of the cemetery could daunt the crowd's barbaric enthusiasm, and Caroline knew she would have the grave guarded until the furor died down.

David had accompanied her, looking pale and sick.

It was his first day outside and he had no business taxing himself so strenuously, but he had insisted. He stood beside her, supported by his crutches, his strained face trying to give her an encouraging smile whenever their eyes met. Chris stood by himself, his hands clenched, his eyes sunken, and Caroline realized he was even more devastated by Hayley's reappearance and death than she, possibly because there was no one in his life to cushion the shock. They'd had no chance to speak since that awful night at the boiler house, and as soon as the service was over, he turned and walked rigidly away.

As Caroline took David's arm to help him down the hill, Lowell Warren strode toward them. He looked ten years older than when Caroline had seen him at a party the Christmas before.

"Mrs. Webb, I know there's nothing to say at a time like this." His voice was tight, and Caroline saw the beginning of tears in his eyes. "I want you to know I loved Tina—Hayley—very much."

Caroline smiled weakly, aware of the lingering hostile crowd who watched her. "Aside from her father and sister and me, I think you're the only one who did."

The vertical lines between Lowell's eyebrows deepened. "We all have a dark side. Hayley's just took control because of the ghastly things that happened to her. But even that monster Longworth wasn't able to completely destroy her spirit. She was still capable of loving me, her little girl, Melinda. That's the side we have to remember, Caroline."

Caroline choked back a sob and impulsively hugged Lowell. He was shaking, but he hugged her back, fiercely. As she helped David to the car, she looked back to see Lowell, hands in his pockets, star-

ing at the coffin that would soon be lowered into its
cold grave.

For two days after the funeral Caroline lay list-
lessly in her bedroom, the strain of the past few
weeks having finally taken their toll. They had decided to keep Melinda home from school for a week
to give the scandal a little time to die down, and the
child, who seemed to have bounced back remarkably
after her experience, was playing self-appointed nurse
to both parents, bringing juice and chattering non-
stop.

"Fidelia's gonna be all right, you know," she told
her mother one morning. "Daddy said some little
bone in her neck was cracked but not broken. She
was unconscious because she had a concession."

"A concussion," Caroline said, sipping cranberry
juice through a striped elbow straw.

"Yeah, well, I talked to her on the phone and she
said she wants to see me as soon as she gets well."

"Maybe I can take you to see Fidelia when she
gets home," Caroline said.

Melinda brightened. "That'd be neat. Do you want
your pillow fluffed?"

"No, honey. You just did that ten minutes ago."

David had given her an old stethoscope, which she
now donned in order to listen to her mother's heart.
Caroline sighed and submitted. "One hundred and
fifty beats a minute," Melinda announced after a con-
siderable search for the heart. "Just right."

"I'm glad." Although she seemed to be in such
good spirits, Caroline was worried about the effect of
the kidnapping and Hayley's suicide on Melinda. So
every now and then she asked a few cautious questions. "Melinda, why did you go with Joy that day after school?"

Melinda sat down on the side of the bed. "When she came up, I told her to go away because I thought she was a ghost. She giggled and told me to touch her. She said if she was a ghost, my hand would go right through her. It didn't. Then she said she'd come to tell me George got loose and got hit by a car. She said she'd take me to him." Of course it had to be something like that, Caroline thought. Fear for her adored pet would make Melinda forget a thousand warnings that had been drummed into her head. "When we got there Tina, or Hayley, was in her car. She jumped out and said you'd already taken George to the vet's, and she'd take me there."

"Did she hurt you or Joy?"

Melinda looked down. "No. But she had a gun and she pointed it at us. That's how she made us hold still till she tied us up."

"Were you very frightened?"

"Very, very." Melinda looked up, frowning. "But way deep down I didn't think Tina'd really hurt us. Even when she put on the wires and said they were hooked up to dynamite, I didn't think she'd blow us up. I thought she was mixed up. She kept talking to herself and she kept calling me Valerie."

"Valerie was her own little girl who died."

"Oh, that's sad. Then Valerie would have been my . . . cousin?"

"Niece. Does it bother you to know Hayley was your sister?"

Melinda lifted her shoulders. "I don't know. She was pretty. And she was nice before, even if she got mixed up later. I know she didn't mean to hurt Fidelia or Daddy or your first husband. And she didn't hurt George. People who are good to animals are good people." Her eyes filled with tears. "But she shot herself in the head!"

"Did you see it?"

"No. I had my eyes closed. But I heard it."

Caroline wrapped her arms around the child. Some day soon she and David could take her to a psychiatrist to see just how much emotional damage had been done, but for now it seemed best simply to give her a lot of reassurance.

"What you have to remember about Hayley is that she's all right now, Lin," she said softly. "She's probably a lot happier than she was when she was alive."

"You think?" Caroline nodded. "Is that because she's in heaven with Valerie?"

"Yes, I'm sure she is."

"Then she'll probably be real glad to see you and me and George when we all get to heaven, too." She sighed. "Do you want another blanket?"

"Sure. That would be great."

By the next day Caroline told herself she'd spent enough time languishing in bed. Hayley was dead, but she had a husband and two children who were very much alive. She decided to make the morning a festive occasion, and when she reached the kitchen bright with winter sunshine she found them already gathered. Greg sat at the table while Melinda bustled around her father asking if he wanted her to take his pulse. "Kiddo, I'm fine," he said good-naturedly. "Why don't you sit down and stop acting like Florence Nightingale?"

"I'm not Florence Nightingale. I'm Nurse Hot Lips Hoolihan from *M*A*S*H*. Do you want your temperature taken?"

"You've taken it three times this morning. Go take Greg's."

"He didn't even get shot. Come on, Daddy, just once more?"

Groaning, David acquiesced. After a few seconds Melinda removed the thermometer. "Two hundred and ten degrees."

"I thought I felt a little warm," David said.

"Squirt, if Dad's temperature were that high he'd ignite," Greg said, laughing.

Melinda looked at David in alarm. "Are you going to catch on *fire?*"

"I haven't heard of any cases of spontaneous combustion lately. I think you might have read the thermometer wrong."

"Oh." Melinda looked in puzzlement at the thermometer.

"Okay, here's the first batch of blueberry pancakes," Caroline announced, forcing gaiety into her voice. Try as she might, she couldn't fight off the darkness that had descended when Hayley put the gun to her head. "Greg, would you get the sausage off the stove?"

"This looks great, Caroline," David said.

"We even have blueberry syrup to go with the pancakes."

"Be sure to save some for George," Melinda said. "He *loves* pancakes with butter and syrup."

Melinda sat down as Caroline returned to the skillet. "Honey, aren't you going to eat?" David asked.

"In a minute. I'll just get another batch going here." Actually, she felt as if she were going to cry. She'd tried this too soon. She couldn't be lighthearted when she had just buried her daughter three days before. Maybe she would never be lighthearted again.

"Well, let's dig in," David said heartily.

"Wait!" Melinda said. "The blueberry syrup!"

"It's on the counter, sweetie," Caroline told her absently.

Melinda hurried over to the counter near the phone. Then she screamed.

Caroline's heart skipped a beat and Greg jumped up from the table, their nerves wrecked by the horrors of the past few weeks. "What is it?" David shouted. "What's the matter?"

"It's Aurora!" Melinda held up the pot bearing her bean sprout. "She's alive!" She ran over to Caroline and thrust the pot in her hands. "Look, Mommy, she's *growing!*"

And sure enough, there stood a tender green sprout. Greg got up and came to peer at the plant. "Amazing," he said softly. "I thought for sure the thing was dead."

"Oh, I always knew she wasn't," Melinda said confidently. "It just wasn't easy for her. She had to have lots of care and attention. She had to know somebody loved her. Mommy told me that, didn't you, Mommy?"

Caroline's eyes filled with tears. She gazed at grinning David, shining-eyed Melinda, strong and handsome Greg. They looked right together, the three of them. And maybe with lots of care and attention, maybe with lots of love, they could all put the memory of the past few weeks behind them.

She looked at David and smiled.

MARY JANE CLARK

CLOSE TO YOU

In front of the camera, as anchorwoman for *KEY Evening Headlines*, she's savvy, sexy, and sophisticated. But when she steps out of the spotlight, Eliza Blake is far more vulnerable than her devoted viewers would ever imagine. Single-handedly raising a young daughter, she's finally found a safe haven: a dream house in the suburbs, where nothing can ever threaten her again . . .

It begins with a venomous letter. No stranger to the occasional hate mail that mingles with glowing correspondence from adoring fans, Eliza is at first unaware that this time, the writer isn't a harmless nutcase. Then come the menacing phone calls. Now that her serene suburban life is shattered by fear, Eliza must face the chilling realization that the stalker is closer, and more lethal, than anyone ever suspected . . .

"An excellent psychological thriller."
—*Publishers Weekly*

"Clark's story retains its suspense throughout."
—*Newark Star-Ledger*

"A frightening—and firsthand—look at the darker side of celebrity."
—*Sun Herald* (Colusa, CA)

THE CHASE

BRENDA JOYCE

NEW YORK TIMES BESTSELLING AUTHOR

CLAIRE HAYDEN has no idea that her world is about to be shattered: at the conclusion of her husband's fortieth birthday party, he is found murdered, his throat cut with a WWII thumb knife. He has no enemies, no one seeking revenge, no one who would want him dead. But the mysterious Ian Marshall, an acquaintance of her husband's, seems to know something. Because someone has been killing this way for decades. Someone whose crimes go back to WWII. Someone who has been a hunter . . . and the hunted. As Claire and Ian team up to find the killer, they can no longer deny the powerful feelings they have for one another. Then Ian makes a shocking revelation: the murderer may be someone Claire has known all her life . . .

> **"Joyce excels at creating twists and turns
> in her characters' personal lives."**
> —*Publishers Weekly*

ON SALE JULY 2002
FROM ST. MARTIN'S PRESS

CHASE 10/01